ORPHANS

of the

TIDE

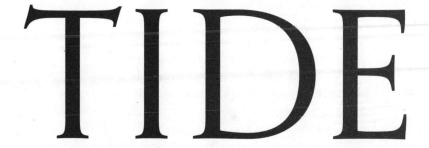

STRUAN MURRAY

HARPER
An Imprint of HarperCollins*Publishers*

Library of Congress Control Number: 2021942278
ISBN 978-0-06-304311-4

Typography by Jessie Gang
21 22 23 24 25   GV   10 9 8 7 6 5 4 3 2 1
❖
Originally published in the UK in 2020 by
Penguin Random House Children's
First US Edition, 2021

For Ruaraidh, Robbie, and Nona

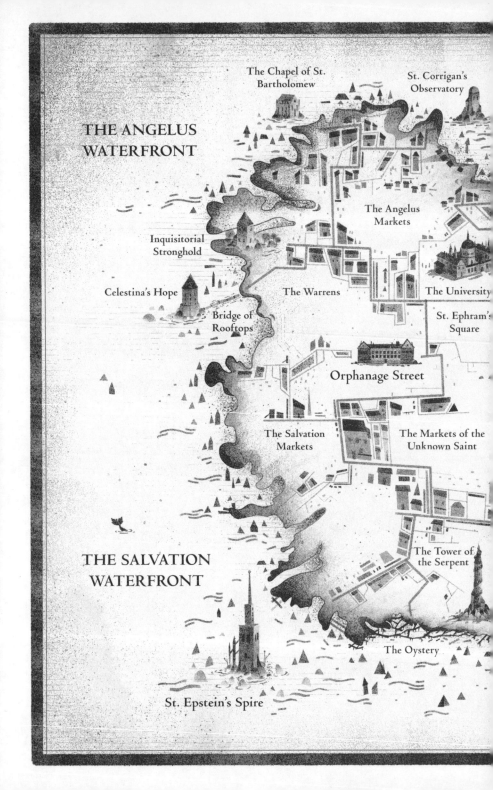

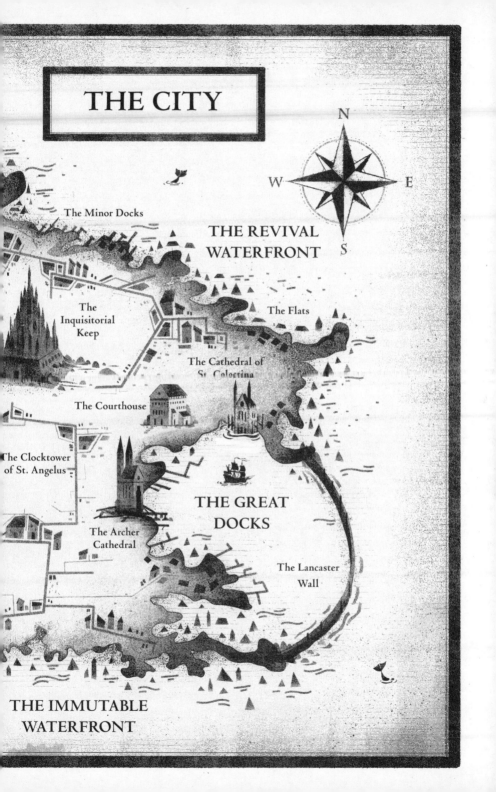

ITS LAST SONG

The City was built on a sharp mountain that jutted improbably from the sea, and the sea kept trying to claim it back. When the tide rose, it swallowed up the City's lower streets. When the tide fell, it spat them back out again, but left its mark. Fresh mussels clung to windowsills. Fish flailed on the cobblestones. That gray morning, once the tide had retreated, a whale was found on a rooftop.

A crowd gathered along the top of the seawall, to gape at the roof below.

"It's an evil omen!" yelled the old preacher, his breath steaming in the air.

"The Enemy didn't do this," snorted a sailor. "It must have got stuck there at high tide."

"It's dead," said a merchant. "Do you think we can sell it for meat?"

The whale lay on its belly, stretched from one end of the roof to the other. It had beached itself on the Chapel of St. Bartholomew, whose rooftop poked above the waves at low tide. Four stone gargoyles stood at each corner, two of them digging sharply into the whale's skin. Hungry seagulls screeched overhead.

The crowd were so engrossed that none of them noticed the girl's arrival. She had tired eyes and tangled, dirty-blond hair, mussed up from a night of broken sleep. She leaned over the seawall and bit her lip.

"It's too big to be out of the water," she said, speaking more to herself than anyone else. "It'll have crushed its lungs just by lying there."

A tiny, wide-eyed boy next to her looked up in horror. He nestled close to his mother's side, watching the girl warily. Her face was pale, with three red scratches down one cheek, and she smelled faintly of fireworks. What was worse, she was dressed like a man, and not an upstanding one either. She wore a frayed crimson scarf, and a coat that was long and hooded, stitched together from weathered cloth and gray sealskin.

"Wh-Who are you?" said the boy, his lips quivering.

"I'm Ellie," said the girl distractedly, rummaging in her coat pockets. She pulled out a magnifying glass, an onion, and finally a penknife with a razor-sharp edge. The boy reached for his mother's hand.

"If we don't cut this whale open soon," said Ellie, holding up the knife, "it will explode."

The boy began to cry.

"Watch your mouth, girl!" said his mother.

"No, really, it will!" said Ellie, raising her hands. "Dead whales start to decay from the inside. There will be a dangerous buildup of gas."

The mother turned away, covering her mouth with the back of her hand.

"I *know*!" said Ellie. "There'll be guts everywhere. And you wouldn't believe the smell! Hmm," she added, staring down at the penknife. "On second thought . . ."

Ellie turned to a girl standing behind her. She looked to be the same age, twelve or thirteen maybe, with a mess of curly ginger hair. She wore a huge woolen blue sweater, heavy black boots, and a bored expression.

"Anna, I need you to run back to the workshop and get my flensing tool," said Ellie.

"What's a flensing tool?" said Anna, yawning.

"It's a sharp blade on the end of a long pole," said Ellie. "It's in the loft beside the bookcases, hanging below a telescope and a rifle."

"*You* have a rifle?" said Anna, leaning forward, suddenly interested. "And bullets?"

"Just hurry, all right!" said Ellie, and Anna rolled her eyes and slouched off up the street.

Ellie hopped onto the seawall, then dropped down the other side. The crowd gasped as she landed on the roof of the chapel ten feet below.

"What is she *doing*?" said a woman.

Ellie held out her hands to steady herself, stepping along the rooftop like a tightrope walker. The whale's eyes were closed, eyelids wrinkled and creased like those of an old man. She knelt, drawing one hand delicately along the whale's side. Its skin was hard, covered in white barnacles and crisscrosses of scar tissue.

"What's going on here?" said a voice above. Ellie glanced up and saw a young city guardsman nudging his way through the crowd, gawky and big-eared, dressed in a black cap and dark blue greatcoat.

"There's a whale on the roof," said a woman.

"That girl's gone down to it," said another.

"What?" the guardsman said, then he looked down and noticed Ellie on the roof. "What . . . what is she doing?" He clapped his hands to his head. "Watch out, miss! That whale will eat you!"

"Whales don't eat people," Ellie sighed, but no one heard. They were all talking over each other now.

The whale's massive body rose and fell beneath her hand as it drew a ragged breath.

It was still alive!

Ellie looked around, wondering if it was possible to get the whale back in the water. A ship might have been able to pull it free when the tide came back in, but that was hours away.

"I'm sorry," she whispered. "I wish I could help."

As she spoke, Ellie thought she heard something faint coming from inside the whale. The clamor of the crowd made it impossible to be sure.

"Get away from it!" the guardsman yelled, though he seemed too afraid to climb down to the roof himself.

"I think you should drag her off."

"Someone call the Inquisition!"

"Please, I'm trying to listen!" said Ellie.

"The preacher said whales could breathe fire."

"Please!" Ellie yelled but no one paid her any attention. She pulled a marble-sized device from her pocket, wrapped in yellowed paper. With a flick of her wrist she hurled it up at the seawall. There was a *crack* and a flash of light, and a riot of frenzied screeching as the seagulls fled. The crowd staggered back and shielded their eyes, shocked into silence.

Ellie held up her hand. *"Listen,"* she said.

And so they all did.

And in the silence they could hear it, drifting toward them.

It was the whale.

The whale was singing.

It was a mournful, melodious rise and fall, reverberating from deep within the creature. Ellie had heard whales sing before, but never one out of water. She had thought it was part of some mating ritual, yet here was this dying whale, singing, for whose benefit she could not guess.

They all listened in awe, for many long minutes.

Then the whale opened its eye.

"Incredible," Ellie whispered. The eye was the dark blue of a cold sea. It focused on her—she could have sworn it—and all she knew was its gaze, and that song. And for those few, wondrous moments, all the pain inside her seemed to go away.

The song grew quieter, as if it were drifting off to the horizon. The eye closed. The tail stopped moving.

And all was silent, even the sea.

"I've got it!" yelled Anna triumphantly, pushing her way to the seawall, holding the flensing tool over her head. The crowd turned to look at her. "What?" she asked, then handed the tool down to Ellie, blunt end first.

"What are you going to do?" the guardsman called.

Ellie pointed to the whale's belly. "I'll have to cut it open, low down. That will prevent any gas building up inside."

Ellie rested the tool upon one of the many grooves that

ran lengthways along the whale's white belly, and pressed. The skin was tough and thick and she was soon sweating from the effort. Finally, the blade punctured the skin, and Ellie almost lost her balance as it sank into the soft organs underneath. A rank smell seeped from the wound and Ellie held her breath. She worked the flensing tool back and forth, cutting down the creature's side. The flesh parted, purple guts drooping from the opening.

"*Ooh*, look at all that blood," called Anna. "Can I have a go?"

"It smells awful," said Ellie. "But I suppose so. Just be—"

She stopped.

"Anna, what's wrong?" she said.

Anna's face had contorted, her eyes fixed in disbelief.

"Sweet mercy," said the guardsman, his hand at his mouth.

There was a confused muttering from the crowd. An old lady screamed. For some reason, Ellie found she couldn't move.

Her body stiffened. The flensing tool fell from her fingers. She looked down.

Something was holding her by the ankle.

It was skinny and trembling and slicked with thick blood.

A hand reaching out from the cut in the whale.

2

FROM THE BELLY OF THE WHALE

The old preacher flung his hands skyward.

"It's back!" he shrieked, fleeing along the seawall toward the streets above. "The Enemy has returned!"

"Oh no, oh no, oh no," a woman kept saying, her hands clasped around the symbol of St. Celestina at her neck. A young man fainted to the cobblestones.

"P-please, everyone, stay c-calm," stuttered the guardsman. "There's no need to panic!"

And all Ellie could do was stare at the hand.

It gripped her ankle, freezing cold against her skin. She jerked her leg away and it slapped down hard upon the slate, leaving a bloody smear on her sock. Ellie swallowed, kneeling to inspect the hand, and the arm it was connected to. The hand was groping across the roof, as if searching for something else to hold. The arm was lean and wiry and led back into the whale, vanishing between fat purple organs.

"Hey!"

Ellie turned to see Anna clambering over the top of the seawall.

"Stop!" the guardsman shouted, squeezing through the crowd toward Anna. "Come back here!" He lunged toward her and managed to get hold of her woolen sweater.

Ellie touched the hand with the tip of her finger. It flinched away from her like a skittish animal. Ellie took a deep breath, then grabbed it. It was sticky and crusty against her fingers. She dug her heels into the rooftop and pulled.

The hand stopped struggling and the fingers curled around hers. She didn't want to pull too hard, in case the person inside was caught against something. But the rest of the arm came easily.

Then a shoulder came too, bony and bloody.

Then tangled black hair. A head. A face.

A boy, gasping for breath.

The crowd cried out. Anna broke free of the guardsman's grip, dropping down from the seawall and skidding toward Ellie. She stared at the boy in shock.

"What *is* that?"

The boy rolled onto the roof, trailing ropes of whale entrails. He was entirely naked.

"Are you dying?" Ellie said, shaking his shoulders. His eyes were closed, and he didn't seem able to breathe. His mouth kept opening and sucking at the air, but it was like he'd never drawn breath before.

"I think he's dying," said Anna.

"Look at me!" Ellie said to the boy. "Open your eyes!"

But he just thrashed back and forth in a tangle of limbs. Ellie pressed down on his shoulders to hold him still. His skin was sticky and smelled of iron filings.

"Get his legs!" she shouted, and Anna fell down flat on his kicking feet. Ellie sat on his chest, his nails clawing blindly at her coat. Grimacing, she put her thumb and finger to his eyelids and forced them open. The eyes stared upward, rolling back like a blood-maddened shark's.

"Look at me," Ellie said.

The boy growled.

"Look at me!"

His eyes flashed down and found her. Ellie gasped.

Gray-blue. The color of a cold sea.

She blinked hard, trying to focus. "Listen," she said as calmly as she could manage. "I need you to do as I do."

She inhaled slowly through her nose, exaggerating the sound, a hand on her chest to demonstrate how it rose with her breath. She exhaled gently through her mouth, and could see him trying to copy her. But his nostrils flared uncertainly. It wasn't working.

"Keep him still," she told Anna. She knelt by his side and pinched his nose, holding tight even when he shook his head furiously. She clamped her lips to his and breathed deeply into his mouth.

A woman shrieked from the seawall.

"What are you doing!" the guardsman cried. He had at last managed to scramble down to the rooftop, but stood paralyzed by horror. Ellie came up for breath, then put her lips to the boy's again. He stared at her as she did it, his eyes wide. A third time she drew a deep breath and shared it with him, and a fourth, and a fifth.

Then, as she took a sixth breath, the boy's mouth opened, and he sucked in a lungful of air. Ellie laughed in relief. The boy drew deep, shuddering breaths at first, then sped up, gulping the air hungrily.

"Slow down," she warned, breathing slowly again to remind him. "Like this. Now stand up and put your hands on your hips like I'm doing. It'll open up your lungs."

He stared at her intensely, his face sharp and menacing. Slowly, he seemed to understand, and placed his hands on his hips. Ellie looked down to check he was doing it right, then covered her eyes.

"Sorry!" she said. She'd forgotten he was naked. "Um, um . . . . Could someone get us a blanket!"

The crowd shrank back. The young guardsman kept staring at the blood, his face turning paler. Ellie sighed and took off her scarf.

"Here," she said. "You can wrap this around your . . . waist."

The boy stared at the fabric, blinking in confusion.

"I'll do it!" said Anna, snatching the scarf from Ellie's hand and rushing at him.

"Anna, be careful!"

The boy's eyes flashed and he leapt at Anna, grabbing her shoulders and pushing her away. Anna tumbled into Ellie, and the boy staggered. His legs didn't seem to work properly.

"Get away!" he yelled hoarsely and fell back against the whale.

"You can talk!" Ellie cried, helping Anna to her feet.

The boy picked up Ellie's scarf. After a moment's hesitation he wrapped it around his waist, tying it on one side.

"How did you—?" Ellie stammered. "What were you—? Why were you in that whale?"

But the boy wasn't listening. He turned and looked at the hole in the whale, seemingly unaffected by the smell. He noticed the crowd watching him in silent horror. He shivered, and Ellie remembered how cold his skin had felt.

A faded blue greatcoat landed at her feet with a thump. The young guardsman was standing ten feet away. He was deliberately not looking at the blood-covered boy, his hand held firmly over his mouth.

"Thanks," said Ellie. She approached the boy and he tensed, clenching his fists. She took another small step, holding out the coat. He was skinny, yet muscular-looking, and his body heaved with every breath he drew. Ellie stepped cautiously to his side and draped the coat around his shoulders.

"What's your name?" she asked.

The boy opened his mouth, closed it, and seemed disturbed by the lack of words that came out in between.

"I think we should call him Seth," said Anna.

"He's not a pet," said Ellie.

"It's a good name. It sounds like the sea."

Ellie shrugged. "Well, I suppose it will do until you remember your real one. Mine's Ellie," she added. "Ellie Lancaster."

She put out her hand for the boy to shake, and he stared at it and did nothing.

"Here, let's get that whale blood off you." Ellie retrieved a handkerchief from her pocket and soaked it in water from her hip flask. "Do you mind?" she said, the cloth poised by his face.

Again he did nothing, which Ellie took to mean he didn't mind. With careful movements, she wiped his brow, his cheeks, his chin, revealing a boy around the same age as

Ellie and Anna, his face unblemished save for tiny crinkles at the sides of his eyes, like he smiled a lot, and a single crease on his brow, like he frowned a lot too. He had thick black eyebrows and a mess of black, blood-soaked hair. He had a prominent, high-bridged nose, wide cheekbones, and his skin was light brown. He stared at her with his large sea-blue eyes, and Ellie found she couldn't look away.

Anna barged her with one shoulder.

"Ow! Right, um, we should get you somewhere warm."

The boy glared at his hands. "Where am I?" he asked. His voice was harsh like sandpaper.

"The Angelus Waterfront," said Ellie.

"Waterfront . . ." he said. "Waterfront of what?" This boy really was confused.

"Of the City."

"Which city?"

Ellie stared at him, puzzled and a little frightened. There was only one City.

She pointed upward, so that he could see it towering above them. The City. A mountainous gray roost of ancient buildings, swarming with squawking seagulls. The boy's gaze flitted from chimney to gargoyle, following the serrated lines of streets and stairways that cut down from the peak of the City to the sea. He stared at three little rowboats tied to metal hoops, swaying in the gentle tug of the waves. He looked out to the horizon, then winced.

"What's that noise?" he said. "Where is that noise coming from?"

He put his hands to his ears, gritting his teeth. Anna and Ellie shared a glance.

"Where are my brothers and sisters?" he asked.

"Um . . ." Ellie scratched her head. "I . . . I don't know?"

There was a commotion on the seawall. Ellie could hear the old preacher returning from the streets above, talking eagerly in his shrill voice.

"It's the Enemy!" he screeched. "I was just leading a funeral at the Church of St. Horace, you see, Master Inquisitor, when I heard all this uproar."

"What's happening?" said Seth.

"An Inquisitor's coming," said Ellie, toying nervously with a hole in her coat sleeve. "But don't worry, you'll be fine. Unless it's—"

The crowd parted. People were falling over each other to keep their distance from the new arrival.

"Oh no," said Ellie.

A powerfully built man appeared at the seawall, taller than anyone in the crowd. He wore a black sealskin greatcoat that spilled down to his ankles and a silver chain across his chest. He had a thick neck and broad shoulders and a face that was pale and puffy, haunted by a shadow of handsomeness that had been lost along the way. His eyes were deep, dark pits, and held no expression. He looked like a corpse for whom death was a small inconvenience.

Seth raised an eyebrow. "Who's that?"

"He's . . ." Ellie's mouth was dry. "Inquisitor Hargrath."

"I had just arrived," the preacher prattled on, "when this *boy* burst from a whale. It must be the work of the Enemy."

"Silence," Hargrath rumbled. "I will judge that for myself."

A balding, diminutive man dropped to his knees in front of Hargrath. "Saint Killian!" he cried. "Save us!"

"On your feet," Hargrath said. "I'm not a saint yet. Only dead men get to be saints."

He vaulted over the seawall, his black boots crunching slate as he landed on the roof. His eyes swept from Seth, to the hole in the whale, then back again.

He took two steps toward Seth, but after a moment's pause took a small step back. It was odd to see such a monster of a man hesitate before this skinny, barely dressed boy, yet Ellie almost thought she saw fear flicker in Hargrath's dead eyes. With his right hand, Hargrath rubbed absently at the empty left sleeve of his greatcoat, which lay folded in half against his body, held by a silver pin. The arm that should have been inside it had since been taken from him.

"What do you want?" said Seth. He spoke like a grown man, in a serious, commanding tone.

"What were you doing inside that whale?" said Har-grath.

"Sir, the boy's done nothing wrong." Ellie stepped quickly between them. "He was stuck in that whale—I had to rescue him."

Hargrath showed no sign of hearing Ellie or seeing her either. His eyes drifted impassively over Seth, like a butcher deciding how to carve up a carcass. "Do you see it, child?" he asked Seth in a quiet growl.

Seth frowned. "See what?"

"The Enemy."

"Who?"

"The God Who Drowned the Gods. It's been speaking to you, hasn't it? It saved you from this whale?"

"*I* saved him from the whale," said Ellie. Still Hargrath ignored her.

"Only the Vessel could survive being inside a whale," he said.

"What's the Vessel?" said Seth.

"You are," said Hargrath.

"That's ridiculous," said Ellie. "What would the Vessel be doing inside a whale?"

Hargrath's hand moved toward the hilt of his sword. Ellie breathed in sharply. Seth's whole body tensed, his hands clenching to tight fists.

Hargrath reached past his weapon and into his coat pocket. He took out a small pistol, and Ellie barely had time to cry out before he pointed it at Seth and pulled the trigger.

"No!"

There was no gunshot, just a sharp hiss, and something embedded itself in Seth's neck with a thick thud. Seth clutched at it—a metal dart protruding by three inches. He fell to his knees. Ellie caught hold of him, but he was heavy, his eyes shut, and he tumbled through her arms to the slate.

"What did you do to him!" she cried, putting two fingers beneath his chin to check he still had a pulse.

Hargrath returned the pistol to his pocket. "A sedative," he said. "Your mother's greatest invention. If the Vessel is unconscious, he can't ask the Enemy to save him when we burn him on the fire."

Ellie's stomach twisted. "He's *not* the Vessel," she said. "You're making a mistake."

"Don't try my patience, Lancaster." He shoved Ellie away from Seth, and Anna ran to catch her. Hargrath lifted Seth easily with one hand, draping him over his shoulder, then strode back toward the seawall. Ellie chased after him, her heart pounding.

"This is all wrong! He's not the Vessel—he's just a *boy*. You're . . . you're just frightened of a little boy! Coward!"

Hargrath stopped. He looked up at the crowd, who watched him with their hands to their mouths. He dropped Seth roughly at his feet, and the crowd jumped back as if the boy were a live firework. He turned and strode back to Ellie. His hand shot out and gripped her by the neck, driving her to the edge of the roof.

"You've never seen the Enemy, child," he said, lifting her so they were face-to-face. "But I have. I saw it burst out of the Vessel. It took my arm, even as I plunged my sword through its throat. While my friends lay dead around me. I see it still when I close my eyes. And the worst part . . . is that I *knew* that Vessel. He was a good, kind man. Yet from him emerged a creature of nightmare."

Hargrath gripped Ellie's neck tighter. She batted desperately at his arm, coughing for air.

"Anyone can be the Vessel," he said.

Out of the corner of her eye, Ellie saw Anna rushing at Hargrath, only to be knocked back by a nudge of his shoulder, sending her tumbling. Ellie's vision crowded with white dots. Her thoughts turned hazy.

"*Anyone.* Little boys, little girls. And I'd kill them all to keep the City safe."

And with that he smiled and dropped her into the sea.

From the Diary of Claude Hestermeyer

After the funeral, I didn't know what to do with myself. I left St. Horace's and walked back to my dusty study at the university—the study I'd shared with Peter. I sat at my desk, staring at his empty armchair. My heart felt like a small, hard apple in my chest.

I was so distracted that it was a moment before I noticed the man standing by the door. I couldn't see his face. He was wearing a black veil for some reason.

"Excuse me," I told him, "I appreciate you coming to offer your condolences, but I said all there was to say at Peter's funeral. Now please leave me in peace."

"Professor Claude Hestermeyer," said the man in a deep voice.

"That's my name, yes," I replied. "Saying it does not excuse the rude way you've barged into my office."

"Don't you recognize my voice?"

I didn't, but I *did* notice the way my fingers were trembling, and the tingling sensation running up and down my spine.

"Sir, I'm afraid I must insist you leave," I demanded.

"That's not how this arrangement works," said the man.

"Arrangement? What arrangement? Is this some cruel joke? Peter Lambeth was cremated today—show some respect!"

Tears trickled hotly down my cheeks. I stood up and marched around my desk, prepared to use force if necessary. But before I got close the man pulled the black veil from his face.

I snapped the pencil I was holding.

There, standing before me, was my dear friend Peter Lambeth.

THE BOY IN THE GREEN
VELVET WAISTCOAT

Ellie could hear distant shouts from above. Seawater filled her mouth.

Her leg had scraped against the edge of the roof when she'd fallen, tearing her trousers and cutting her skin. She squirmed as the sea salt stung her leg.

She looked into the murky depths. Ghostly spires and rooftops rose from the gloom like an underwater skyline. Most of the City had been drowned a long time ago.

Ellie scrabbled for the surface, but her coat dragged her down. She cursed herself—the pockets were too full! She'd crammed them with wrenches and compasses, telescopes and oil canisters, penknives, screws, and matches. A smoke bomb and a pocket watch floated past her head. She was about to wriggle out of her coat when she heard a deep, watery *clunk*. She looked up and her heart leapt.

The pole end of the flensing tool!

With a surge of strength, Ellie grabbed hold and was hoisted up immediately. The sounds of the surface crashed in around her and she was blinded by the sudden light. She spluttered for breath as she was hauled onto the roof of the chapel.

"Ellie!" Anna cried, dropping down next to her. The young guardsman was there too, clutching the flensing tool.

"Hargrath's taken the boy, hasn't he?" said Ellie. She coughed, and seawater dribbled from her mouth.

Anna nodded. With great effort, Ellie hauled herself to her feet.

"Ellie, sit down or you'll throw up," said Anna, stepping back hastily.

But Ellie shook her head. She wiped her lips with the back of her hand, and staggered forward, weighed down by her sodden clothes. She held her hand out to the guardsman. "Thanks for saving me."

The guardsman looked uneasily at her hand. It was the one she'd just wiped her mouth with.

"You need to go back to the workshop and change," said Anna, peeling seaweed from Ellie's neck. "Here, let me take this," she added, tugging at Ellie's sopping-wet coat.

"No, I'm fine," said Ellie, pulling it protectively around herself.

"You'll catch a cold!" Anna insisted.

"All right, all right," said Ellie, shedding the coat resentfully. "But I can't go to the workshop yet—I have to get to the Inquisitorial Keep. Someone needs to defend that boy. He's not the Vessel!"

"Ellie, if the Inquisitors want to kill him, then we probably shouldn't get in their way."

"But the Vessel always *knows* they're the Vessel, according to the books I've read, and that boy didn't even know his own name! Also, the Vessel always looks ill, but Seth seemed very healthy. Well, under all that blood anyway. Now listen, I need your help on an important mission."

Anna's ears pricked up. When getting Anna to run an errand, it was important firstly to never call it an errand, and secondly to dress it up with the promise of sailors. And violence, if possible.

"I need you to go to the Great Docks and see if any sailors have heard about a boy falling from a ship, and maybe even getting swallowed by a whale."

"Why?" said Anna.

"Because, if we can find out *who* Seth really is, it might help us clear his name. But just be careful—they're having a walrus fight by the docks today, and those can turn violent."

This was a lie, and it worked excellently: Anna turned and ran off. Ellie limped after her, shoes squelching with every footstep. She passed alongside the whale, its eye peacefully closed. One of the gargoyles was pressed hard against its tail and looked about ready to break off and tumble into the sea. Funnily enough, it was in the shape of a whale.

Blue eyes, Ellie thought, then felt a sharp pang as she worried what might be happening to Seth. What if the Inquisition had already decided he was the Vessel, and were even now throwing him on a bonfire? She sped up, clambering over the seawall and squeezing through the crowd, racing toward the cobbled street above.

The business of morning was fully underway as Ellie ran up through the City. The Angelus Market was packed with shoppers, merrily haggling their way from stall to stall. The rooftops were lined with hungry gulls, the air thick with the stink of fish. Three bearded musicians played a mournful tune on their cellos, while an old lady heckled them from a window above, throwing a boiled turnip at them and demanding they play something more uplifting. A street magician with a bulging woolen cap and a gray smock performed an illusion for a group of clapping children, who cheered even louder as the trick went wrong, and the seal pup he'd been trying to pull from his cap leapt out and bit his finger.

Ellie slowed down, rubbing at the cut on her leg. It was still stinging terribly from the salt water.

"Nellie!" called a happy voice.

She looked up, and grimaced. A smiling boy was walking jauntily toward her, dressed in a fine leaf-green velvet waistcoat and a black cloak.

"You're all wet," he said, looking her up and down. He had short golden curls, a sprinkle of freckles across his cheeks, and bright blue eyes that stared intently. He was slightly younger than Ellie, and pretty—he looked like a cherub that had grown up and shed its puppy fat; some angelic boy who mothers would coddle and priests would steer eagerly to the front of the choir.

"Yes, I've just been swimming," she said, trying to sound cheerful.

He noticed the tear in her trousers, frowning in concern. "Are you okay?"

"Fine." Ellie took a deep breath. "What do you want?"

"Oh." The boy seemed surprised by Ellie's bluntness. He fiddled with the silver chain around his neck, from which dangled an assortment of trinkets: keys and seashells and brass figurines. "Well, I heard a boy came out of a whale."

"I don't have time for this, Finn," said Ellie, and she hastened up the street. She passed a priest standing on a wooden platform in his black robes, yelling to the sky.

"Trust not your neighbor!" he cried. "For the Great

Enemy could be lurking behind his eyes. Trust not in your family, or even yourself. But fear not! The gods may be gone, but the saints watch over us, and have sent the Inquisition—brave men to keep us safe from ourselves."

"How do you think he was able to breathe in there?" said Finn, skipping at Ellie's side.

"Where?"

"The whale of course!"

"Oh, *I* don't know, Finn. Maybe he stuck a tube out of its blowhole?"

"You don't have to be rude; I was only curious. Where is he now?"

"Hargrath took him," said Ellie. "He thinks the boy's the Vessel."

"Oh, I'm sorry. Can I help?"

"No," said Ellie flatly. "I'm going to speak to the Inquisitors."

"Girl! GIRL! Come here this instant!"

An old man was shuffling through the crowded market, wheezing and hugging a large mechanical device to his chest. It looked sort of like a metal crab but was the size of a small pig. He glared down at Ellie. His glasses were so large they magnified his eyes to twice their normal size.

"Now listen here, this oyster-catching machine of yours

is broken, and every moment it's not working is time *I'm* losing business."

"I'm afraid I'm really busy at the moment, sir," said Ellie politely. "There was this whale—"

"Whale?" the man snapped. "I don't care about whales— oysters, girl, oysters! Now, you built this machine, so you can fix it!"

She sighed. "I didn't build that machine."

The man squinted. "But you're Hannah Lancaster, aren't you? The inventor?"

"I'm Ellie. Her daughter."

"Oh." He readjusted his glasses. "I thought you were shorter than I remembered. So where can I find your mother?"

"Nowhere. She's been dead for five years."

"Oh," said the man again, rocking back on his heels in surprise. "Well, um, I still need this machine mended! And I expect you to do it."

Ellie grimaced, looking up to the City peak. Every second of delay put Seth in more danger.

"Shame she's dead, though," the man muttered to himself. "I doubt we'll ever see her talents again."

With a sigh, Ellie took the oyster-catcher and placed it belly-up on the cobblestones.

"I can help with that if you like," said Finn, but Ellie ignored him. She fished out a screwdriver from her wet trouser pocket, shoving it into the oyster-catcher's under-side and prying off a metal panel. She peered inside, prodding the countless cogs that made up the machine's innards.

"Blockage . . ." she muttered.

Rummaging in her pockets, she pulled out a brass key, a walnut, and finally a long pair of tweezers. Biting her tongue in concentration, she extracted the blockage—a glittering, moon-white pearl.

"That's mine!" said the man. "It was in my machine—give it to me."

Ellie rolled her eyes and dropped it in his outstretched hand. "Fine."

She wound the handle on the back of the oyster-catcher until its six legs twitched, then laid it on the cobbles. It waddled along the stones, gathering up imaginary oysters with its two tiny arms.

"Bye!" Ellie yelled, darting back into the marketplace, between a girl leading a goat and a handcart laden with fresh sardines. Unfortunately, she had failed to shake off Finn.

"*I* could have fixed that in half the time," he said proudly. "Say, remember when I helped you build your boat? The one that goes underwater? We should really fix it one day."

Ellie turned sharply left. Four burly men came down

the street, carrying a dead tiger shark on a plank, its toothy mouth lolling open. Ellie slipped around them, leaving Finn on the other side.

"So this boy," he said, reappearing next to her, "what can he do? Is he really clever or something? You're not hoping to replace me, are you?"

"As what?" said Ellie. "You're nothing to me."

Finn shook his head, smiling like she'd made a joke. "So why *are* you trying to save this boy's life then? You seem so on edge, Nellie. Why are you bothering?"

"Because he didn't do anything wrong!"

Ellie squeezed through a crowd gathered eagerly at the feet of another preacher.

"My friends, know this—whenever the Vessel returns, a brave soul will rise to destroy it, and take his rightful place among the saints. Why, he could be one of *you*."

The crowed *oohed* appreciatively.

"Hey!" cried a tall young man with copper hair, bouncing gleefully at the edge of the crowd. "Guess what? They've found it—they've actually *found* it!"

"What?" said a scowling old woman.

"The Vessel!" cried the man, ruffling his hair with excitement. "Hargrath caught him just now! He truly is a saint!"

The crowd cheered. The copper-haired man hugged the old woman, and she grimaced and swatted him away.

Ellie felt a surge of fresh panic and wriggled free of the throng, then groaned when she found Finn still walking right next to her.

"Everyone seems so happy," he said. "Maybe you should just let them get on with it? It's not your job to help strangers."

"My job has nothing to do with it. It's about what's right," said Ellie.

Finn's eyes narrowed. "Huh. I don't think that's the real reason, Nellie."

"They could *execute* him, Finn. An innocent boy."

"I see. You feel guilty. That's why you're doing this, isn't it?"

Ellie felt her tummy twist. She swallowed. "Stop it, Finn."

Finn's eyes went wide. "I'm right, though, aren't I? You feel guilty for what happened before and think that if you help *this* boy then you'll make everything okay again."

"Finn."

"I'm not sure how you think you can rescue him, though. You're just not that good at saving people."

"Shut *up*, Finn!" Ellie said, hurriedly climbing the stone staircase that led past the university.

"Sorry," said Finn, skipping after her. "But, just so we're clear, I am right, aren't I? You're trying to make up for that nasty business with—"

Finn's smile flickered and died as Ellie grabbed him by his lapels, shoving him up against the wall. The trinkets around his neck jingled.

"Listen to me, Finn," she told him. *"Leave the boy alone."*

"But I just want to help! I like helping you."

"I will *never* need your help again."

She let go, and Finn sank down the wall, fussing over the loose buttons on his waistcoat. Ellie carried on up the stairs.

"Sometimes, Nellie," he called after her, "I wish you were nicer to me."

She turned to look back down at him.

"And sometimes, Finn, I wish I could kill you."

THE WHALE LORDS

Ellie had been out on whaling ships before and had seen the City from afar. It looked like a spear tip, rising sharply to the sky, gray-black against the horizon. She tried not to think about how impossibly steep it was as she raced up alleyways that were almost vertical, her chest tight from running, her throat thick with phlegm. She hurried past a line of gossiping schoolchildren.

"Did you hear, did you hear!" one girl cried, her voice a mix of excitement and terror. "They've found it—they've found the Vessel!"

The words raked at Ellie's stomach as she clattered up a metal staircase. Foolishly, she glanced over the railing, her legs weakening as she saw the City spilling out in all directions beneath her: ten thousand slate rooftops, growing greener with moss and whiter with gull droppings as they got nearer the sea. An army of statues clung to them, gray angels and animals, their faces pocked by centuries of wind, rain, and sea spray. It was sometimes joked that there were as many statues in the City as there were people. Far below, Ellie could see the Warrens, a maze of narrow winding streets where hundreds of fishermen had once lived in a hive of snugly packed houses—until the Enemy had burned down the entire district.

Ellie staggered up the stairs, along a final street, and into St. Ephram's Square, the highest point of the City. Gleaming white mansions lined its sides, the gold-leaf walls of the council chambers glittered in the sun, and rising from the middle was an ornate fountain decorated with marble dolphins. It was nearly a beautiful place. Nearly.

The Inquisitorial Keep reared high over the square. A hundred jagged black spires made up its body, growing taller toward the center, clustered together like the pipes of an organ. At its base, a vast archway formed the entrance, above which stood a crowd of gray, blank-faced statues—men, women, and children, holding hands side by side and staring down with empty eyes.

At its very peak, carved from white marble and casting a shadow across the square, was a young man. Handsome and tousle-haired, the statue was as tall as the whale had been long. He stared down adoringly at the bundle in his arms. He was cradling a baby.

In gold lettering, at the base of the statue, were written the words:

AND IT SHALL CLAIM EVEN THE INNOCENT

As a child, Ellie had always thought the man looked at the baby so caringly and held it so carefully. She had considered the statue very lovely. She didn't realize until later that the man was the Enemy, and the baby was its Vessel.

She hurried up the steps of the keep, toward the double doors. Two axes swung together right in front of her, and she stumbled and almost fell backward.

"No entry to the Inquisitorial Keep," one of the two guardsmen announced. They didn't so much as look at her.

"But I *need* to speak to the Inquisitors."

"No entry to the Inquisitorial Keep."

"But—"

"Ellie, what are you doing? Get down from there!"

Ellie spun around. She'd been so determined to get inside the keep that she had failed to notice the cluster of men arguing nearby.

It would be hard to find a more eclectic-looking group anywhere in the City. Some were expensively and absurdly dressed in silk shirts with puffy sleeves, sporting large, elaborately styled mustaches. Others were towering and muscle-bound, their faces weathered from driving rain, their bare arms like tightly wound ropes of iron, fashioned from a life spent at sea. Some were dressed in vests, others animal furs. One wore a stuffed eel around his neck like a scarf. Another wore a wooden hat that resembled a ship.

A tall, broad-shouldered man was marching up the steps toward her. He had dark brown skin, a short black beard and mustache, and wore a long trailing coat of crushed red velvet. He carried a cane made from the tusk of a narwhal, and the pelt of a gigantic, shaggy black wolf was draped on his shoulders, its head dangling off to one side.

"They've taken my friend—" she began breathlessly, but before she could protest further the man had scooped her up in one arm and was carrying her down the steps.

"Hey, put me down!" she cried as the world spun around her. "I mean, sir, please could you put me down?"

She was placed gently at the foot of the steps. Lord Castion raised an eyebrow.

"Repeat after me," he said softly. "He's not your friend."

"Fine," Ellie admitted. "He's not—but they're making a huge mistake. He's not the Vessel."

Castion glanced at the keep, then put a finger to his lips. "Ellie, he *is* the Vessel, until the Inquisition say otherwise. And until they do, he's not your friend and never was, all right? You never even saw the wretch."

"But I *did*," Ellie said. "I rescued him from that whale!

And he couldn't breathe, so I—"

"*Ellie*," said Castion, kneeling down so their eyes were level. "The Inquisitors will ask him the questions and perform the tests. If he is proved to be the Vessel, he'll be burned alive, right here in this square. And anyone who helped him will be imprisoned. Or worse. So, please—promise me you won't get involved."

Ellie was shocked by his seriousness. Castion was normally such a kind man, quick to joke and laugh.

"I won't," she lied after some hesitation.

Castion removed one of his many rings from his finger to show her. This one was silver and had a little emblem of a spanner on it, her mother's personal symbol.

"I couldn't live with myself if anything happened to you," he said. "The Enemy hasn't taken a Vessel in more than twenty years; you don't know what it's like when that thing is at large. Distrust seeps through the streets. Friends turn on friends. The City is about to become a very different place."

Castion gave her a long stare, and she nodded uncomfortably.

"Is now really the time to be befriending street urchins, Castion?" said a snide voice. The other whale lords had paused in their arguing, and the one with the model ship on his head was staring at Ellie disdainfully.

Castion sighed and pushed himself upright on his cane.

He had lost his left leg as a young man—bitten off by a shark, or so the rumors went. Ellie's mother had built him a mechanical leg and foot, which clicked like clockwork when he walked.

"Show some respect, Archer," Castion said. "This is Hannah Lancaster's daughter. She's been fixing your harpoon guns for two years."

"That must be why they keep breaking," said Lord Archer. "The damn things miss most of the time. She's not a patch on her mother, clearly."

Ellie felt her cheeks go hot. She shuffled behind Castion, holding the sleeve of his coat. Castion squeezed her arm.

"That's funny," he told Archer lightly. "They never miss when I'm using them."

"We were discussing an important matter when you rushed off," said Archer. "Or weren't you listening?"

"My most sincere apologies," said Castion. "It's just difficult to take someone seriously when he's wearing a ship on his head."

Archer's lip curled. There was a bang, and they all turned toward the Inquisitorial Keep.

Hargrath was storming out of it.

"Ah, Inquisitor Hargrath," said Archer. "Just the man we wanted to see. We've been told by one of your lot that we're not allowed to collect the whale on top of St. Bart's Chapel."

Hargrath marched straight past them, looking tired and distracted.

"I say, Killian? What's the meaning of this?"

Hargrath paused momentarily, then turned, like a harassed parent speaking to a persistent child. "That whale had the Vessel living inside it."

"You mean, it was the vessel of a Vessel?" joked the youngest of the whale lords, with a nervous giggle. It seemed he had tried and failed to grow a mustache to match those of the others—it looked like bits of dog hair glued to his face. The other whale lords glared at him and he blushed.

"This is no laughing matter, Duncan," said Archer, turning back to Hargrath. "You took the Vessel out of the animal, though? That's good whale meat going to waste."

Hargrath chewed his tongue. "The whale has been tainted by the Vessel's presence and is not safe to eat."

"Ah, but see here," Archer continued, stepping over to Hargrath. The man was much shorter and leaner than the Inquisitor and Ellie thought he was either very brave or very stupid to get so close. "A beast that size is worth a lot of money. Twenty barrels of whale oil at least, and enough meat to feed an entire district for days. We're the whale lords—it's our job to catch whales."

"You didn't catch that whale," Hargrath growled. "A chapel did."

"That's besides the point," snapped Archer. He looked like he was about to say more but fell suddenly silent. Hargrath had placed his hand on the side of the whale lord's head.

Archer's voice went up an octave. "Just what do you think—" he began.

In one swift motion, Hargrath removed the whale lord's ship-hat. He gripped it in his broad gloved hand, then crushed it to tiny splinters. Archer stared in horror.

"N-now listen, I have many p-powerful friends," he stuttered furiously.

"Are any of them Inquisitors?" said Hargrath.

"No, but—"

"Then you have no powerful friends."

"Gentlemen," said Castion, stepping between Hargrath and Archer. "There's no need for an argument here." He rested his hand on Hargrath's shoulder.

"Don't touch me," Hargrath whispered, with such venom that Ellie was surprised he didn't run Castion through with his sword.

"Why so tense, Killian?" Castion asked. "The Vessel has been caught. Should we not be celebrating?"

Hargrath glowered resentfully. "The High Inquisitor is conducting his own tests on the boy. Until he is proved to be the Vessel, and until he is dead, there is no cause for celebration."

Castion smiled warmly. "Ah, but should the Enemy come you can just kill it again, can't you? Like last time."

Hargrath stared at Castion, a look of purest hatred in his eyes.

"Yes, we're in safe hands with you, Hargrath!" cheered the young whale lord with the patchy mustache. Hargrath snarled and took a step toward him, and the whale lord's face paled instantly.

Castion hurriedly patted Hargrath's shoulder. "He didn't mean anything by it, Killian. A poor choice of words, that's all. Now come, we won't touch the whale, as you command." He bowed deeply, flashing the same brilliant smile that had made him so beloved in the City. "The Guild of Whale Lords exists to serve the people. We are grateful to the Inquisition for all it does to keep the people safe."

Hargrath scowled. "You exist to serve yourselves. And only because the Inquisition allows it. You'll tow that whale five miles out to sea on the next tide and let it sink there. If I hear that any one of you has so much as skinned its tail to make a fancy coat, I'll have you rotting in a cell in some bleak corner of the City, until your own family has forgotten your name."

He marched away, pushing past Ellie as he went. "You should really get somewhere warm, Lancaster. You'll freeze to death in those wet clothes." He paused, and a nasty smile twisted his lips. "On the other hand, if you wait here long enough, there's bound to be a big fire."

And with that he strode off across the square and vanished into the streets.

The whale lords started squabbling again, arguing over who should tow the whale out to sea. As they did, Ellie looked up at the Inquisitorial Keep, trying to imagine what tests they'd be performing on Seth, picturing macabre torture instruments with sharp points and saw-toothed edges. She wondered if there was any way of rescuing him—some secret route into the Keep from the sewers and tunnels below. She would have to consult the architectural drawings in her library, she decided, slipping quietly away while Castion was distracted.

But Finn was waiting for her at the corner, wearing that pretty, angelic smile she hated so much.

"That didn't go well, did it?" he said.

"No," she snapped, without sparing him a second glance. He skipped after her, the trinkets around his neck jangling merrily with each step.

"So they're going to kill him?" he asked.

"They're still doing tests. But probably."

Finn shook his head. "That's terrible."

Up and down the market street the wealthy were out on their morning errands. Aristocrats, merchant barons, surgeons, and lawmen, dressed in fine waistcoats of crushed velvet, their coats lined with the furs of seals or red foxes from the hunting islands. Their wives patrolled alongside, festooned in strings of pearls, elevated on high-heeled boots. Finn could have passed for any one of their sons, what with his hale, rosy cheeks, clean golden locks, and the happy twinkle in his eyes.

"At times like this, it would be nice to have someone you can rely on," he said. "Someone clever and trust-worthy. It's not as if *Anna* can help you. And last time I checked, you don't have any other friends."

"I don't want your help, Finn."

"Oh," he said, looking crestfallen. "You mean you've figured out a way of rescuing the boy yourself?"

"I'll come up with something."

Finn nodded sincerely. "Yes, I'm sure you'll find a way to rescue him, Nellie; you're so clever, after all. I'm sure you'll find a way of rescuing an imprisoned boy from the most heavily guarded building in the City."

"He won't be in there the whole time. If they execute him, it's going to be public."

Finn stamped his foot hard on the cobbles. "Well, that's excellent. There you go—you can just whisk him away to safety while ten thousand people watch you do it! Simple!"

Ellie quickened her pace again, dodging a cartful of glistening mackerel pulled by two fishmongers.

"Do you think they'll be merciful?" said Finn. "I doubt

it, right? They'll want everyone to see the Vessel suffer. I'm sorry, Nellie—that will probably be difficult for you to watch. I'm so sorry. Will they do what they did to the twenty-ninth Vessel, do you think? With the hooks and the rats? Or maybe they'll dip him in pig's blood and throw him to the sharks?"

"They're going to burn him."

Finn sighed. "Well, that's definitely not the *worst* way they could do it. That's something at least. Maybe you shouldn't be so sad about it?"

Ellie wound in between tall aristocrats, some of whom wrinkled their noses at her. The upper parts of the City were home to only the wealthiest, and Ellie looked out of place in her wet, torn clothes stained with splotches of paint and grease, her hands covered in cuts and bruises.

Just then, a red-faced woman burst into the marketplace, her neck hidden entirely by gleaming pearls. "They've found it!" she cried. "They've found the Vessel!"

The aristocrats lost all composure. One threw her fox pelt into the air; another started to sing. Ellie winced and snuck off down an empty alleyway, but Finn nipped in after her, laughing to himself.

"Honestly," he said breathlessly, "it's like you're *trying* to lose me."

"I *am*!"

Ellie pulled a metal chestnut-sized sphere from the

pouch at her belt and hurled it down hard between them. There was a hiss and a heavy gray cloud of smoke spilled upward, filling the alley with a sharp, acrid smell.

Ellie could hear Finn's furious cries as she sped across the cobbles.

"D'you think that trick works on me, Ellie? Do you think I can't still find you? Fine, FINE! Abandon me again—leave me all alone! You're good at that. But you'll need me soon, you'll see!"

From the Diary of Claude Hestermeyer

I backed toward the wall. I kept trying to speak but no words would come.

"Claude, it's me," said Peter.

"No," I whispered. "No, it can't be. Peter died. He died in front of me."

"Yes, I did," said Peter.

"Get out."

"Claude—"

"Get out!" I yelled. "Whatever you are, GET OUT!"

I reached for the first thing I could find—an ink-pot. I hurled it at Peter but missed. The pot seemed to sail straight through him, spraying black ink across my books, my shelves, and the floorboards. Somehow, there wasn't a spot of ink on his crisp gray shirt.

I stared at him in disbelief. I steadied myself against the desk. "I must . . . I must get some rest. I'm seeing things."

"I am real, Claude," said Peter. "Very real. Come, let me prove it to you."

He held out his hand toward me. I hesitated, then took hold of it. His grip was firm, warm.

"But the inkpot?" I said.

"Is just an inkpot." He placed his other hand on top of mine. "We are bonded, you and I."

"But . . . you're an illusion. You're inside my head. You're not *real*."

"No, I'm real *and* I'm inside your head," said Peter. "I put myself there."

"Well take yourself out again!" I cried, wrenching my hand from his. I couldn't bear to look at him. His eyes were cold and distant, where Peter's had been sweet and compassionate.

"Again, I'm afraid that's not how this arrangement works."

I rummaged in my desk for the bottle I kept there. My head was swimming.

"Would you . . . like some whisky?" I said, sitting down. "Or would it pass straight through you?"

"I'm afraid I wouldn't even be able to lift the glass," said Peter. "Not unless you asked me to."

I buried my face in my hands. My heart hammered painfully.

"You're real, but you're in my head. You're in my office, but not really here at all. And you can move things, but only if I tell you to."

Peter nodded. "You know what that means, don't you?"

I did know. I knew the signs better than anyone—before this fateful day, my research had focused on studying the history of the Enemy.

I sipped some whisky and stared at the man who'd once been my best friend.

"It means I'm the Vessel."

5

ELLIE'S WORKSHOP

Ellie had grown up in her mother's workshop, in the wealthier upper parts of the City. When she was eight, her mother had died, and Ellie and her brother had moved into the orphanage down on Orphanage Street. When she was ten, her brother had died, and Ellie had moved into the abandoned blacksmith's across the way, to build a workshop of her own.

It had been Castion's idea. The City needed someone to carry on Ellie's mother's work. Hannah Lancaster had been a genius, transforming the City with her inventions; by the time she died, the City relied on her machines to catch whales, gather oysters, filter seawater, and more besides. Ellie didn't know much about her mother's inventions, not really, but she knew more than most, so Castion had convinced the City councilors to pay her a small wage to keep the machines in working order, and to create her own inventions too. Ellie's first invention had been a small rocket, powered by gunpowder, which she had proudly demonstrated in the workshop in front of Castion and Anna, aiming it out of the open window. Her second invention had been a sprinkler system.

The workshop was at street level, with a library in the loft and a small metalworks in the basement. It was a dizzying, confusing place, looking as it did like the insides of a busy and unfocused mind. It was a tall, unevenly shaped room, lined with shelves that towered to the rafters. The floor and the walls were wood-paneled, though a visitor would be forgiven for not realizing this, since there was little wall or floor space that wasn't covered in some way. Despite the size of the workshop, it had a musty, close feel, smelling of damp and paint and old books. It creaked and groaned beneath its own weight.

At no point did it appear to have been tidied. Discarded projects congregated in the corners, swept in that direction by their maker's changing moods, picked up months later, then thrown back again. Slab-like workbenches rose from the clutter of scrap metal, fallen paint pots, and open books. Delicate instruments for charting the weather lay strewn carelessly around. Glass jars stood in ranks upon splintery shelves, filled with dead things floating in yellow liquid: the coiled-up intestines of a giant sea bass, the barbed tail of a stingray. Reams of ink-smudged papers trailed from the wall to the floor, covered with drawings of bodies and faces and hands, of whales and icebergs and ships. Of things that wandered Ellie's dreams, and contraptions she'd built, or half built, or would build one day.

The door to the street was a large oak-paneled shutter. Mounted above it was a stuffed sunfish, its mouth parted perpetually in a vacant O, its glass eye drooping slightly from its socket. The skeleton of a giant turtle hung from the ceiling on iron chains, suspended from the thick brass pipes of the water tank. In the back right corner, a spiral staircase curled toward the loft: a half-floor Ellie had built as a library to accommodate the many books her mother had left her. The collection had since swollen to twice its original size, so the shelves of the library were packed to bursting.

On the ground floor, taking pride of place upon the central workbench, was a large harpoon gun. On the other benches were a brass telescope, a chemistry set, and a device that could generate electricity. Lying on the floor, meanwhile, were an open crate of fireworks, a working model of the solar system and—tonight at least—Ellie, who was curled up asleep on a pile of maps.

There was a knock at the door, and she startled awake, spitting out a mouthful of her own hair. She hadn't dried it properly after being dropped into the sea, and it had become a messy tangle that scratched against her face, crunchy with sea salt.

"Just a second!" she cried. She had fallen asleep, fully dressed, while examining the layout of the City sewers. She hobbled clumsily toward the door, cursing herself for having fallen asleep when there was a boy who needed her help. It was already dark outside the window.

The knock came again, louder this time, as if someone were banging their whole head against the door.

"I'm coming, Anna!"

Ellie set about undoing the many bolts on the front door, then rattled it along to one side on its metal wheels. There was a ripple of giggling and three tiny figures hurried in from the darkness. They were followed by Anna, who nodded lazily to Ellie and slouched inside.

"Hi," she said.

The three younger orphans—Fry, Ibnet, and Sarah—ogled the workbenches with wide eyes. Within seconds there was the crunch of something breaking underfoot.

"Watch where you're stepping!" Ellie scolded.

"Maybe if you cleaned up occasionally you wouldn't have this problem," said Anna.

"Don't *you* start. I've seen the state of your bedroom," said Ellie, rushing over to Ibnet, who was brushing his hair with a stuffed hedgehog. "I wish you'd warn me when you're bringing visitors." She pulled the hedgehog from the boy's grip. "Did you find anything out by the docks?"

"Yeah, I met this sailor called Darrius and he's going to teach me how to kill a seagull with just a—"

"I meant about *Seth*," Ellie said, whispering the name.

"Oh right, him. No, nothing. Don't touch those, Sarah."

The orphans were standing on tiptoe to inspect the glass jars, marveling at the dead things floating inside. Ellie glowered meaningfully at Anna.

"I couldn't disappoint them," said Anna, picking up an apple from one of the workbenches. "They said they wanted to see what 'crazy old Ellie' was up to."

"*Old?* I'm the same age as you! Careful with that!" she added—Fry had picked up a thick black clay tube from the ground, which had a whale carved on its side. She put the tube to her lips and blew. A horrible rasping sound trumpeted out the other end. The other two children covered their ears.

"Look, I'm busy right now," said Ellie, snatching the tube from Fry's hands. "I have work to do."

"You know you've got a sock in your hair, right?" said Anna, plucking it from on top of Ellie's head. "So have you figured out how to rescue Seth?"

"Who says I'm planning to rescue him?"

"It's obvious," said Anna, biting into her apple. "You've got that wild look in your eye. You get it when you're about to start work on a new invention."

Ellie looked at the orphans to make sure they weren't listening. "I've been thinking about it." She pointed to the open maps on the floor. "There are sewer tunnels running right under St. Ephram's Square, where Hargrath said the execution's going to be. It might be possible to get up *underneath* the bonfire and rescue Seth from on top of it."

Anna stared at Ellie, then spat out an apple seed. "You *are* crazy. There's no way that'll work. Why *do* you want to save him so much anyway? He didn't even seem that interesting."

"He'd just come out of a whale! How much more interesting do you want? They're going to kill him! If one of the orphans was drowning, you'd jump in to save them, right?"

"Yeah," said Anna, "but they're *my* orphans. He's not your responsibility; it's not like it's your fault he was caught."

"Yes, it is!" Ellie cried. Anna gave her a confused, disgruntled look. "I should have done more to save him."

"What more could you have done?" said Anna. "Hargrath threw you in the sea. You're being stupid."

But Ellie wasn't listening. Her thoughts were haunted by the image of Seth, trapped inside a cell, being kicked and punched by Inquisitors. Her tummy ached. "He'll die without my help."

"I heard he's the Vessel," said Fry, puffing her chest out proudly.

"I heard they're going to kill him!" said Sarah.

Ibnet giggled. "Yeah! Kill the Vessel! Kill the Vessel!"

"You're the Vessel!" Fry cried shrilly, pointing at Ibnet, and the two girls chased him around the workshop, cornering him between two bookshelves.

"Stand back!" Ibnet cried. "The Enemy's about to burst out of me!"

He performed a gruesome pantomime, falling to his knees with a horrid gurgling sound, clutching his chest like it was about to pop open. Sarah and Fry fell about, laughing hysterically.

"Will you shut up!" Ellie yelled. "This isn't a joke—a boy is going to die!"

"We heard you kissed him, Ellie?" said Fry, grabbing a book of anatomical drawings from the shelves and leafing through it. "I hope you didn't get corrupted by the Enemy."

"It wasn't a kiss—it was mouth-to-mouth resuscitation," said Ellie wearily. "Besides, that's not how it works—the Enemy is only ever inside *one* Vessel at a time. It can't move between people as it pleases. Once it's chosen a Vessel, it's stuck in that person until they're executed, or until the Enemy can take its own physical form."

"We *know* that," said Fry, rolling her eyes.

"Ellie, is it true you've built a boat that can swim underwater, like a fish?" said Ibnet, rattling a brass telescope against his ear.

"It's *supposed* to swim underwater," Ellie muttered. "Only it kind of, well . . . sinks."

"Can we have a go in it? We won't break anything," he said, rattling the telescope so hard it slipped from his hand.

There was another knock at the door. Ellie groaned. She felt uncomfortable with so many people in her workshop. "Who else did you invite?" she said, glaring at Anna, who had cleared a space on one of the workbenches and was now slumped across it.

"Nothing to do with me," she said, her mouth full of apple.

Ellie rolled the door aside and Castion came hobbling in from the darkness, droplets of rainwater on his beard.

"Good evening, Ellie," he said, bowing. "And Anna too, I see! And who are these mighty heroes?" he added, smiling at the three younger orphans, who'd fallen silent, staring at Castion with wide eyes.

"Problems with your leg?" Ellie asked.

"Yes," Castion sighed.

Lord Castion's left leg was the pinnacle of Ellie's mother's engineering. Every time Ellie was called upon to fix it, she was both awestruck and distressed by its intricacy. Its insides were made up of tiny cogs and counterweights and moving rods, arranged in a mechanism so complex it made her eyes water. She tried her very best to mend it, but always with mixed results; Castion had never walked so well since Ellie's mother died.

He pulled off his boot and rolled up his trouser leg, revealing the brass shell of the leg and foot, like part of a suit of armor. He undid the straps and yanked the leg off without ceremony, glancing about for some free workbench space to put it on. Ellie shooed Anna off the workbench she'd been lying across and took the leg carefully from Castion.

The younger orphans sidled over, gazing up at Castion in reverent silence. Ellie wondered if they had ever seen a whale lord up close. Sarah examined the wolf's head on his shoulder, touching its nose. Castion removed a killer whale's tooth from his coat pocket and placed it in her hand.

"A present," he said, and the three orphans gawped at the tooth like it were some holy relic.

"Sir?" said Sarah, unable to contain herself. "Have you ever nearly drowned?"

Ibnet shoved her aside. "Did you ever ride a ship through a storm?"

Fry shoved him aside. "Is it true you killed a giant squid with your bare hands?"

Castion held his hand up to silence them. Then he leaned down, favoring them with a slow, brilliant smile. "Of course I did," he said. "How do you think I lost my leg?"

They watched him in wonder, their eyes glistening. But the silence was too brief; with a violent shriek they fell on each other in a heap, wrestling for the whale's tooth.

"I thought you lost your leg to a shark," Ellie grumbled, unscrewing the mechanical leg's outer casing. She was still angry with Castion for not helping her earlier.

He shuffled his stool closer with a squeak of wood. "Listen, I'm sorry I was so stern with you up in the square," he said. "Are you all right?"

"They're going to kill that boy," she said.

Castion grimaced. "They might find him innocent," he said. "Ellie, you didn't know him before today, did you?"

"No."

"So why do you care about him so much?"

"I think she fancies him," said Anna, who was now stretched out on the floor. Ellie grabbed a blanket and threw it over Anna's face.

"It's because he's just a *boy*," she told Castion. "He's innocent—it's not fair."

Anna was laughing underneath the blanket, making it wobble up and down.

"Stop it. I do *not* fancy him!" Ellie cried, giving Anna a light kick.

"Children!" said Castion, slamming his hand against a workbench.

Ellie and the other orphans fell silent. Anna pulled the blanket from her face, holding it meekly to her chest. Castion's eyes were wide in the flickering lamplight. "You need to understand how serious this is. If he *is* the Vessel, then you must forget you ever met him, and you must *not* do anything to help him. People who associate with the Vessel are not looked on kindly by the Inquisition." He took a deep breath. "After the twelfth Vessel was executed, his family was hanged too, because they'd been hiding him in the cellar of their house. His whole *family*, Ellie. Except for his eight-year-old daughter."

"Because she was so young?" said Anna.

Castion's gaze fell to the floor. "No. Because she was the one who told the Inquisition where to find him."

Ellie felt her chest tighten. Anna looked at the younger orphans. "That's horrible," she said.

"No, it's *necessary*," said Castion. "You don't know the power of the Enemy. You've never seen it."

He turned his cane over in his hands. He was silent for a long time.

Ellie took a tiny step toward him. "Sir . . . have . . . have you seen it?"

But Castion just continued to stare down at his narwhal-tusk cane. Ellie noticed his fingers were trembling. Then he sat up straighter and looked to the door.

"What's that noise?" he said.

Ellie heard it too. People were shouting outside. She felt a chill in her heart and rushed to slide open the door. The cheers swept in with the freezing night air.

"It's him!"

Girls and boys were running along Orphanage Street, crying up to the windows and balconies above. In the distance, a mighty bell began to toll.

"It *is* him! It *is* him!"

One girl skipped across the cobbles, trailing in the wake of her bright-eyed friends. Ellie grabbed her arm as she raced past. "What's happening?" she said urgently.

"That boy they found in the whale. He's the Vessel! The High Inquisitor says so. Now they can kill him and we'll be safe again for years and years."

Ellie's stomach twisted worse than ever and she thought she might be sick. Seth was going to die. He was going to die and it was all her fault. She had to do something—she *had* to save him—even if he was to be executed the very next morning.

"When is it going to happen?" Ellie said. "When will the execution take place?"

The girl grinned happily in the glow of the oil lamps. "Why, it's happening now."

6

JOY AT AN EXECUTION

Drops of rain flecked Ellie's face. The children rushed by and she stared and wasn't sure any of it was really happening.

Castion squeezed her shoulder. "I'm sorry, Ellie," he said, "but this *must* happen. The Vessel has to be killed before the Enemy can use him to take its own physical form. Once that's done, it might be decades before it claims another Vessel. Years of peace and safety."

"I need to go!" Ellie cried, breaking into a run.

"*Ellie,*" Castion yelled. "You don't want to see this!"

As Ellie raced down Orphanage Street, other city folk appeared in doorways, throwing on coats and scarves. Everyone was smiling. Overhead, fireworks erupted in the cloudy night sky. Ellie was dismayed at the sight of them—they were fireworks *she'd* designed, exploding in swirling, corkscrewing showers of gold and silver.

"Oi! Wait for me!"

Anna crashed after her. "Put this on," she said, draping Ellie's coat across her shoulders. It was almost dry now after spending the day by the boiler.

"What do I do, Anna?" said Ellie. "They're going to kill him." She patted her trouser pockets. "Oh no, I forgot my keys!"

There was a clinking of metal. "Here they are," said Anna.

"Where were they?" Ellie said, relieved.

"In your trousers. Five minutes ago, anyway."

"*Anna!* I've told you to stop pickpocketing me! And stop smirking too. This isn't funny—an innocent boy is going to die!"

She picked up her pace. The dark streets seemed much more menacing than usual, their cragged spires and chimneys like broken bones. Children skipped and danced in the drizzling rain. Stifling clouds of smoke filled the alleyways as vendors tossed fish into pans of burning oil, racing to turn a quick profit. As Ellie and Anna neared St. Ephram's Square, the crowd grew thicker. Ellie tried to squeeze through but kept treading on people's feet.

"Hey, watch where you're going!"

"Careful!"

Ellie stood on tiptoe but failed to see over the shoulders

of the people around her. She had no idea how many there were—she felt like she was stranded in an infinite sea of revelers. They smelled of tobacco and wine, their breath coiling over their heads. At last Ellie pushed forward into the square, where a pile of logs sat atop a high platform.

The bonfire.

Ellie's head spun; she didn't know what she was going to do when she reached the bonfire. She just kept going, nipping between boisterous sailors and smiling old women and parents with children bouncing on their shoulders.

"Ellie!" Anna called. "Ellie, slow down!"

She was bigger than Ellie and seemed to be having a harder time weaving through the crowd. She was less reckless too—already Ellie's cheek burned from where she'd been bashed by an elbow. She shoved and ducked and the pile of logs grew taller and taller overhead.

"Hello."

Finn was standing next to her. There was a smudge of soot on his face and he had a spanner in his hand. His cheeks were rosy and he looked even more pleased with himself than usual.

"What are you doing?" Ellie whispered.

"Helping!" Finn said cheerily. "I've got everything planned out, you see. Gosh, look how happy everyone is! Almost seems a shame to spoil their fun."

"I told you, Finn, I *don't* need your help."

"Why not?"

"Because your help always comes at a price!"

"Well, it's not like you have a choice. Unless . . ." He raised an eyebrow. "Unless you *want* him to die? Now listen, I was watching when they built that platform"—he turned the spanner over in his hand—"and I've got it all figured out. Imagine the greatest magic trick you've ever seen—this will be even better."

"Finn, I told you, I—"

"Don't need your help," he said, imitating her in a childish voice. "Saints, you're so boring, Nellie. Fine, just let me know when you change your mind."

And he turned and darted into the crowd. Ellie watched him go and was so distracted that she failed to notice two men gripping each other and jumping so gleefully that they crashed into her and knocked her to the ground. She fell onto all fours, smacking her head on someone's knee on the way down.

"Ellie!"

Warm hands lifted her, and her heart leapt as she caught the familiar smell of Anna's blue sweater.

"You're going to get yourself *killed*," said Anna, hugging Ellie firmly as if to stop her from running off again.

"We have to do something!"

"We *can't* do anything!"

There was a sudden, jubilant, deafening roar from all

around that could only mean one thing—Seth was being brought out.

"Anna, I need to get on your shoulders!" said Ellie. Anna grumbled but knelt down, and Ellie clambered awkwardly onto her back.

"Ow, you're pulling my hair!" Anna complained. She stood up, and Ellie rose above the heads of the crowd, the icy wind biting her cheeks. A firework illuminated the entire square, revealing just how many people there were: ten thousand at least, spilling out in every direction across the square and into the streets beyond. Ellie felt sick at the sight, like she'd opened a cupboard to find a nest of woodlice within.

Then Ellie saw the doors of the Inquisitorial Keep swing open. A procession emerged.

At its head was the drummer, a brawny man with beaters the size of a blacksmith's hammer in each hand, the drum strapped to his front. Then came the High Inquisitor—an old man in a long black greatcoat—followed by a host of other Inquisitors, including Hargrath. Behind them came a cage carried by four guardsmen. The crowd cheered and hissed, flecks of spit filling the air.

Inside the cage was Seth.

Ellie bit her fist. Seth's skin was bruised and cut. His hands were bound to an iron pole, and they'd hosed the whale blood off him and dressed him in a tattered pair of trousers. He was awake, though barely—his eyes were half closed and he looked at the crowd as if in a dream. Twenty crossbows were pointed at him.

The cage was hauled up the stairs of the platform to the peak of the bonfire. The drumming continued. The crowd fell silent.

Seth blinked. He seemed to be waking up, and stood tall inside his cage, arms tensed like a cornered animal. In the glow of the torchlight, Ellie saw tears flowing freely down his cheeks. He must have realized he was surrounded by madmen. He must have realized he was alone.

He lurched forward, baring his teeth, and hundreds of people in the crowd screamed. Hargrath calmly pulled his dart-gun from his pocket. He fired, and Seth grunted. His head drooped and the crowd sighed in relief.

The High Inquisitor climbed the platform, to stand at the base of the bonfire. He was so old that his skin was stretched like a mask across his skull. He paused for breath, then spoke in a rasping voice that echoed around the square.

"In the name of the Twenty-six Saints and Their Most Holy Inquisition, I pronounce you Vessel, corrupt and diabolical host to the Great Enemy of Humankind, and sentence you to die."

Ellie hugged her stomach, her fingers trembling. A desperate impulse crept in, her thoughts flashing like lightning. She wanted to be rid of this feeling. She looked around, and found Finn quickly, easily recognizable by his shining golden hair. He was hanging from the statue of an angel at the edge of the square.

He was looking right at her.

Ellie toyed with the hole in her coat sleeve, nervously pushing her thumb through it. She took a deep breath, burying her lingering doubts.

Then she nodded.

Finn grinned, leaping down from the statue and skipping into the crowd. Ellie waited, counting the moments in painful heartbeats.

But nothing happened. One guardsman stepped toward the bonfire with a burning torch, holding it to the kindling at the bonfire's edge. It caught, and orange sprites of fire danced up the wood, sending off wisps of curling smoke. Ellie dug her nails into her palms. The crowd held their breath in anticipation.

Then there was a hiss, and a ripple of bangs like cannon shots. Fireworks streaked upward around Seth's cage, spurting showers of sparks into the crowd with a sound like rushing water. The noise became deafening, the thundering blaze so bright it appeared as a single column of blinding light, like a star being born at the center of the crowd.

Ellie couldn't see Seth's cage through all the light.

Somehow, Finn had managed to slip fireworks *inside* the bonfire. A young man barged past Anna as he tried to flee, and Ellie was forced to slide off her shoulders before they both fell.

Without warning, the light vanished all at once, leaving a thick blanket of smoke that rolled out into the crowd, filling the square with coughs and panicked cries.

"Secure the cage!" roared Hargrath somewhere close by. Ellie tried to waft away the smoke around her, eyes watering.

Please, please let him be gone.

"Watch out!" someone cried.

The fireworks had set the logs alight, and now the flames were spreading. Hargrath leapt up one side of the bonfire, climbing to its peak. Ellie clenched her teeth. Hargrath hauled himself to the top just as the last of the smoke cleared.

The cage stood with its door hanging open.

It was empty.

Ellie sank gratefully into Anna's side. She felt suddenly exhausted, like all the substance had gone from inside her.

"He's escaped!" someone cried.

"NO!" screamed another.

A woman next to Ellie scooped up her wailing child, pleading for the sailors behind to let her through. A bottle was dropped and crushed underfoot. There were shouts and screams as the crowd was seized by panic, lurching like a herd of startled sheep.

Anna huddled close to Ellie, frightened by the change in the crowd. Ellie grabbed her hand and gripped it tightly.

"It's okay," she said, summoning the strength to move. "We'll be okay. Come on, let's go."

All around, children were crying for their parents. An old man tripped and was sucked down beneath the press of bodies. Three pale Inquisitors raced by without stopping to help. Ellie rushed Anna from the square, into an alleyway so narrow their arms brushed the sides. They squeezed by a preacher, staring vacantly at the bonfire like a man in a daydream. He dug his hands into his hair, and terror poured into his eyes.

"The Enemy!" he cried. "THE ENEMY WALKS AMONG US!"

FROM THE DIARY OF CLAUDE HESTERMEYER

There is some great commotion in the City tonight. I can hear fireworks and shouting. Smoke rises above the rooftops. I have locked myself away in my office for some peace and quiet—I feel compelled to record my experiences of being the Vessel. I am a scholar after all, and this is a unique opportunity to further the learned community's understanding of the Enemy.

After our first encounter, I was shaken. I have lived my whole life being afraid of the Vessel, like any good citizen, but now that I *am* the Vessel, I can't see any reason why people should fear me. I'm not strong, I'm certainly not in the best of health, despite being only twenty-five, and I'm not nearly so clever as I like to pretend.

Two days after the funeral, I was sitting by the fountain in St. Ephram's Square, staring up at the statue of the Enemy on top of the Inquisitorial Keep. Then I realized the *actual* Enemy was sitting right next to me.

"So, nobody can see you but me?" I said to him.

"That's correct," he said.

The Enemy looks just like Peter. Reading back

over my diary, I see I first described him as cold and distant, but that must have been the shock, because this Peter is just as warm as I remember the real Peter being.

We went for a stroll to the burnt-out Warrens, where gangs of ragged children were play-fighting in the ruins. I tried to imagine what the Warrens might have looked like before the Great Fire, when the Enemy set light to a vat of whale oil, stalking through the streets, killing hundreds of people as the fire drove them from their homes.

"You've been kind to me so far," I said, watching a flock of gulls wheeling above us. "But I know how this works. You won't stay inside my head forever. I know you'll eventually assume a form of your own, emerging from my body. And I know I won't survive the process."

"And how do you know that?" said the Enemy.

I laughed. "Because that's what always happens! The Enemy is a parasite. Like one of those crook wasps that lay their eggs inside other insects."

"How poetic."

"The egg hatches, and the larva feeds off its host, until eventually it grows large enough to *kill* its host, then spreads its wings and flies away. But . . . I don't *feel* like you're feeding off me."

"Maybe the stories are all wrong," said the Enemy. "Maybe I'm not so evil as everyone says."

I shook my head, pointing around us to the crumbled husks of three hundred little buildings.

"The evidence is against you there, I'm afraid."

IT WALKS AMONG US

The bell of the Inquisition tolled above, a cold, heavy sound that startled roosting seagulls into flight. Doors banged, keys rattled, heavy bolts thudded into place. Children were hushed, shutters were closed. Prayers were muttered to the saints. High overhead, a cloud of firework smoke drifted across the rooftops, hiding the moon from view. Ellie and Anna scurried across the cobblestones, splashing through puddles. The streets were a blue-gray haze of mist and rain.

"He just . . . vanished," said Anna. "He *must* be the Vessel. How else could he have gotten off that bonfire? Unless—" She looked at Ellie in horror. "Oh no, you didn't—"

Ellie's throat tightened. "Of course not," she said weakly. Anna couldn't know—she *couldn't*.

"You did, didn't you?" said Anna. "The fireworks were exactly your style—you found some secret passage beneath the square and used the fireworks as a distraction and broke him out of the cage and—"

"*Shh!*" Ellie hissed, glancing at the tenements around them. Who knew who might be listening from behind locked doors? "I was with you the whole time, remember?" she whispered. "And I was in the workshop all afternoon."

But Anna didn't look convinced. She stared across the street, at the cramped, dismal-looking coal cellar next to the orphanage, its door hanging from its hinges. She sighed. Her eyes were big and glossy in the moonlight.

"You would tell me if you were up to something, right? I don't want anything bad to happen to you."

Ellie nodded, and felt a painful stab of guilt. Anna was her best friend but there were some things she could never know about. Finn was one of them.

"I'm tired. I should go to bed," Ellie said. It was true—she felt like she would collapse at any moment.

Anna looked her up and down. "Yeah, you look terrible—I think you've caught a cold. I told you to dry off after Hargrath dropped you in the sea. Why don't you sleep in the orphanage? It's much warmer than your freezing workshop."

Ellie hesitated.

"You wouldn't have to use your old room," Anna

continued, seemingly encouraged. "Emma's got lice and they've quarantined her in a room by herself, so there's a free bed next to mine. But there's no lice in it now!" she added hastily.

Ellie shook her head. "Thanks, but I'll be better in my workshop."

Anna glumly dragged her toe through a puddle. "Knew I shouldn't have mentioned the lice," she muttered. They hugged goodnight, and Ellie squeezed Anna more tightly than she would normally have done.

Ellie was still unlocking the workshop door when she noticed two guardsmen walking up the street toward her.

"Um . . . hello?" she said nervously.

"Eleanor Lancaster?"

"Yes?"

"Lord Castion's asked us to stand watch outside your workshop tonight."

"Oh. Why?"

"He didn't say."

Ellie scowled, wondering how much Castion had paid them. He was probably worried that Seth would come looking for her. She muttered a goodnight, then slunk inside, heaving the door closed and slamming the heavy bolts into their latches.

"I have to find him," she whispered, fiddling with the hole in her coat sleeve. She fished out a match from her pocket, lit the whale-oil lamp hanging by the door, then darted across the workshop, weaving in between work-benches, towers of books, and piles of scrap metal. She bounded toward the door of her bedroom, flinging her coat on the back of a chair and tying her hair up. Escaping her workshop without the guardsmen noticing would be no problem—there was a door in the basement that led to the sewers. First, though, she needed some sort of disguise, so she could move through the City unrecognized. She lit another lamp by her bedroom door, then stepped inside.

Seth was lying unconscious on the floor.

Ellie scrabbled for the doorframe, a hand to her mouth. He was still dressed in ragged trousers, his black hair wild as ever. His feet were scratched and dirty and the bruis-ing on his chest and face looked terrible up close: angry blotches of red and purple. Ellie looked over her shoul-der, fully expecting to find Finn lurking somewhere in the workshop, waiting to surprise her. But she couldn't see him anywhere. She gazed back at Seth in amazement, until a sharp instinct pressed in on her.

He was in her bedroom.

She had to get him out again.

She bent and tried to lift him, but he was much too heavy—the moment she had him up, her whole body was wrenched back down. Ellie eased him to the floor, none too gently, his head lolling toward her. His face was startling, his large, closed eyes and wide cheekbones giving him an appearance that was almost feline. She slid her arms under his, his trousers rustling as she strained and heaved and dragged him across the floor. She hauled him out of her room, sweating already, and his eyes opened.

They caught each other's gaze, and it was like they'd both woken from a nightmare. Ellie fell backward, smacking against a workbench. Seth leapt to his feet, breathing heavily. His eyes darted around the workshop, pausing on the skeleton of the giant turtle, on the mountain of books clustered at the center of the room, on the harpoon gun, its sharp point glinting in the lamplight.

"Where are my brothers and sisters?" he whispered.

"Um . . . I don't know," Ellie said. She wondered if his memory was coming back. "Did you see them in the crowd? Do you know their names? What do they look like?"

Seth stared at his feet, frowning. "I can't remember." He looked at her seriously. "But I think they need my help."

All of a sudden, he clutched a hand to his throat, like he'd been slapped there. "Water," he yelled hoarsely. "Water!"

"Don't *shout!*" Ellie hissed. "There are two guardsmen right outside."

Seth shook his head. "So?" he wheezed. "What can they do to me?"

Ellie screwed up her face, confused by his confidence. "Kill you, that's what."

"I'll tear their heads off with my bare hands."

"Oh yeah, I bet you would," she said scornfully. "Don't be stupid—they'll arrest you and march you right back to the bonfire."

"I'd like to see them try."

Ellie frowned. "They *did* try. And they would have succeeded if I hadn't rescued you."

But Seth had doubled over, wheezing and pawing at his throat. Ellie supposed he hadn't had anything to drink all day.

"All right, wait," she said, and hurried toward a sink in the corner. There was a chime of glass against glass and she turned to see that Seth had removed a jar of yellow liquid from one of the shelves. It had a dead rat in it.

"What are you doing?" she said. He had taken the lid off, pressing the edge of the jar to his lips. He coughed and held the jar out at arm's length, causing the rat to swish to one side. Liquid spilled over the edge.

"What *is* that?" he spat.

"It's preserving fluid, you idiot! I'm *getting* you some water."

"Why do you have all these dead animals?"

"I'm studying them, obviously," Ellie said. She filled a mug with water and rushed back to Seth, shoving it in his hands and carefully returning the dead rat to the shelf. "The experiments are really interesting, actually—"

"More," said Seth.

Ellie stared in disbelief at the empty mug. "How did you drink that so fast?"

Seth just stared back at her. "It's you," he said. "You were there this morning. On the roof."

"Of course I was," Ellie said resentfully. How could he have forgotten that she'd *saved* him from suffocating to death inside a whale?

"You saved my life," he said, and shook Ellie's hand in both of his. "Thank you . . . Ellie?"

Ellie nodded, then her stomach turned as Seth pulled her sharply forward, so his mouth was right next to her ear.

"Ellie, I need to get off this island," he whispered. "Everyone seems to want to kill me, and I don't think I can stop them all, if I'm honest."

"You can't stop *any* of them," she said, shoving him roughly away. She was starting to regret risking so much to rescue this boy. He seemed half wild, and entirely unpredictable. "And you can't get out of the City, either."

"Why not?"

"Because there's nowhere else to go."

"There must be other cities."

"Other cities?" Ellie said in astonishment, taking a step

away from him. "Of course there aren't any other cities! There's just *the* City."

For emphasis, she pointed at a faded yellow map pinned to the wall. A single large, jagged shape took up a third of the paper. It was simply labeled THE CITY.

"Doesn't it have a name?" Seth asked.

"It might have, thousands of years ago. It used to be much, much bigger. Most of it's underwater now."

"What about these?" said Seth, pointing to a scattering of other, much smaller shapes around it.

"Those are the farming and hunting islands," said Ellie.

"I can live on one of them, then. I bet I'm good at hunting."

"You wouldn't last a day. Also, farmers live on the farming islands, and they'd be just as afraid of you as people are here."

Seth squinted at the map. "You get all your food from *these* tiny islands? But there were thousands of people in that square."

"The whale lords get most of the food for the City. They have these huge ships that they use to fish and hunt whales. It means they're very powerful. They practically rule the City."

"Those men who put me in the cage . . . were they whale lords?"

Ellie shook her head. "They were Inquisitors. They

protect the City from the Enemy. They really *do* rule the City, although you don't see them very often. Well, until now. What's wrong?"

Seth was clutching his head and gritting his teeth. "That noise." He looked around. "Where is it coming from?"

Ellie frowned. "What noise?"

"*That* noise," he said, looking at her with wide eyes. He pointed to the ceiling. "Listen, it keeps rising and falling. What is it?"

"What does it sound like?" said Ellie uncertainly.

"Like a . . . *voice*. A voice shouting, only I can't figure out the words. You can hear it, can't you?"

Ellie listened, but heard only silence. She grimaced in apology. "No . . . Um, Seth, did you tell the Inquisition you could hear this voice?"

"What? No. I don't think so. Maybe. I can't remember a lot of it. They spent most of the time"—he looked briefly ashamed—"hitting me."

The memory of this seemed to come flooding back to him. "That man with one arm. He *beat* me!" he roared, his whole body trembling with rage.

Ellie pulled him by the elbow. *"Shut up,"* she hissed, looking at the door. "You'll get us both caught!"

"I have to get out of here," said Seth. "Right now." He rushed toward the door, but only managed three long paces before tripping. "Ow!"

"Be *quiet!*"

Seth grabbed his foot and held it up, revealing a bloody gash across the sole. He picked up a jagged curl of metal, one edge now glistening with blood, then glared resentfully around the workshop.

"Don't you ever clean up?" he said, pointing to a crumpled dress smeared with paint. Ellie's clothes were strewn everywhere, together with half-empty glasses of water, cups of tea, scraps of orange peel, and slivers of apple core. He stared at a sheet of paper nearby. A stick of charcoal lay on it that had since been stepped on, a fine black powder sprayed across the floorboards. "How can you stand to live in this mess?"

"Listen, they *will* kill you if you go out there."

Seth paused. "Because I'm the 'Vessel,'" he said, remembering. He sat down on the edge of a workbench, inspecting the cut on his foot. "They said I had the Enemy inside me. Who's the Enemy?"

Ellie sighed. "The last god."

"What happened to all the others?"

"They drowned the world," said Ellie. "Only the Enemy tricked them, and they ended up drowning too. The City is all that's left. It was built on one of the highest mountains—the only parts that still stick above the sea."

"So where *is* the Enemy?" said Seth.

"Well, it depends." Ellie leaned against a bookcase.

"Sometimes it's floating around in the air, as just a harmless spirit. But eventually it chooses a Vessel. Then it lives inside the Vessel's mind, growing stronger and stronger, until it gets so strong that it can burst out of the Vessel in its true physical form. It's called 'manifesting.'"

"What's that like?" asked Seth.

Ellie shrugged. "I've never seen it—the last time it happened was twenty-three years ago. But apparently the Enemy's true form is terrifying—stronger than ten men and much, much faster. That's why the Inquisitors try to find and kill the Vessel *before* the Enemy can manifest. But, if it does, the Inquisitors have to destroy it. Usually it kills a lot of people first. The person who defeats it gets to become a saint when they die."

"And what happens to the Enemy?"

Ellie shrugged again. "No one really knows. It goes away for a while. Sometimes many years. But it always comes back eventually."

"So they think I have this Enemy inside me," Seth said, putting a hand to his heart. For the first time, he didn't seem so sure of himself. "That's why all those people were so happy to watch me die?"

"Unfortunately, yes."

"But . . . how do I know I'm not the Vessel?"

"You'd know if you were. You'd be able to see the Enemy. That's the Vessel's 'gift.'"

Seth thought about this for a moment. "Well then, I know what I have to do," he said.

"What?"

"Find the real Vessel and kill him."

Ellie's breath caught. "*What?* No, that's stupid."

Seth rolled his eyes. "Well, of course it wouldn't make sense to you. You don't have an entire city trying to kill you. I'm leaving and you can't stop me." He headed for the door.

"Wait!" Ellie raced to cut him off. "If those guards outside see you, the Inquisitors will *know* I'm helping you and I'll probably get burned alive too. That's not the kindest way to repay me for saving your life twice in one day."

"Twice?" said Seth, frowning.

Ellie folded her arms. "Who else do you think rescued you from that bonfire?" she said, feeling another twinge of guilt at this sort-of lie.

"*You* rescued me?"

"Well, I had a . . . friend," Ellie said. "He was able to get you out."

"How? In front of all those people?"

Ellie scrunched up her face. She didn't like talking about Finn. "He's good at that sort of thing."

"He must be a wise man."

Ellie shifted uncomfortably. "He's a boy. A very clever boy. But not always nice."

"Then why did he save my life?"

"Because I asked him to. We've known each other a long time. And he enjoys proving he's cleverer than me."

"What's his name?"

"Oh, um . . . Finn," Ellie said, swallowing.

"He must have risked his life to save me. Can I meet him?"

"No," Ellie said flatly. "He's, um, he's got a terrible temper. Better not to be around him."

She was worried Seth would keep asking questions, but he seemed to have lost interest. His eyes drifted around the workshop, then rested on the window above. It was set into the sloping roof, and had a ladder leading up to it.

"I bet there are no guards out there," he said with a wicked smile.

"Don't you dare," said Ellie.

But he was already racing toward it, nimbly bounding over workbenches and leaping between Ellie's chemistry set and the shelves of bottled powders. He reached the ladder.

"Stop!" Ellie yelled.

Seth turned. "What are you doing?" he sighed. Ellie had grabbed the harpoon gun and was aiming it straight at him.

"Miss Lancaster?" came a muffled voice from the street. "Are you okay in there?"

"I'm fine, thank you!" Ellie called. "Just dealing with

some, uh . . . rats." She looked pointedly at Seth. "Ungrateful rats."

"What's that?" said Seth.

"A harpoon gun, obviously. My mom built it. The whale lords use these to kill things much bigger and less annoying than you."

"You won't shoot me," he said.

"I will."

Seth peered curiously into her eyes, then laughed. "No, you won't. I can tell."

He started to climb. Ellie's hands trembled on the harpoon gun, then she groaned and let it go. Looking around, she spotted a brass contraption by her foot. It resembled a small, portable cannon with a clockwork winding mechanism on the side.

"I'll use this instead!" she announced, pointing it at him, finger on the trigger.

Seth sneered. "Did your mom make that too?"

"*No*, I did. It's ingenious—it fires a big net. It's meant for catching bears and wolves, but you'll do."

Seth snorted. "I don't believe you. You don't seem very smart."

"I am smart!" Ellie bristled furiously. "I spent months on this. And I didn't get any help—I didn't even use my mom's books!"

Seth kept climbing, and Ellie muttered a curse then pulled the trigger.

There was a loud *thunk* and a screech of metal and something smacked Ellie hard in the nose. Pain exploded across her face.

"Ow!" she cried, dropping the net-cannon and clasping her hands to her nose. "No, no, *no*," she muttered. She heard the rungs of the ladder juddering—Seth must have gotten away. Her stupid, worthless invention!

A hand touched her shoulder, making Ellie yelp in surprise. She looked up into Seth's dark eyes.

"Oh," she said.

"Are you all right?"

Ellie stared at him, astonished. Seth leaned in close, touching his hand gently to her face. "Does it hurt?"

She nodded, noticing blood on Seth's fingers.

"I think you've broken your nose," he said.

"What?" Ellie moaned, touching it lightly with her fingers. "Are you sure?"

Seth nodded. "It's sort of . . . turned to one side."

"It already did that!"

"Oh," said Seth. "Well then it's not broken. Here." He picked up a brass cylinder from the ground. "This is what burst out of that net-thing."

Ellie grabbed it from his hand. "Why are you still here?" she said sourly, picking up a cloth and pressing it to her nose to stem the bleeding.

Seth looked up at the window. "I don't know. Maybe you're right. You seem very . . . persistent."

He winced and put his hands to his temples.

"The voice again?" Ellie asked.

He nodded. "It won't go away." He squeezed his eyes shut. "It keeps crashing and crashing. How can you not hear it?"

"Look, you can't go out there," said Ellie. "There's too much you don't understand."

Seth nodded distractedly. "Pinch your nose. It will help stop the bleeding."

"How do you know that?"

Seth thought about this. "I'm not sure," he said. He looked exhausted—the skin around his eyes puffy, his forehead clammy. He slumped down on the floor, leaning against a workbench. "What sort of city tries to burn a boy alive, Ellie?"

There was shouting in the street as a crowd clamored by. They sounded afraid.

Ellie looked down at Seth and shrugged in apology. "This one."

From the Diary of Claude Hestermeyer

I have learned some upsetting news.

Peter—the *real* Peter—was fond of gambling. Much too fond. I had thought he'd learned to control his habits; we had worked hard at it together. But it seems he had carried on in secret and incurred a large debt. Now, the moneylenders have come to collect.

From Peter's father.

I went to visit him today, to see how he'd been coping since the funeral. He had not been coping. His face was badly bruised and he needed my help to walk from the front door to his chair. He winced with every step, clutching his side.

"Who did this to you?" I asked. I could not bear to see him this way—first for him to lose his son, and now this. I felt somehow that it was my fault, for failing to help Peter deal with his problem.

I returned glumly to my office that night, trying to figure out how I could raise the money to clear the debt.

"I could help," said the Enemy as we walked up the street toward the university.

"Hmm?" I said distractedly.

The Enemy smiled. "You remember who I am, don't you?"

"But you can't *do* things," I said. "You can't even hold a glass of whisky."

"I thought you studied the Enemy for a living? I *can* do things if you ask me to. Try it," he said. "Ask me to pick up that starfish."

I stared down. Sure enough, there was a starfish lying on the cobblestones, gray and long since dried up.

"All right," I said. "Pick up that starfish."

To my amazement, he bent over, picked up the dead starfish, and put it right in my hand. It wasn't an illusion—I could feel the weight of it. I found myself suddenly light-headed.

"Now try to think bigger," the Enemy said. "*Much* bigger."

I considered this for a moment and, though a part of me screamed not to, I kept picturing Peter's father's bruised face. I had failed to help Peter, but perhaps I could help him.

"Get the money he needs," I said. "However you can."

THE CATHEDRAL OF
ST. CELESTINA

Ellie stumbled groggily from her bedroom the next morning. She rubbed her eyes and the workshop settled into view, sunlight streaming down from the window, dust motes drifting in the beams. There was no sound from the basement, where she'd cleared Seth a space to sleep, providing him with an old mattress and a pillow she'd improvised from a bundle of rolled-up sweaters stuffed inside a potato sack.

Ellie looked around, hoping Finn hadn't crept in during the night, but there was no sign of him. She was about to climb to the roof to water her plants when there was a knock at the door.

She undid the bolts and pulled the door open an inch, afraid the guards might still be outside. But it was just Anna, dressed in her usual blue sweater, black skirt, and mismatched socks. She was making whooshing sounds, swinging her hand back and forth like she was wielding a sword. She looked Ellie up and down. "You're still in your nightgown."

Ellie cleared her throat. "Oh, I . . . um . . . I slept in."

"You never sleep in."

"I didn't sleep well. You know, because they nearly burned Seth alive?"

Anna continued making her whooshing sounds. "You're still bothered about that?" she said. "So what are we up to today?"

"Well, if you don't mind, I wondered if you could run me some, uh, errands," Ellie said distractedly.

Anna raised an eyebrow, then fished an apple from her pocket. "For what?"

"Well . . . for some, uh"—Ellie glanced around the floor for inspiration—"screwdriver . . . tips, and, um, apple . . . cogs."

"Okay," said Anna.

"Really?"

"Yeah." Anna took a huge bite of her apple. "And then you can tell me where you're keeping Seth."

"What?" said Ellie.

"Well, you're blocking the door so I can't come in, and you're acting even weirder than usual."

"I'm tired, that's all," said Ellie.

Anna peered over Ellie's shoulder. She was taller than Ellie and barely had to stand on tiptoe.

"Why's there blood on the floor?" she said.

Ellie turned in surprise. Anna used that moment to nip under her arm.

"It's everywhere!" she cried, following the trail past the book pile, where she found the scrap of metal Seth had cut his foot on.

"Anna, don't," said Ellie, as Anna dropped to the floor and tried to inspect the soles of Ellie's feet. "Get off!"

"You didn't cut yourself!" said Anna.

"It's . . . paint."

Anna scowled at her. "You think I can't tell the difference between blood and paint?" She rushed across the workshop, vaulting a pile of books. She looked at Ellie's bedroom door, then back at Ellie.

"Don't go in there," said Ellie sternly. Anna shrank away from the door; she knew better than to try Ellie's patience where her bedroom was concerned.

"Is he in there?" said Anna.

"Who?"

Anna rolled her eyes. "Seth."

"No!"

"But he *is* here?"

"*No!*"

But without meaning to, Ellie let her gaze flicker to the basement door, and it was all Anna needed.

"No, Anna, don't go down there!"

But Anna rushed over, pausing only to frown at the floor. "Why's there a puddle here?" she said, wrinkling her nose. Carefully, she stepped over it and put her head inside the door.

"Anna, listen," Ellie spluttered. "You can't—"

"So where is he then?" said Anna, reappearing. Ellie stared at her in shock, then peered down the stairs into the cramped basement.

The mattress was empty.

"But . . . where's he gone?" said Ellie in a tiny voice.

"So he *was* here?" said Anna, but Ellie was already racing back into the workshop, checking under tables and behind bookcases. "But you said it wasn't you who rescued him! You lied to me!"

"I *didn't* rescue him, he just showed up here last night and I let him sleep in the basement. He tricked me!" she cried. "I can't believe it, that little *monster*."

"Hmm, he probably hypnotized you or something," said Anna thoughtfully. "I bet the Vessel can do that."

"He's *not* the Vessel," Ellie snapped. "Ugh, I'm such an idiot! Last night he said he was going to try to find the real Vessel. I bet that's what he's done."

Anna rubbed her hands on her skirt to get rid of the apple juice. "Well, I guess that's that, then. No more Seth. Have you had breakfast?"

"No, we have to find him! *Especially* now that I've interfered. What if he tells Hargrath that we helped him?"

"We?" said Anna, appalled. "I haven't done anything."

"Exactly. You're not turning me in to the Inquisition right now. That makes you an accomplice."

"I told you not to get involved in the first place," Anna said, crossing her arms. Ellie grabbed a tin of whale oil from the shelves and poured some of it into a lamp.

Anna screwed up her face. "It's daytime, we don't need a light."

"Shh," said Ellie. "I took some precautions before bed, in case Seth did decide to run off."

She carried the lamp to a workbench, where she cleared aside a saw, a paint-splattered shirt, and a sheep's skull, until she found what she needed: a curved piece of violet-stained glass. She placed the glass over the oil lamp, then lit the lamp with a match so it emitted a faint, purple-blue light. Anna watched her, perplexed.

"Pretty clever, isn't it?" said Ellie.

"I have no idea what you're doing."

"I'll show you. I have this special tincture—I think my mom invented it or found it on one of the hunting islands. I think it's called, uh . . ."

"Just tell me what it does," Anna groaned.

"It *glows*, but only under the right color light. I left a puddle of it outside the basement door last night, in case Seth decided to escape. I knew he wouldn't try the front door because of the guards, *but* . . ."

Ellie ran over to the basement door. She shone the lamp down, and a puddle of pale violet liquid appeared on the floor.

Anna frowned. "So?"

Ellie bit her lip in anticipation and raised the lamp higher.

There, on the floorboards, were more blotches of pale violet, crossing the workshop, then climbing the ladder to the window, alternating from left to right on each rung.

"Footsteps!" Ellie explained delightedly, bouncing on the balls of her feet. "And they'll lead us straight to Seth."

Ellie thrust the lamp into Anna's arms, then pulled on a sweater and trousers over her nightgown, grabbing her coat and yanking on a pair of boots. They clambered up onto the rooftop.

"It's too bright out here," said Anna, pointing the lamp down toward the slates, searching for more violet splotches.

"Hold on," said Ellie, taking off her coat and using it to give them some shade. Purple footprints dotted across the rooftop, right to the edge. Ellie and Anna peered down into the street.

"He *jumped* down?" said Anna. "Maybe he fell," she added hopefully.

"He's actually quite athletic for a boy who lived inside a whale," said Ellie. "Come on."

They picked up the trail of violet splotches in the street behind the workshop. The marks led them downhill, along several alleyways.

"He's heading for the sea," said Ellie, furrowing her brow. "Why?"

"Maybe he's looking for a whale to climb back into," said Anna.

As they followed the trail, the salty tang of the sea grew stronger, along with the reek of old seaweed. Around one corner, they found an old man praying frantically.

"Oh saints, grant us the wisdom to find the Vessel. Oh saints, give us the strength to defeat the Enemy."

He stopped at the sight of Ellie and Anna, watching them suspiciously as they hobbled by, bent double beneath Ellie's coat.

In the next alleyway, a young girl was crying.

"Don't worry," her father said, hugging her close. "The Inquisitors will find him. They'll find him and kill him."

"You promise?" the girl said tearfully.

Down another alleyway, an Inquisitor was knocking on someone's door. A terrified young man answered, swallowed, then led the Inquisitor into his home. His neighbors watched from the windows above, gossiping darkly to each other.

Occasionally, Seth's trail swerved sharply into an alcove, or behind a stack of fishy-smelling crates. Ellie pictured him ducking out of sight as people passed by. At least that meant he was being careful, she thought.

The footprints led them into an open market where people were hurrying briskly about their morning errands. Overhead, the ruined Clocktower of St. Angelus poked above the rooftops. The tower had been smashed open from inside by the Enemy twenty-three years before, the last time it had manifested. Ellie noticed that people were lowering their gaze as they went by, to avoid looking at the broken clock face.

Farther down, they passed a gray, gargoyle-covered building with boarded-up windows and a spike-crowned roof. Ellie had always thought it was abandoned, but now there was an ornate silver lock on its front door, which seemed wasted on an otherwise moldy ruin. As they approached, the doors crashed open, and Ellie pulled Anna aside as Hargrath stormed out, four Inquisitors scuttling in his wake.

City folk hurriedly darted from his path, but one old woman yelled at him from a side street. "You failed us!" she cried. "You were supposed to keep us safe, and you failed us!"

Hargrath turned his head slowly, staring at the woman with cold, dead eyes. He began to march steadily toward her, and she turned and hurried into the alley.

When he was gone, Ellie and Anna crossed the street and picked up Seth's trail again. The violet splotches were getting fainter, but they were still able to follow them along the cobbled road, down to where the Great Docks spilled out from the side of the City.

The docks were not nearly so old as the city they'd grown from. When the City had been built, long ago, the sea had been miles below. Now, hundreds of ships were moored to a collection of submerged towers and hollowed-out mansions. The City's largest ship, the *Righteous Archangel*, was anchored within the ruins of a massive church. Smaller ships huddled around the outsides of the buildings, or else were moored along the strips of floating platforms that branched out to sea.

Masts and rigging rose up all around Ellie and Anna, and soon they were surrounded by the shouts of sailors and the creaking of elaborately decorated ships. The whale lords loved to outdo one another, and each ship had been ornamented in some way, with gold leaf or murals or carvings of ferocious sea creatures.

Ellie and Anna stepped uncertainly onto the wooden platforms that bobbed up and down with each movement of the waves. They slowed their pace, unsteadied by the motion, skirting the occasional gaps where the boards had rotted through.

"Careful you don't slip," Ellie warned.

Anna rolled her eyes. "I *can* look after myself, Ellie. I come down here all the time without you."

There were sailors everywhere, their songs and their laughter ringing across the docks. They bounded easily from platform to platform, their soaking boots drenching the wood with salt water and washing away any chance Ellie had of picking up Seth's trail. "This is no good," she said. "How are we going to find him now?"

They paused beside a robust ship being tied up against the dock. Sailors winched a long, heavy-looking bundle down from the deck. It was the length of three men, and as thick as a rowboat, wrapped in a great swathe of canvas that tapered at one end. Ellie and Anna stared at it curiously.

Castion leapt from the rigging, his long red coat fluttering behind him like a cape. He began working his way down the canvas, stripping it aside in rough, sudden movements. A fin could be seen first, then a streak of charcoal gray and a dead black eye. He flung the canvas to the ground, revealing the colossal body of a great white shark.

Anna gasped. "Whoa, it's huge!" she said.

The shark lay slumped on one side, its thick, snarling gums curled around rows of pointed teeth. There was a deep gouge in its side.

His sailors all cheered, though Castion himself looked grim and distracted. As his men gathered around to shout his name, he cut them short with a chopping motion of his hand.

"There's nothing to be happy about today," he told them, pulling a knife from his belt and kneeling down at the side of the shark. "The Enemy walks among us."

Ellie grabbed Anna by the arm and pulled her away before Castion could notice them. They wandered around, scanning the docks for any sign of a slinking shadow.

"Look!" said Anna excitedly.

Ellie's heart leapt into her throat. "What?"

"Those sailors over there are so handsome."

"Oh, for goodness' sake, Anna," Ellie groaned. "There are more important things to worry about!"

Anna sighed, mournfully watching the sailors. "I should have brought some flowers to give them."

Ellie dragged Anna back onto dry land. She had almost given up hope of re-finding Seth's trail, when she spotted a tiny smudge of purple on the stones by her feet.

"I've found them!" Ellie cried. The trail led them out of the Great Docks and along a narrow alley, before depositing them in the shadow of an immense, lopsided cathedral that had half crumbled into the sea. Ellie felt a cold thrill of nerves in her chest.

"What has he gone in *there* for?" she said.

"It doesn't matter—we can't follow him," said Anna. "It's not safe."

"It's perfectly safe. It's not like the Enemy's still *in* there."

It had probably been an impressive, awe-inspiring building once, but history had treated it poorly. Great gouges had been torn from its sides, and its roof was pockmarked with soot-ringed holes, as if geysers of fire had erupted from inside. A wooden notice stood by the dismal archway that served as its entrance.

This is the hallowed site upon which St. Celestina and the Holy Inquisition defeated the first manifestation of the Great Enemy: the God Who Drowned the Gods NO ENTRY, EXCEPT ON INQUISITION BUSINESS

Ellie knew the sign was inaccurate—her mother had told her as much. There had been no Inquisition back then, just a gang of desperate survivors fleeing the Enemy's destruction, and Celestina hadn't been a saint yet, but a fearless woman with a fishing spear and perfect aim. Ellie told all this to Anna, and Anna let out a great yawn.

"Stop showing off."

Ellie crept inside, warily eyeing her surroundings. The Cathedral of St. Celestina looked just as it must have at the time of that first battle, seven hundred years before. Thick pillars rose to the rooftop, though two had fallen and now lay scattered in segments. The building sloped down, and the sea had spilled through the holes in the wall, drowning half the floor. A towering stained-glass window poked out of the water.

"Ellie, I'm telling you, we shouldn't be in here," said Anna.

"Like you've never been in here before," said Ellie, pointing to a gray stone wall, where the words ANNA WAS HERE were drawn in red chalk.

"That could have been any Anna. It's a very common name."

"If you're frightened, you can stand by the entrance and check that no one's coming."

But Anna just scowled. They crept onward, following the line of fading purple marks that led down to the water. They couldn't see Seth anywhere. They passed a cluster of tall statues of robed men and women, three of which had been smashed aside, resting against the far wall of the cathedral in many pieces, leaving just the legs and feet behind. Four times Ellie and Anna passed the strange shadow of a figure on the walls, like a large charcoal drawing, spread up the stone with its arms flung wide. Elsewhere they saw deep scratches in the stone, as if human fingernails had raked through the rock like it were butter.

Ellie found it hard to conceive that the Enemy had actually stood in this place—not in its Vessel but its actual, *physical* form—destroying both the cathedral and the people who'd fought against it, until at last a fishing spear was hurled straight at its head. She shivered. Anna was standing very close to her, her hand hovering by the sleeve of Ellie's coat.

Ellie inspected the floor. The splotches were barely visible now, just tiny flecks of purple, no bigger than a raindrop. She followed them around a pillar that had survived the Enemy's attack. The purple dots vanished into the water.

"He's gone *into* the sea," Ellie said, astonished.

"No," said Anna in a hollow voice. "He's up there."

Ellie looked up, then took a step back.

Seth was fifteen feet above them, perched on top of a disfigured church organ that rose straight out of the sea, a tangled mess of brass pipes topped with gold angels. He was crouched among the angels like a cat preparing to pounce, glaring at the sea beneath him.

"What is he doing?" Ellie whispered as she and Anna

watched from the cover of a fallen pillar. She wasn't sure why she was whispering, exactly, only it felt somehow that they had intruded on something private. The cathedral was silent save for the quiet lapping of the sea against the stone. That became a quiet rumble.

Then a much louder one.

The sea began to bubble, almost as if it were boiling. Anna clutched Ellie's arm.

Seth was staring at the sea with such intensity, his knuckles pale as they gripped the organ pipes. Tentatively, he raised one hand. The sea rippled and began to *rise*—a column of water breaking from the surface. Seth's fingers trembled, his eyes wide. Ellie gasped—Seth was *drawing* the water toward him until it nearly touched his hand.

"How . . ." Ellie whispered. "How is he doing that?"

"What do you want from me?" Seth yelled suddenly. "Get out of my head!"

He was shaking with fury, a vein throbbing on his brow. The sea thrashed, then rose up all at once in a huge wave, crashing down against the church organ. Ellie leapt forward to help, only when the sea washed away, Seth was nowhere to be seen.

"Seth!" Ellie cried, rushing to the water's edge.

"Did you see that?" said Anna. "He *is* the Vessel."

But it had seemed to Ellie more like the sea had *attacked*

Seth, like an unruly dog biting its master. "Help me find him!" she yelled. She dug in her coat pockets for the pair of special glasses she'd made for seeing underwater, slammed them on her face, then flung off her coat. She jumped into the water.

Seth was lying below the surface. He was unconscious, draped across the rubble of the shattered cathedral floor.

Something was moving on his skin.

For a moment, Ellie thought it was the shadows from the dappling sunlight breaking through the roof. Then she realized it was *inside* him—dark blue shapes swirling up and down his bare arms and on his chest where his shirt had ripped open. Ellie put an arm around Seth's neck, and another around his back, pushing off toward the surface.

"Thanks for *helping*," Ellie said to Anna, dragging Seth onto the dry stone.

"He's dangerous," said Anna, staring in horror at the blue swirls on Seth's skin. "I don't think you should touch him."

"He's not dangerous," Ellie said.

As she spoke Seth came to life, gasping for air and smacking Ellie in the face with a flailing hand.

"Ow!"

She staggered backward, while Seth rolled onto his front and coughed up water.

"Are you all right?" Ellie said, rubbing her cheek.

"I was trying to get it to be quiet," he said.

"He's completely lost it," said Anna.

"What do you mean?" Ellie asked him. "What were you doing?"

"SHUT UP!" Seth roared again, glaring at the sea as if it had just tried to insult him. The water rumbled in response.

"Shh!" Anna warned, glancing nervously up at the entrance. "If they find us here . . ."

"Seth, you need to keep your voice down," said Ellie.

"Me?" Seth raged. "I'm not the one making all that *noise*!" The water thrashed and spat again.

"You're the *only* one making noise," said Anna.

"Seth, it's all right," said Ellie, crouching down beside him. "We're here. Maybe, um, maybe you should take some deep breaths?" she added, eyeing the unsettled water, worried it might lash out again.

Seth glared at his hands, then took three long gulps of air. As he did, the water began to still, then was calm. A tiny crab scuttled from the shallows.

"Why did you come here?" Ellie asked.

Seth screwed his eyes shut, like he was trying to banish a headache. "I had to know what was making all that noise—and I couldn't do it out *there* where everyone wants me dead." He waved his hand around vaguely.

Ellie paused, trying to find the right way of phrasing her next question. Whatever words she chose sounded too bizarre. She looked at Anna, then back at Seth.

"Seth, did you just *move* the sea?"

"I told you, I was trying to get it to be quiet!" he yelled, as if yelling at the sea was a normal thing to do. Again the sea rumbled.

Anna backed away, motioning for Ellie to do the same. "We have to turn him in," she said. "He's the Vessel—he'll kill us."

"He's not the Vessel," said Ellie.

"Then how come he made the water bubble up like that?"

"And even if he *was*—which he isn't—then if we turned him in they'd probably throw us in prison for trying to help him in the first place."

"*I* didn't try to help him," Anna grumbled.

"So you want me to get locked up?"

Anna scuffed one foot violently against the stone floor. "No," she said quietly.

Seth stared at the sea. He took a threatening step toward it, and Ellie grabbed his wrist.

"*Stop it,*" she said. "Don't you see? Somehow, when you get angry, the sea gets angry too." A sudden frustration flared up in her chest as she remembered what it had cost her to rescue him in the first place. "I can't believe you! You left the workshop, even after I *told* you how dangerous it was. You really are stupid!"

"Don't call me stupid," Seth growled. Behind him, the sea growled too.

"We're *not* taking him back," said Anna firmly. "I don't want him anywhere near the orphans."

"We have to," said Ellie. "He's not safe here."

Anna stared at Ellie in disgust. "You want to study him, don't you? He's like . . . an experiment, isn't he? Like one of your dead rats."

"I'm not a rat," said Seth, rounding on Anna. "Who are you anyway?"

Anna clenched her fists. "The person who's going to turn you in to the Inquisitors if you're not careful."

Seth took a step forward, and Anna squared up to him, her face inches from his. Ellie squeezed in between them. Again the seawater rumbled.

"Go stand over there," Ellie told Seth. To her surprise, he obeyed, slumping down next to one of the statues and closing his eyes. He looked like he hadn't slept at all.

"It's not safe, Ellie," Anna whispered, squeezing Ellie's arm. "He's—"

"He's *not* the Vessel," Ellie said wearily. "I can prove it to you."

"Then what is he?"

Ellie looked at Seth, his eyes closed but his brow furrowing every time a wave washed in, relaxing when it went out again.

"Something else."

From the Diary of Claude Hestermeyer

Peter's father got the money he needed. It just appeared in his sitting room that very day, though his doors and windows were all locked. At first, I was delighted. The moneylenders would leave him alone now. The next morning, though, I wandered into the dining hall, and saw the master and the treasurer of the university sitting together, looking worried and confused.

Apparently, some gold had vanished from the university vaults. It wasn't a huge sum, but its disappearance was a concern for my fellow scholars. And for me.

"You took the money from *us*?" I raged, marching up and down my office.

The Enemy was sitting comfortably in Peter's armchair. He smiled an ugly smile while I shouted at him, one that I couldn't remember ever seeing on my old friend's face.

"It had to come from somewhere, Claude," he said. "Be glad I didn't take it from the orphanage."

I slept that night on the floor of my office, too tired to go home. After I asked the Enemy to get the money, I'd found myself suddenly exhausted, in body and mind. When I awoke, I could barely rise from the floor, and when I finally *did* stand, I felt like my brittle legs would snap. I stumbled over to the mirror and saw that I was paler, and thinner.

"Is this something to do with you?" I asked the Enemy, who was still sitting in the armchair. He looked sleek and relaxed, as if he had enjoyed dinner and a perfect night's sleep.

He shrugged. "You asked me for my help," he said. "That's a side effect."

"It's *you*, isn't it?" I said accusingly. "You're sapping my energy—I've made you stronger!"

I scowled and went to brush my hair, but when I did, several brown strands came away in the brush.

"What's happening to me?" I groaned, sitting down at my desk. "I should never have asked you to get that money."

The Enemy looked at me for a long time, saying nothing. I felt he was looking right into my soul. Finally, he leaned forward.

"No," he said. "You really shouldn't have."

9

EXPERIMENTS WITH SEAWATER

"*Sign of the Vessel number four,*" Ellie read aloud, holding the book in her hands. "*The Vessel's skin is of a pale, sickly hue, unusually prone to scratches and bruising, and often damp to the touch.*"

"Do we really have to do this?" Seth complained. He was standing on a stool in the middle of the workshop while Ellie inspected him. Anna stood on a workbench nearby, both hands firmly gripping the harpoon gun, pointing it directly at Seth. It was the only way Ellie had been able to persuade Anna to let her bring him back at all.

"Yes," said Ellie. "But not for much longer. Castion should be here any minute with a special delivery." She turned back to Anna. "As I was saying, he doesn't look sickly. And he's not damp at all," she added, putting a hand to Seth's forehead. Seth wrinkled his nose.

"What about those blue marks that appeared on his skin?"

"Those weren't sickly—they were just weird. Now let's keep going. *Sign of the Vessel number five. The Vessel will often seem distracted by a voice in his head. This is in truth the voice of the Enemy.*"

"But he *does* hear voices," said Anna.

"Yes, but we already know that's the sea he's hearing, not the Enemy," said Ellie.

Seth stifled another yawn and got down from his stool. He picked up a loaf of bread and began tearing huge chunks out with his teeth.

"Ugh, he's so disgusting," said Anna. "And not in a good way."

Ellie scanned down the page. "*Sign of the Vessel number eleven,*" she read, feeling pleased with herself. "*The Vessel will have a severely reduced appetite.*"

Anna glowered at her.

"*Sign of the Vessel number twelve,*" Ellie continued. "*His hair falls out easily.*"

"Hey!" Seth complained as Ellie tried unsuccessfully to pull out some of his thick black hair. "You've proved your point," he said, shoving her away.

Anna motioned for Ellie to come closer, keeping the

harpoon gun trained on Seth. "Let me see that."

Ellie reluctantly handed her the book. Anna barely glanced at the page.

"*The Vessel likes to eat a lot of bread*," she said.

"Anna, you've got the book upside down," said Ellie.

Anna thrust it back into Ellie's hands. "I don't care what some stupid book says! He's the Vessel and he can't stay here. Not with the orphans across the street."

There was a knock at the workshop door. They all tensed. Anna stabbed her finger at the basement door.

"I'm going," Seth grumbled, batting the harpoon gun aside on his way past.

"Ellie!" came Castion's voice. "It's me. Are you in?" There was a moment's pause. "That spider hasn't escaped its cage again, has it?"

Ellie hurried to the door and flung open the bolts. Standing in the street behind Castion were four of his sailors, their foreheads slick with sweat. Between them was a large iron trunk, like a massive bathtub with a lid on top.

"Your delivery, as requested," said Castion with an ironic smile. After so many years of being called to the workshop, with requests for odd materials at even odder hours, he had long since stopped asking questions.

"Ooh, thank you," said Ellie, eyeing the tub excitedly.

"Though you didn't need to come yourself, sir."

"No, but I wanted to check you were okay, after all that business with the Vessel."

"That's really, um, nice of you," Ellie said. "I'm fine, thanks."

"I hope you've been staying indoors—there's a nine o'clock curfew in place now. So don't go, you know, *looking* for him."

Ellie felt her face go red, feeling suddenly trapped. She had no choice but to lie, even though Anna would *see* her lie. She could feel her glaring at her already. Ellie waved her hand, trying to seem casual.

"Oh no, I'd never do that, sir, I'm not stupid. I've been right here the whole time, working away. I've got a lot of, um, inventor stuff to do."

"Good. Good," said Castion. "I'm glad you're not putting yourself or anyone else in danger."

"I'm going," Anna announced suddenly, glowering at Ellie.

"Really, Anna?" said Castion. "But I've just got my hands on an antique throwing dagger—I thought you'd love to see it."

Anna gnawed her lip. "Sorry, sir, the younger orphans have an, um, painting competition. They want me to judge it."

"What?" said Ellie. "I thought that wasn't until next week?"

On her way past, Anna picked up a spare harpoon and placed it in Ellie's hands. "You should probably keep hold of this," she muttered, her eyes flicking meaningfully to the basement door. "In case that big, ugly spider *does* come back. Better to just get rid of it before *someone gets hurt.*"

Castion swallowed. "But I thought you caught that spider? You've not been feeding it, have you?"

Anna stormed from the workshop, and Ellie hurried after her.

"Anna?" she called. Anna turned, looking at her hopefully.

Ellie opened her mouth, then glanced back at Castion. She felt her throat constrict. "I'll, uh, I'll see you later?" she said feebly to Anna.

Anna's hopeful look vanished, replaced by an expression of exhaustion and disappointment. She rushed across the street toward the orphanage, slamming the door behind her.

"The orphans must be scared," said Castion. "After last night."

Ellie rubbed at a pain in her chest. "Has there been any news, sir?"

"Well, there was a fire out by the Revival Waterfront

last night—a woman thought the Vessel was in her attic, and started a fire to try to trap it. And someone in the Anchor Tavern accused another man's son of looking just like the Vessel, which started a pub brawl, which turned ugly, which alerted the Inquisition, who put a stop to it." Castion rubbed his eye. "The longer the Vessel remains uncaught, the more these sorts of things will happen. So just be careful. Now, all rested, gentlemen?"

The four sailors groaned, then hauled the metal container inside the workshop. Ellie hurried to clear a space.

"What's it for, then?" said Castion.

"Oh, just an experiment," Ellie replied, kicking aside some books.

"And what sort of experiment calls for twenty gallons of seawater?"

Ellie shrugged awkwardly. "Um, a very important one?"

"Well, let's leave the genius to her *very important* work," Castion said with a smile. He bowed deeply, then strode from the workshop, the four sailors hurrying after him.

Ellie rushed excitedly to the basement door, knocking three times quickly, then three times slowly. Seth slunk out, eyeing the tub suspiciously.

"What have you brought *that* here for?" he said, his lip curling. He put a hand to his head. "Take it away."

Ellie beamed. "So you *can* hear it?" she said, bouncing on the balls of her feet. "Even seawater that's been taken *out* of the sea? That's excellent."

Seth gave her a dead-eyed stare. "Why?"

"Because you can use it to practice," she said, flipping open the lid.

"Practice?"

"Yes! To figure out what this connection is between you and the sea. If we can learn more about *that*, maybe we can figure out who you are!"

Seth looked back at the tub and the still seawater inside.

"What happens if you put your hand in it?" Ellie said eagerly.

Seth's black eyebrows angled sharply. "I'm not doing that."

"Why not?"

"Because I almost drowned before!"

"Yes, but there's not enough water here to drown you. Probably."

"I said *no*," Seth said firmly, and the water in the tub bubbled slightly.

Ellie clapped with glee. "See? That was you! That's incredible. Okay, now please will you touch it?"

Seth growled. "All right, all right—if it will shut you up!"

He stormed over to the tub, which was still bubbling,

and thrust his hand into it. The water splashed and rumbled immediately, and Seth cried out in shock as it flowed up his arm, engulfing it like a sleeve.

"Let *go* of me," he snarled, only this seemed to make the sea hold on tighter. It was *pulling* him now, dragging him in almost to his shoulder, his free arm straining against the tub to keep him upright. Ellie rushed forward, wrapping her arms around his waist and trying to pull him away. But his arm might as well have been stuck in stone. Sweat rolled down his neck.

Ellie's mind raced. She hurried toward her shelves of chemicals, grabbed two bottles of colorless liquid, then rushed back to Seth, unstoppering one bottle and shoving it under his nose.

"Quick, breathe in!" she cried.

"What is it?"

"Just breathe in!"

Seth inhaled sharply, and his eyes glazed over. His arms and shoulders relaxed and the water seemed to let go of him. Ellie had to help him into a chair.

"What . . . what *is* that?" he said dopily.

"Ether," said Ellie, restoppering the bottle. "It's a sedative. Look, it's calmed you right down."

"But"—he'd gone cross-eyed—"why did the water let me go?"

"I think because it calmed down too. It seems to respond

to your emotions. Here." She pulled the other bottle from her pocket. "Smell this now."

Seth inhaled, then leapt up, eyes wide. He began to cough. The water in the tub bubbled.

"That's spirit of ammonia," Ellie said proudly. "It smells terrible, doesn't it? Now listen, back in the cathedral you were able to control the water, do you remember? Before it attacked you. How did you do that?"

"I don't know. It just . . . felt right."

Ellie nodded. "But then you got too angry, and so the *water* got angrier, and it attacked you. But maybe, if you can control your emotions, then you can control the sea too!"

Seth gave her a look that still had far too much emotion in it, and Ellie held out the ammonia bottle in threat. "Why don't you keep trying?"

So he tried again, holding his hand out above the water each time, and whenever he got too frustrated he would stand back and take several deep breaths until the water calmed down again. Very soon the floorboards were drenched.

"I can still hear it," said Seth, lying spread out on the floor, chest heaving in exhaustion. The same blue, mist-like splotches had appeared on his skin.

"What *are* those?" Ellie asked, kneeling down to inspect

them under a magnifying glass. They swirled and shifted like skittish fish.

"Why can I hear the sea in my head?" said Seth. "It's so angry. Or is that *my* anger?"

Ellie tucked her knees under her chin, watching him thoughtfully. "Maybe you need to inhale some ether and *then* try to control the water," she said.

"*Ellie*, you're not listening!" said Seth.

"I am!" she protested. "Only you're getting all emotional and it's not helping. You need to *control* your emotions."

"That's what I'm trying to do!" Seth cried, and seawater sloshed angrily over the edge of the tub.

"Well, try *harder*," said Ellie. "Maybe you need a way to focus. Sometimes, when I'm angry, I paint a picture. It's usually a very angry picture, but by the time I'm done I don't feel so angry anymore."

"You don't get it," said Seth, standing up and running his hands through his hair. "I keep thinking about all those people in the square that night, and how they want me dead. And I think about how I . . . I don't *know* anyone, and I feel so lonely, and that makes me angry too!" He turned sharply, and the water in the tub spluttered. "And then I think about how I *did* have someone once—lots of someones, my brothers and sisters—only I can't remember who they are. And that makes me—"

He screwed up his face, his hands clenching into fists. Water boiled up and splashed over the sides of the tub.

"Um, maybe we should take a break," said Ellie nervously. "Here, you should eat something." She grabbed an apple from a workbench and tossed it to him.

Ellie got the feeling he wanted to be alone and wandered over to the far side of the workshop. Here, thousands of pieces of paper had been stuck, one on top of another, until nothing of the wall underneath was visible. She stared at a drawing she'd sketched the day before—a diagram of a humpback whale, with a boy inside it.

Seth finished his apple and came to join her. He seemed calmer now—the water in the tub was silent. He leaned over to inspect the drawing. "Is that supposed to be me?"

"Yes," said Ellie.

He frowned. "Why is my head so big?"

Ellie huffed. "It's a study of a whale's digestive system. I'm trying to figure out—"

"How I survived inside a whale," Seth finished, his eyes scanning the drawing. "Why?"

"What do you mean *why*?" she said. "Because it's a mystery! It seems impossible, but you managed it, so it must be possible."

"But it doesn't help us catch the Vessel, or figure out who I am."

"Maybe not, but it's still *interesting*. I am an inventor, you know."

"I thought you just fixed your mom's broken stuff."

Ellie bristled. "Fixing things is hard! And I *do* make new things. Like the net-cannon, or that cherry-picker over there. It gets cherries down from high-up branches," she said, puffing out her chest.

"But I haven't seen any trees on this island—"

"And we need to figure out who you are," said Ellie, cutting him off. "If we know how you survived, we might be able to work out how you got in that whale in the first place." She pulled the drawing from the wall to show him more closely. "I'm fairly sure I dragged you out of the whale's stomach. Now, human stomachs are full of acid, and you certainly wouldn't want to live in one. But I think a whale's stomach is more like a cow's— Seth?"

Seth was staring quizzically at a yellowed piece of paper that had been hidden beneath the drawing of the whale.

Ellie felt an icy stab in her chest. "Seth?" she repeated. But he kept staring.

It was a drawing of a girl and a boy in a rowboat, out at sea. Though it was easy to tell that the girl was Ellie, with her long, messy hair and her nose that curved a little to one side, it was harder to say who the boy was.

"Who's that?" said Seth, pointing at the boy.

"Oh." Ellie's mouth was suddenly dry. "That's my brother."

"Why doesn't he have a face?" said Seth. "Why is it left blank?"

Ellie felt a chill run up her spine. "Because . . . because I can't remember it," she said. It was only partly a lie.

"I didn't know you have a brother," said Seth.

Ellie let out a deep breath. "Had," she said in a small voice.

"I'm sorry," said Seth. He stared at his feet for a long while. "I wish I could remember my brothers and sisters too."

"I know," said Ellie.

Seth closed his eyes. "I feel like, if I could remember them, I'd feel warm again. Like nothing could hurt me, because they wouldn't let it . . ." He trailed off, then shrugged. "Do you feel that, when you think of your brother?"

Ellie realized there was a tear on her cheek and angrily wiped it away. She tried to visualize that day in the boat, when they'd gone out fishing together. But immediately a terrible, painful cold filled her body.

"No," she said. "I don't feel warm. I don't feel that at all."

"Did you not get along?"

"Of *course* we got along," said Ellie, feeling her temper flare. "He was my little brother. Only . . ." She stared at the drawing, and the blank-faced boy with his fishing rod. "I was supposed to keep him safe. And I didn't."

FROM THE DIARY OF CLAUDE HESTERMEYER

I have begun locking my office door at all times, terrified that someone might come in and find this journal, or some piece of evidence I've overlooked. My door closes on its own, thanks to one of those clever door-closers of Hannah Lancaster's invention, and locks by itself too. Once, when my life was less fraught with peril, my door was always propped open, so my students felt free to speak to me whenever they wished. Now, I hide myself away, and ignore anyone who comes knocking.

Not that many do. I am much more irritable these days, and ever since I asked the Enemy to get that money, I have been tired and withdrawn. Even holding a conversation is difficult, so my office has become like a sanctuary to me. Or a prison.

On Tuesday, I returned after lunch and saw that my door was ajar. I looked down, and saw something unusual propping it open:

A dried-up gray starfish.

I frowned, wondering what in the world this might mean. Then I jerked upright as the door opened fully. It was one of the servants, a freckle-faced young man called Thomas. He must have seen that my door was open and assumed that meant I wanted the room cleaned. He bowed slightly, then walked past me, striding briskly along the corridor.

I watched him go, then shot into my office, locking the door behind me.

"You're not going to like this," said the Enemy, who was draped in his usual armchair.

I followed his gaze. Icy water trickled down my chest.

There, sitting on my desk in full view, was a large pile of gold coins.

10

THE ORPHANAGE

The orphanage was home to thirty-two children, at Ellie's last count. This was no great number, and most of the bedrooms were unfilled; there hadn't been any terrible storms since the Evercreech Hurricane, and the Enemy hadn't walked the City in twenty-three years.

It was a cozy place, with low ceilings and a long, winding corridor that branched off to the bedrooms, the bathrooms, the games room, the art room, and the kitchen. It smelled of cotton blankets and woodsmoke and was always much warmer than the workshop. The matrons even kept Ellie's old bedroom free, just in case, though she never went in there.

As Ellie hurried down the corridor, a frustrated, tired-eyed matron rushed past her, pursuing a tiny boy.

"Ian, Edward says you licked him—is that true?"

The boy turned, his nose wrinkling. "Ugh, why would I *lick* him? He tastes horrible."

Ellie found Anna in the games room, patting the head of a little girl with frizzy hair and tears in her eyes. As Ellie watched, Anna hugged the girl, whispering something in her ear. The little girl laughed, and Anna gently pointed her at the door and she skipped eagerly from the room, rubbing her tears away.

Then Anna saw Ellie, and the smile dropped from her face. She slumped down in an armchair, picked up a bowl of dried figs, and propped her feet on a stool, looking for all the world like a queen on her throne.

The younger orphans lay about on the floor, rolling dice and accusing one another of cheating. The games room was home to some of Ellie's earliest inventions— an ocean of mechanical whales, sharks, dolphins, and fish hung from the ceiling, each one made from many segments of polished steel so that they glittered in the firelight. A cabinet held stacks of different board games that Ellie had made, each one based on an idea of her brother's. She watched a redheaded brother and sister sitting by the fire, playing a game of Kill the Kraken. Ellie remembered it well—each player took control of a ship, and had to do battle with a mighty, many-tentacled sea monster that moved across a clockwork board. The boy laughed in triumph as his sister's ship was swallowed up by the monster. They fell about giggling and play-fighting, and Ellie had to look away.

She picked her way through the room, careful not to tread on any small toys or small children. Anna didn't look at her, but put a fig in her mouth, chewing it with intensity.

"Why didn't you come over this morning?" said Ellie.

Anna threw a second fig into her mouth.

"I could really use your help—Mr. Mayhew's flood-drainer isn't working again. He says he's got jellyfish in his kitchen."

Anna tossed a third fig into her mouth. A tiny freckled boy sidled up to Ellie, his eyes wide and pleading, clutching a silver, mechanical toy puppy. He wound it up and placed it on the floor, where it staggered dismally in a circle then fell over. Ellie picked it up, pulled a screwdriver from her pocket, and prodded exploratively at the puppy's cogs. The boy watched approvingly.

"I can't fix the flood-drainer by myself," she told Anna. "I need a—" She nearly said "second pair of hands" then thought better of it. "I need your expertise."

Anna swallowed loudly. "Why don't you ask your new *friend* to help you?"

Ellie glanced nervously at the other orphans. "He can't be coming around the City with me," she whispered. "I have to *protect* him."

Anna's eyes bulged. "Protect him? You . . . He . . ." she spluttered. She looked at the other orphans, who were all now listening in on their argument. Anna snatched a clockwork mouse from the floor, winding it up. "A penny to whoever catches this!" she announced, then flung the mouse across the room.

There was an immediate eruption of noise—every orphan gave chase to the speeding mouse as it darted beneath chairs and tables. It was like being in the middle of a flock of demented seagulls. Ellie dropped the mechanical puppy on Anna's chair and went to cover her ears, only Anna grabbed Ellie by both arms and pulled her close. She took a great, gulping breath. "You don't care about saving Seth's life," she hissed. "And you don't care that he might be the Vessel! He's just another puzzle for you to solve, so you can prove how clever you are." She picked up the mechanical puppy and thrust it at her.

Ellie flinched, her eyes prickling. "That's *not* true," she said.

The noise died down as a round-faced girl put the mouse proudly back in Anna's open palm and was rewarded with a single bronze coin. Anna fixed Ellie with a deathly stare.

"You don't even care that you're putting everyone in danger," she whispered.

Ellie picked up her screwdriver. "So you're not going to help me, then?" she said, her throat hurting. "In the workshop?"

"Not while he's there."

"But I already proved that he's not, well, *that*. Look—just come over and . . . I'll let you have the rifle in the library?"

Anna ground her teeth. There was a scuffling at the door, and Fry and Ibnet staggered into the room, wrapped up together in what seemed like a cuddle, but was, on closer inspection, a headlock. Ellie watched them curiously, until the tiny freckled boy at Ellie's side climbed up her arm and tugged on her ear, pointing at the puppy. Ellie continued fixing it.

"They're mine, I want to show her!" said Ibnet, his voice muffled by Fry's arm.

"I found them!" Fry protested, raising a large brown-stained pillowcase in her other hand.

"I did most of the work," said Ibnet, trying and failing to wriggle free of Fry's grip. Both their faces were grubby, their trouser cuffs caked with dried dirt.

"Oh, what do you know, paint-eater?" said Fry.

"I told you, I wasn't *eating* the paint," said Ibnet. "The brush just fell in my mouth."

Anna pulled the pair apart. "Fry, Ibnet, be quiet. Let's see what you found."

Fry eagerly untied the grubby pillowcase, and a hundred grimy trinkets clattered to the floor. Ellie glanced down at them. It was a favorite pastime of the orphans to go down to the Flats at low tide, hunting for treasure. The Flats were a wide expanse of submerged rooftops off the east coast of the City. When the tide went down, it left all sorts of curiosities poking from chimneys and gutters. Mostly old shoes and discarded tobacco pipes, but once in a generation, a lucky orphan might chance across some ancient relic dating from before the Drowning, and their name would become part of orphanage legend.

Fry held up a thin piece of wood with a round bit on the end, "This was a mirror belonging to an ancient prince," she boasted.

"It's a hairbrush," sneered Ibnet. "The bristles have fallen out. Anna, look at this watch I found."

He held up a golden pocket watch on a glittering chain.

"*You* didn't find that," Fry spat. "I stole it from that rich old . . ." Her voice trailed off as Anna raised an eyebrow. "I mean, um, oh hi, Ellie, I didn't see you there! Say, can we have a go in that underwater boat of yours?"

"Yeah, I want to go under the sea!" said Ibnet. "Think of the treasure!"

Ellie opened her mouth to say no but Anna spoke over her. "Why don't you leave these things with me to go through while you two get cleaned up? Before the matrons see you."

Fry and Ibnet nodded eagerly, then scarpered from the room. Ellie put her screwdriver away, wound up the mechanical puppy, and placed it on the floor, where it trotted in a perfect straight line. The little freckled boy clapped in delight, and Anna nodded at him encouragingly. She turned her face to Ellie, and her expression dropped.

"If you keep him," said Anna, turning over the clockwork mouse in her hand, "you're putting the orphans in danger, just so you can show off."

"I told you, *no one* is in danger." Ellie pressed her fingers into her palms. "I'd never put you or the orphans in harm's way. I just need to fix this for him—and I'm *sure* I can fix it, if only I could—"

Anna's face twisted. "TWO PENNIES THIS TIME!" she bellowed, and hurled the wind-up mouse at the floor again.

The orphans burst into a new round of squealing, even louder than before. Ellie growled in frustration and marched out of the games room, sidestepping a matron as she rushed to see what the racket was.

Ellie kicked a stuffed seal toy on the floor. She wanted

to shout and rage and punch things. She steadied herself against a door, and it was a moment before she realized which door it was. Her breath caught.

There was a whale carved into the wood and, above it, two little stick figures sitting in a rowboat. A girl and a boy.

Ellie reached out her hand, her fingers trembling over the doorknob. But then her chest tightened and flooded with ice water. She pulled her hand away and hurried out of the orphanage.

11

THE THREAT

Anna didn't show up to the workshop at all for the next few days, so Ellie went about her duties alone, criss-crossing the City to fix drainage pumps and whalebone saws and fish-gutting machines. But she was distracted and tired, and it was showing in her work—twice she'd had to go back to mend a device she'd failed to fix properly the day before.

The mood in the City didn't help calm her nerves. Three days earlier she'd seen a fight break out when a wealthy merchant was accused of sheltering the Vessel in his wine cellar. The merchant and his accuser had wrestled each other to the ground in broad daylight, until an Inquisitor arrived and arrested both men.

To make matters worse, Seth was constantly pestering her with questions. Sometimes they were overly personal:

"What happened to your parents?"

Ellie grumpily stripped the outer casing from a harpoon gun. "My mom died of a wasting sickness when I was eight. I never knew my father—he was some playwright. He died when I was one. I'd rather not talk about it."

Sometimes they were about Anna:

"So is she your assistant or something?"

Ellie carefully inserted a lens into a telescope. "Don't let her hear you say that if you want to live. She just helps me with my work now and then. She's my best friend."

"Oh," said Seth. "Then why's she not talking to you?"

"I'd rather not talk about it."

Other times they were about the City, or the Enemy, or the Inquisition. But especially, they were about Finn·

"So where does he live?"

"Oh, the other side of the City. Forget about him—he's really not that interesting."

"But he went to all that effort to save my life, just to show off? What if he'd been caught?"

"He's very arrogant. Look, I'd rather—"

"Not talk about it," Seth grumbled. "Yes, I know."

Ellie tossed and turned that night. Her mind was a swirling mess—the same dark thoughts churning endlessly. With a huff, she threw off her clammy sheets and crept from her bedroom, trailing a blanket after her.

The workshop was ghostly in the twilight, a sea of glinting metal and half-hidden shapes. Ellie tiptoed across the floorboards in her nightgown, toward the giant mound of books in the middle of the room. She stooped to pick one up.

A History of Executions the title said.

She winced and threw the book aside, then hunted around until she found one more to her liking. She stared at the cover. It was some sort of storybook.

Ellie flicked through its pages. It was mostly text, but there were several illustrations. One showed the hero standing tall at the prow of a ship, a spear raised in his hands. She was certain the book had belonged to her brother— he'd been obsessed with the sea, and everything in it. The walls of their bedroom in the orphanage had been covered with drawings of sea creatures, though she struggled now to remember what they'd looked like. Ellie searched the pages for anything her brother might have left, like a doodle in the margins, but found nothing.

She sighed and closed the book carefully, then returned to her task, clearing a wide space on the floor. Next, she collected a stack of books, wedging them under her chin and carrying them over to the space she'd made. She built a wall of books that came up to her knees, as long as she was tall. Then she built another, parallel to the first, with enough room in between for her to sit in.

She connected the two long book-walls with a shorter one, making a rectangle with only three sides, then completed the shape by adding a pointed end to the rectangle from two more short walls of books, like an arrowhead. Finally, she added a pile of three large books inside, forming a seat, and then three more to form another. She nodded, pleased with her handiwork, then climbed in and sat down on one of the seats. She stared at the other.

From the floor, Ellie picked up a broom handle. She held it across her lap, in both hands, then began to drag one end back and forward in a rowing motion, never quite letting it touch the floorboards. She tried to imagine the sound of the sea, lapping gently against the boat. She tried to imagine the cold of the wind on her face. She tried to imagine the presence of another person in the seat across from her. She tried to imagine his smile, the sound of his voice, his laughter.

She tried, and tried, and tried.

Then she put the broom handle back down and sighed. She hugged her legs, her pulse resounding through her whole body. She counted thirty beats, then sat up. The other seat was still empty. Words formed in her chest, spiny and sore.

"Where are you?" she said. Her tiny voice filled the workshop.

"What are you doing?"

Ellie cried out and spun around, sending several books

flying. Seth was sitting cross-legged on top of the giant turtle skeleton that hung from the ceiling, framed in moonlight.

"What are *you* doing?" Ellie hissed.

Seth looked at the strange arrangement of books around her. "You were talking to your brother," he said.

"I wasn't," said Ellie adamantly.

"There are tears on your cheeks."

"I *wasn't* talking to him. Shut up." Ellie climbed out of the book-boat and turned away. "What are you doing up there?" she said curtly. "You should be in the basement."

"I like the way this sways," he said, leaning from side to side so the skeleton swung slightly on its chains.

Suddenly hot and embarrassed, Ellie conspicuously picked up a screwdriver and leaned over the broken net-cannon. Her nose still ached whenever she looked at it.

"I couldn't sleep," she said.

Seth stood up, balancing effortlessly on the turtle. He dropped catlike to the bookcase below, then to the floor.

"You *were* talking to your brother."

"Seth, just shut up, all right?" said Ellie, violently prying open the side of the cannon.

"I'm sorry. It's just . . . I don't have anyone to talk to, except you."

"Then we can talk about *other* things." Ellie reached for a pair of pliers and pulled out a bent cog. "Here, help me fix this. Make yourself useful for once."

He took the cog and held it still while Ellie strained to bend it back into shape with her pliers.

"If I'm going to live here," he said, "you're going to have to talk to me. Is that why Anna's angry with you? Because you don't tell her things?"

Ellie picked up the net-cannon. "What do you care about Anna? She hates you."

Seth shrugged. "Doesn't mean I hate her," he said, following Ellie to another workbench, where there was a large vise. "Every time I ask you about yourself, you start talking about something else."

Ellie threw down the net-cannon with a clatter. "Well maybe you should take a hint and *stop* asking me. How would you like it if I asked *you* private things about yourself all the time?"

"I'd love it," Seth said simply. "Only I don't know anything about myself."

Ellie opened up the vise and wedged the bent cog inside. "It must be nice," she said bitterly, "not having any memories. Not knowing about any of the bad things that have happened to you. The bad things you did. Hold these," she said. She held out her pliers, but Seth just stared at her. His eyes were wide in the moonlight.

"Please don't say things like that," he said.

Hot guilt bubbled up in Ellie's chest, followed by a rush of anger at Seth for making her feel that way. She turned from him, picked up a large hammer in both hands, and pounded the cog back into shape. She closed the panel on the cannon and risked a glance at Seth. He was looking at his feet.

"I'm sorry," she said. "That was cruel."

There was a long silence that made Ellie's palms itch with discomfort.

"Here, why don't you be the first to test it?" she said, picking up the net-cannon and offering it to him. He looked at it skeptically.

"It won't backfire like last time, I promise. I fixed that little, um, issue. And it's really fun when it's working. Go on, try."

Seth took the cannon from her uncertainly, pointed it at the turtle skeleton, and pulled the trigger. There was a metal *clunk* and a huge black net blasted from the end of the cannon, wrapping itself snugly around the skeleton like a blanket.

Seth looked at her, his mouth a little open. "That *was* fun," he said.

"Help me get the net down and we can do it again."

Seth clambered quickly up the bookcase and snatched the net down. He looked around, eyes darting curiously. Then he vanished into the dark.

"Seth?"

"Let's use this!" he said, reappearing with a ball made

from the skin of a puffer fish. "It'll be more fun with a moving target."

Ellie grinned, feeling a tiny flutter of joy in her chest. They took turns, one of them throwing the ball into the air and the other one trying to catch it with the net-cannon. They kept score, and Ellie didn't even mind when Seth got more points than her. After many rounds, and a score of twenty-one to twelve, she slumped down against a work-bench, out of breath. She finally felt like sleeping.

She realized then that she was sitting with her feet against the boat made of books. She shifted uncomfortably, looking at her lap. Seth sat down next to her.

"My mom used to say that my brother and I were her greatest inventions," Ellie said. "She made a machine that could predict when a storm was coming, three *days* before it happened, can you believe that? But she thought my brother and I were better."

Ellie found that her body was trembling, her chest tight. Seth watched her silently.

"I was supposed to keep him safe," she said. "I was sup-posed to *protect* him. And when he got ill . . . I should have been able to *fix* him."

She rested her head on her knees. "When he got sick, I did everything I could. I went to the university. I scoured every library in the City for a way to save him. But I couldn't. I couldn't figure it out. My mom would have known what to do, but I didn't. And the worst bit was that he was alone. I left him alone in his bed. And when I came back to the orphanage . . ." Ellie took a deep, trembling breath. "When I came back my brother was dead."

She heard the sound of fabric on wood as Seth shuffled nearer. She felt the closeness of his hand as it hovered by her shoulder. Then his hand retreated.

"He needed me, Seth," she said. "I couldn't fix him, and I wasn't there for him when he died. He *needed* me, and I failed him."

"You didn't—"

"I *did*," she said fiercely, turning to look at him, daring him to say otherwise. Seth swallowed, and his gaze dropped from hers. They sat in silence.

After a while, Ellie sighed, angrily wiping away her tears. She got to her feet and picked up the ball from among a pile of books. "Come on," she said, tossing it into Seth's arms. "I'm going to beat your score if it takes all night."

How much longer they played, Ellie wasn't sure, though they quickly started giggling again, and, as they got more and more tired, their aim became abysmal. Ellie laughed so hard her lungs started to hurt. She lay down against a bookcase.

"Giving up, are you?" said Seth.

"I'm done," she said breathlessly. "And I could have beaten you easily. I was just being nice."

Seth tutted, but kept smiling. Then, he looked sharply across the room, like a cat noticing something no one else can see.

"What is it?" said Ellie.

Seth walked over to the large metal tub and pulled the lid aside.

"Hey, what are you doing?" said Ellie, rising cautiously to her feet.

The surface of the water was utterly still. Seth took a deep breath and the water bubbled, ever so slightly. His eyes flicked to Ellie, and it stopped. He put out his hand, holding it above the water.

At first, nothing happened.

Then the water rose, silently, a smooth cone-shape glistening in the moonlight. It touched the palm of Seth's hand, and his face broke into a disbelieving smile. He laughed, and the water sputtered playfully, spraying him before collapsing back into the tub.

Ellie bounced up and down, clapping eagerly. "You did it!" she cried.

Seth looked back at her with wide eyes. "I did it."

When Ellie awoke, her lungs still hurt from laughing. She was lying wrapped in her blanket on the workshop floor. She couldn't remember falling asleep, but it was still dark. She looked around and saw Seth sleeping a few feet away among a pile of books. He looked very peaceful.

There was a tiny noise in the distance. Ellie tensed and sat up.

It was faint, but she'd know it anywhere. It was coming from the street outside, a quiet jangling of metal.

"Please," she whispered. "Not tonight."

She closed her eyes, hoping it would go away. But the sound grew more insistent. She stepped barefoot across the workshop, collecting the oil lamp that hung from the wall. She put her eye to the spyhole to look outside, but the oil lamp in Orphanage Street had gone out and there was nothing to see but the dark.

Nothing to hear but the tinkling of metal.

Delicately, she undid each bolt, as quietly as she could, so as not to wake Seth. She slid the door open, holding her lamp up to the alleyway across the street.

"Oh, hello," said Finn timidly. "I'm so glad you heard me."

He was standing where the street met a narrow alley, twenty paces away from her, drawing one finger across the chain at his neck.

"It's cold," he said, his pretty features lit up with golden lamplight. "I was worried you might leave me out here."

"What is it?" said Ellie, gripping her blanket tighter and pulling the workshop door shut behind her. She didn't want Seth to hear anything.

"I thought you'd want to know how I rescued him," said Finn.

"I don't."

"Oh," he said, looking dejected. "But I thought . . . It was very clever, what I did. I know how much you like clever things."

"I don't care, Finn," she said. "Just go away."

He scratched his head. "I don't understand. You asked for my help?"

"I didn't have any choice. He was going to die."

"I know . . . I went to all that effort to save him. Don't you care?"

"Finn, *no more games.*"

He sniffed and rubbed his nose. "But you always used to like our games. I thought, maybe, now that I've helped you . . . maybe you'd let me forgive you?"

"Stop it, Finn!"

"Why are you being so cruel?" he moaned. "Aren't I your—"

Ellie dropped the lamp and the blanket and ran at him, pushing him roughly backward.

"NO! You are nothing to me. You are nothing!"

Finn's breathing was shallow. "You've got to listen to me! I know you like having Seth around—I know you like the company. And I *know* that rescuing him makes you feel less guilty about all the terrible things you've done."

"Shut *up*, Finn."

"But please, Nellie, you can't keep him—he'll lead the Inquisition straight to you!"

"He's not safe on the streets," said Ellie. "He's staying here. And there's nothing you can do about it!"

Finn scrunched up his face, fat tears dribbling down both cheeks. Ellie fought the maddening urge to comfort him, and turned away instead.

He spoke in a tiny voice behind her. "But . . . there is something I can do, Nellie. You know there is."

The words were like a knife slid between her ribs. Her throat was dry. She turned.

"No. You can't."

He swallowed, sorrow in his eyes. "I have to do *something*. It's for your own good."

"Finn!"

"I'm sorry, Nellie."

"He's innocent. He's done nothing wrong."

"It's not safe for you."

"No, please. I don't want you to!"

"But you need me to. I wish it didn't have to be this way."

"Yes, you do," Ellie snarled. "You *love* to see people suffer. You'll enjoy it!"

Finn stared at her, astonished. "Why would I want that,

Nellie? I'd never be so cruel. I only want what's best for you."

Again, something deep in the pit of Ellie's stomach pleaded for her to comfort him, and again she silenced it. His eyes were still watery, his bottom lip quivering. He stared pitifully at his feet. Then he looked at her.

And the corners of his mouth twitched upward.

He put a hand up to hide his face. Ellie's heart was pounding. "You smiled," she said.

He shook his head fervently. "No . . . no, I didn't."

"You did, I saw you!"

"No, Nellie, really, I didn't smile. I promise."

"You *monster*," she spat, picking up a loose cobblestone from the ground and throwing it at his face. Finn dodged nimbly aside, and then was fleeing, racing off along the alleyway, swiftly lost to the darkness.

FROM THE DIARY OF CLAUDE HESTERMEYER

"What have you done?" I said, staring in horror at the money. "*How* did you do this?"

"Because that's how it works, Claude," said the Enemy, sitting comfortably in his armchair. "What, did you think that the only price for my help is that you feel a bit tired for a while? No, dear friend, I'm afraid it's not so simple. You're the Vessel, and I'm the Enemy. When you make a wish, I get to make a wish of my own. You asked me to pick up that starfish, so I used a starfish to wedge your door open so the servant would go in. You asked me to get money for Peter's father, so I stole some *more* money from the university and put it on your desk."

"But," I began, my breath coming quickly, "that servant, Thomas—he saw the gold. And now he's going to tell the master, I'm sure of it. They're going to think I've been stealing from the university!"

The Enemy leaned forward in his armchair. "Well then, I think you know what you have to do."

I made for the door. "No, I'm *not* asking you for any more favors. I'll see to this myself."

"If you do, it will be too late," he said as I reached for the door handle. "You can't get there quickly enough. But I can. I can stop the servant from talking."

I wiped my sleeve across my brow. I stared at the pile of gold and uttered a silent prayer to St. Celestina.

"*Don't* kill him," I said. "Stop him, but don't kill him."

"It will be easier if I kill him," said the Enemy.

"*No,*" I snapped. "No killing. Just . . . *hide* him somewhere until I can figure this out."

The Enemy nodded, and stood up. "Very well," he said.

I buried my face in my hands. When I looked up again, he was gone.

12

THE OYSTERY

The sun had risen by the time Ellie had worked up the resolve to prod Seth's shoulder. He looked so peaceful asleep, and she felt so guilty for waking him with such bad news.

"I think Finn's going to try and kill you today."

Seth blinked rapidly and eased himself up. "What? Why?"

"He thinks you're putting me in danger."

Seth massaged his temples. "So then why did he save my life in the first place?"

"Look, I told you, he's bad-tempered and he gets these ideas. If he says he wants to kill you then he's certainly going to try."

"But why does he care about me? Why does he care about *you*?"

Ellie grimaced. "It's complicated. He doesn't have many friends so he gets kind of, uh, territorial. As long as you stay here with me, in the workshop, then he can't do anything without risking my safety. But we need to be ready to defend ourselves."

Seth gave her a rebellious look.

"He's a *genius*, Seth. You should be afraid of him."

Seth wrinkled his nose. "Fine," he said bitterly. "You have weird friends, though."

Ellie sighed. "I know. Right, we should still take some precautions—Finn might tip off the Inquisitors that you're here, so we'll need a way to escape the workshop. I've got an idea for some hidden traps."

There was a knock at the door and Seth snuck down to the basement to hide. Ellie opened the door and found Anna standing outside, looking as if she'd rather be anywhere else. Ellie was surprised by the leap of happiness in her chest.

"Anna! I didn't think you'd be coming today."

Anna shrugged. "Someone needs to make sure *he* doesn't get you killed," she said, gesturing at Seth, who had reappeared at the sound of Anna's name.

"Good morning, Anna," said Seth cheerily.

"Ugh," said Anna, blowing a curl of ginger hair aside. "Ellie, it's the Magnus Alderdice Festival today, down in the Markets of the Unknown Saint. Let's go to it. The *whale boy* can stay here and play with the furnace or something."

"Oh, um," said Ellie, flustered. She looked around and spied a broken oyster-catcher. "I've got to fix that this morning," she lied. "The owner wants it finished by noon."

"Oh, all right," said Anna, shrugging. "I'll stay and help you then."

"No, no," said Ellie hurriedly. "You'll have more fun at the market."

"But I want to help," said Anna, a frown forming on her brow.

"It's fine, really," said Ellie. "Seth can help me."

Anna's face fell. Seth drew in air through his teeth.

"Well, I guess you don't need me at *all* then," said Anna, and she spun around furiously and stormed out of the workshop.

Ellie noticed the look Seth gave her. "I don't want her *involved*," she explained. "It's too dangerous."

"I think Anna can take care of herself," said Seth.

"Come on," said Ellie. "Let's get to work."

After an hour spent pulling nails out of the floorboards and attaching hinges so they could make the boards fall inward, Ellie thought she heard a very faint jingling in the street.

"Um, I'm just popping over to the orphanage to talk to

Anna," she said, checking that Seth was busily engrossed with the floorboards. She stepped out of the workshop and closed the door quickly behind her. Finn was leaning against a wall, chin resting lazily on one fist.

"Go away," she hissed. "He's not coming out."

Finn chewed his lip in disappointment. "Fine," he said, scowling. "You win. Unless . . ."

Ellie's heart quickened. "Unless what?"

Finn's scowl softened, then vanished. "Unless I change my plans. I think I need to remind you which one of us is cleverer."

Ellie pressed her thumb through the hole in her coat sleeve. "Finn, you can't do anything. He's safe in here with me."

"I know that," said Finn. "But *she* isn't."

He smiled an angelic smile, then darted around the corner. Sharp pricks of worry stabbed at Ellie's skin.

"Anna."

She rushed across the street and into the orphanage. She checked Anna's bedroom, the kitchens, and the storage room, where the forgotten possessions of past orphans were piled to the ceiling. Anna wasn't in any of them.

Fry and Ibnet were lounging on the floor of the games room.

"Where's Anna?" Ellie asked them.

"She's out," said Ibnet.

"Where?"

"They're having a festival for the anniversary of the seventeenth Vessel's execution," said Fry, holding out a pouch for Ellie to see. "Look, Ellie, Anna's been teaching me to pick pockets. This is Ibnet's purse—I stole it from him, and he didn't even realize!"

Ibnet leapt across the room to wrestle his money away from her, but Ellie turned and raced back to the workshop.

"Anna's not in the orphanage," she told Seth. "I think Finn's going to try and do something to her." Her heart was firing like a cannon in her chest. "I'm going to go and find her. You—"

"Stay here," Seth muttered moodily. "Yes, I know."

The Markets of the Unknown Saint were right on the southern edge of the City, on the Immutable Waterfront. They spilled through a dozen streets and many more alleyways; scores of stalls and hundreds of shoppers. Ellie had to duck and weave between them, eyes darting around for any sign of Anna. She came to an open square where a hungry, raging bonfire had been built for the celebration. But the people standing around it looked glum, the children waving their streamers halfheartedly. Ellie guessed it was hard to celebrate the anniversary of an old Vessel being killed, when a new Vessel was loose in the City.

On the corner of the square, Ellie passed another

massive, sturdy-looking building that she'd always thought abandoned. It had boarded-up windows, a spiked roof, and a shiny silver lock on its front door. As she watched, an Inquisitor pulled along a small man bound in chains. He hurled him inside the building, then went in after, slamming the door behind him.

Ellie leaned against a jewelry stall to catch her breath, looking around anxiously for a bright shock of ginger hair, or a familiar blue sweater.

"Hey, watch what you're touching!" shrieked the stall owner.

Three burly men hurried by, carrying crates of eels, and another elderly shopkeeper yelled at her to buy a wooden carving of the Enemy.

"Burn it in a bonfire!" he screeched. "Banish the Enemy for only twenty pennies!"

Ellie rubbed the sides of her head and tried to think like Anna. Where would she have gone? The market stalls only sold things like earrings and fish, and wouldn't interest Anna. And there were very few sailors for her to pester here, so far from the docks.

"Think, think, think," Ellie told herself. What was the most reckless, dangerous thing someone could do near the Immutable Waterfront?

"The Oystery!" she cried.

Anna loved it there! It combined so many of her favorite

things: a perilous three-hundred-foot drop, seagulls to spit cherry stones at, and grizzled old fishermen who could teach her new swear words.

Ellie broke into a run, darting between a group of musicians and four children flinging sardines at each other. As she got nearer to the seafront, an enormous tower reared up, far taller than the buildings around it. It was called the Tower of the Serpent. It had once been used as a lighthouse, a beacon fire lit on top of it every night. Winding in a spiral around the outside was the vast, graven figure of the sea serpent that gave the building its name, so large that a stairwell ran up its insides. Ellie's mom had often taken Ellie and her brother to the top of the tower when they were little. When her brother had gotten scared of being up so high, her mom had bundled them up and sung to them. On a better day, the sight of the tower would have made Ellie feel safe and warm.

"Anna!" she cried, turning her head wildly. "Anna!"

Ellie burst out of an alleyway and the sea exploded into view, the sound of crashing waves filling her ears. The Immutable Waterfront didn't slope down smoothly to join the water but fell sharply into the sea—a cliff made from a hundred submerged buildings. Every day, when the tide went down, the walls of these buildings were covered in thousands of oysters.

Ellie's mom's oyster-catchers could be seen ponderously

climbing the walls, gathering up the oysters into a compartment in their bellies. From here, the oysters dropped into a sack trailing beneath the machine, like a clutch of insect eggs.

Stretching out from the walls of the Oystery was a sprawling network of wooden walkways and platforms, raised up high above the sea on towering stilts, connected to each other by rope bridges and staircases. Dangling from these platforms on long ropes were hundreds of cages for catching the lobsters and crayfish that swarmed over the rooftops beneath the sea. Fishermen winched the lobster traps back up from the water and carried cagefuls of shellfish back to the City. Some even lived in huts on the platforms, their washing lines tangled with the bunches of mussels that clung to the wooden stilts.

And there, sitting on the edge of the platform furthest from the City, legs waggling back and forth as she stared glumly out to sea, was Anna.

"Anna!" Ellie cried. "Anna Stonewall!"

But her voice was drowned out by the wind. She looked up and down the flat street that wound along the edge of the Oystery, and saw him instantly, sitting on a bench and idly winding a lock of golden hair around his finger.

Finn caught Ellie's eye and waved enthusiastically.

"ANNA!" Ellie roared. She pulled a flash-bang from her pocket and launched it as hard as she could in Anna's direction, only the wind caught it, and it swirled in a graceful loop before plummeting toward the sea.

Ellie gritted her teeth and ran along the closest rope bridge. Wooden planks rattled. Fear stabbed like needles driven into her hands and feet.

"Anna! ANNA!"

At last, Anna looked over her shoulder and saw Ellie. She scowled, stood up, and started walking in the opposite direction.

"No, no, Anna! Come back—it's not safe!"

But Anna couldn't hear, or didn't want to. The wind whipped Ellie's hair painfully against her neck. She ran, and her leg nearly plunged through the gap between two planks in the rope bridge. Behind her, someone was shouting, but Ellie only cared about reaching Anna.

"Go away, Ellie!" Anna yelled above the wind, turning to hurl the words in Ellie's direction.

Then Anna's eyes went wide, as she looked over Ellie's shoulder. Ellie turned, and was hit by a cloud of smoke.

The Oystery was on fire.

13

THE TOWER OF THE SERPENT

Men were shouting and screaming. Somehow, the platforms had caught fire: a hut, two staircases, and a long stretch of platform were already ablaze, and the flames were spreading at a terrifying pace, as if the wood had been coated with whale oil.

"Anna!" Ellie cried.

"Ellie!"

They ran at each other, hugging tightly. Anna had dried tears on her cheeks and smelled of cherries. Ellie looked around the Oystery—already the fire had claimed another platform and was racing down a wooden stilt toward the sea. If they didn't move quickly, there'd be no path back to the City, and they'd have no choice but to jump hundreds of feet into the sea below. Ellie had once read that falling into water from a great height was like falling into solid rock.

She scanned the platforms, trying to figure out a path to safety. "This way!" she cried, taking Anna's hand. Of all the people in the Oystery, they were by far the furthest out to sea. The fishermen were all running back as fast as they could—none had noticed the two girls trapped behind them.

Ellie and Anna raced up a flight of stairs. The fire streaked out in all directions, consuming rope bridges and wood and spreading like a fiery spider's web. Below, Ellie could see flames licking at the dangling lobster traps. She kicked the levers of every winch they passed, dropping the lobsters back into the sea before they could be burned alive.

"It's okay!" Anna said, as they crossed another swinging rope bridge. "We'll make it!"

But then the fire reared up before them, and the bridge lurched beneath their feet. Down to their right, an entire platform collapsed into the sea as its wooden stilts gave way and its rope bridges crumbled to ash.

"No, *no*," said Ellie. She searched the faces of the hundreds of people who'd gathered along the waterfront, watching in horror. Where was Finn? Surely he wouldn't let her die?

She took a deep breath and was about to speak when

she spotted someone she *did* recognize standing apart from the crowd.

It was Seth.

He wasn't looking at them, though, but at the sea far below. His hands were out at his sides. His eyes were wide and wild.

"Ellie," said Anna, tugging at her sleeve and pointing downward. "Look."

The sea was wild too, seething like a pot of boiling water. Waves crashed in all directions, as if some mighty creature were thrashing around beneath the surface. Then, that same beast seemed to hurl itself from the water—a blue-black construction of seawater, the size of a ship and rising upward. Not toward the flaming, crumbling plat-forms, but toward the City. Toward Seth.

Something was wrong. Ellie pulled a telescope from her pocket to get a closer look at Seth, and saw blue misty swirls on his skin again, larger and angrier than she'd ever seen them. Worse, the dark blue of his eyes was bleeding out from the edges, blotting out the pupils and the whites and turning them all one color.

"He's too angry," Ellie said fearfully, watching the sea twist and thrash as it smashed against the stone of the seawall, higher and higher each time. "He's making the sea all angry."

Seth shuddered. His mouth opened, like he wanted to

scream, but no sound came out. His arms fell limp and he dropped to his knees, his body jerking and swaying like flotsam caught in a riptide.

Ellie groaned as she watched the sea climbing toward him: a swirling mass of darkness, spraying white foam in all directions, rising up the side of the City to claim its prize. A rush of heat singed the hairs on her neck; she could *hear* the sound of the fire around her, a strange, sucking sound, like it was gulping up the air.

She reached into her pocket, her fingers trembling as they groped around for what she needed. They bumped into a small spherical object wrapped up in paper. She ripped it out and launched it toward Seth, aiming for a large wooden stake that jutted from one of the platforms between them.

There was a deafening *crack* and a brilliant, blinding blaze of light that eclipsed even the light of the fire. Seth's eyes flicked from the sea toward it, like someone drawn from a dream. His eyes met hers.

Ellie tried to pour all the meaning that she could into her gaze. Seth frowned, his eyes all blue and expressionless, blue mist-shapes curling over his face. He put his hands flat on the ground. He stood up. His pupils returned to his eyes. He breathed in deeply.

The towering column of seawater spun away from him, back toward the fiery platforms. It surged, and grew, and more of the sea rose up to join it, until the entire ocean seemed to be rising. Seth lifted his hands above his head.

"We need to tie ourselves to something!" Ellie cried.

They flung themselves flat on the rope bridge and Ellie pulled a length of rope from her pocket. She threw it around them, then tried to tie a knot. But her fingers were trembling too much, and Anna snatched the rope from her hands and tied it herself.

The water hit, swallowing them up and crashing in on Ellie's eardrums. They were pulled roughly in all directions as the rope bridge twisted and turned upside down. Salty froth rushed up Ellie's nose. A mussel shell cut her ear as it spun by. They were turned around again, and again, until Ellie couldn't remember which direction was up.

At last, the wave fell back to the sea, leaving steaming puddles on the platforms and a mist of swirling vapor. Anna untied the rope and they clambered to their feet, shivering and coughing. Their hair was soaked, slicked flat to their skulls. Ellie could feel the heat from the charred wood through the soles of her boots. She looked around. Rotten chunks of wood had been sucked away by the wave, and the whole structure was now a frail walkway of steaming charcoal and wobbly wooden planks. But if they were careful, they'd be able to climb back up to the waterfront. Ellie wanted to laugh. They had done it! They'd beaten Finn!

Then a cry came from the crowd.

"It was that boy!" a man yelled. "I saw him! *He* made the sea do that."

"Look at his skin. Oh, saints have mercy—that's him!"

"THAT'S THE VESSEL!"

"No!" Ellie cried. She grabbed hold of a blackened stump of wood and used it to vault across a crumbled gap in the platform, racing back to the waterfront with Anna right behind her.

"Get the Inquisitors!" someone screamed in terror.

The crowd shoved and pushed as they tried to flee. Seth swayed and staggered—he looked like he was going to pass out. Ellie ran toward him but got stuck among the surging crowd.

"Ellie!" Anna cried, grabbing hold of Ellie's coat. "Ellie, wait!"

Ellie twisted, shaking Anna off. "Go back to the orphanage—it's not safe here!" she said, pushing farther into the crowd. A chill traveled up her spine as she saw, between the blur of panicked faces, the distinctive black coat of an Inquisitor.

"Out of my way!" he roared.

Ellie was knocked about by the mass of hysterical people. She felt Anna's hand grab hold of her, then get pulled away again. At last she squeezed free of the crowd, the Inquisitor still caught among them.

"Idiots! Control yourselves!" he cried, shoving men and women out of his way.

Ellie saw Seth stumbling into an alley at the edge of the Oystery. She hurtled after him, catching him just as he was about to fall. His hand was ice-cold.

"The Inquisitors are coming," she whispered.

But Seth slumped against the alley wall, eyes closed.

"Come *on*, Seth," said Ellie desperately. She reached up and yanked some hairs from his head. Seth winced and his eyes flashed open. *"Now,"* she said, grabbing his hand and pulling him along the alley.

They turned a corner, and Ellie heard the heavy tread of boots behind. From her pocket she pulled a small, wheeled device with a key sticking in its back, like a child's clockwork toy. She wound it up, then hurled it down a cross street, in the opposite direction from where they were heading. It emitted a high-pitched whistle as it rattled along the cobblestones.

"That will distract them," she said as they hurried onward.

"Won't they know it's yours?" said Seth.

"No. In about thirty seconds it's going to explode."

Ahead, the Tower of the Serpent loomed above them.

"What do we do?" said Seth, searching for places to hide. All the doors around them were locked shut.

"We could get into the sewers maybe?" Ellie said,

glancing around. "Oh, but there aren't any entrances nearby! Come on, this way—we'll hide up here."

At the base of the stone serpent they found the entrance to the staircase, which would take them right to the top. They climbed, winding through the snake's insides. Ellie let out a sigh of relief as they left the streets beneath them.

They emerged onto the flat top of the tower, looking down on the mossy rooftops of the City, a kingdom of nests and gull droppings. Seth collapsed on his front, his hands on his head. Ellie's knees hurt from running, and she had swallowed so much seawater she felt sick.

She looked around the flat rooftop. There were dozens of large crates scattered around, which she didn't remember being there before. Seth staggered to his feet and walked to the edge, looking down at the streets below.

"They're still chasing that whistling thing," he said with mounting excitement. "They're not following us!"

Ellie almost laughed. They'd done it. They'd actually done it.

Then she heard the tinkling of metal.

"I just knew you'd come up here," said a cheerful voice nearby.

Ellie's heart seemed to stop.

Finn was lying on his back behind one of the crates, staring up at the sky. Ellie checked over her shoulder to make sure Seth wasn't watching her, but he was focused on where the Inquisitors were going. Ellie scrambled toward Finn, kneeling down at his side behind the crate.

"What are you doing here?" she whispered. "You can't be here!"

"You've always been so fond of this place," he said. "I thought, if you were going to hide anywhere, it would be here. Isn't it nice to have someone on your side who knows you so well?"

"They're *still* going the wrong way!" Seth cried.

"What have you *done*?" Ellie snarled, grabbing Finn's wrist and squeezing tight.

"Dear, dear, Nellie, such a short fuse," Finn said, then smiled. "Oh, and speaking of which . . ."

Ellie heard it. Somewhere nearby, something was hissing.

She ran toward the crates, kicking one aside and over-turning another. "Where is it?" she cried. "Where's the fuse?"

"Ellie, what's wrong?" said Seth.

"Now it will just be you and me again," said Finn. "I'd say that's worth celebrating. And what better way to cele-brate than—"

Ellie ran toward Seth and pulled him down to the roof-top just as a huge series of thunderous explosions rocketed upward. A hundred fireworks detonated at once from inside the crates, blasting wood in all directions, burning missiles corkscrewing into the air. Finn vanished amid the smoke.

Yells and shouts came from below, barely audible beneath the scream of the fireworks. Seth got to his feet.

"What have you done?" Seth yelled at Ellie at the top of his lungs. "The whole *City* will see us now! We need to get down!"

Ellie's vision swam with blinking lights. The tower was covered in a blanket of smoke, smelling of scorched almonds and acid. Little sparks still fluttered in the crates, doing purple loop-the-loops. She rushed to the edge of the tower. Below, five Inquisitors were heading for the steps. If they went down that way, they'd be caught. But what other way was there? It was a hundred-foot drop from the roof to the cobbles.

"Seth!" she yelled. She could hardly hear herself over the ringing in her ears. "We're going to have to jump."

Seth stared at her in disbelief. "What?"

"Trust me, all right? This will work."

They held one another's gaze.

"Ellie, I know you're clever," he said, "but even you can't trick death."

"Watch me," said Ellie. "Now come on!"

The last of the fireworks spat and fizzled. One whooshed past Ellie's ear; she smelled her own hair burning.

Heavy footsteps echoed up the stairwell. "Here! The Vessel is up here!"

Seth took hold of Ellie's hand.

They stepped to the edge.

And jumped.

FROM THE DIARY OF CLAUDE HESTERMEYER

Last night we had the Feast of St. Emery. Nearly every scholar was there, young and old. The good silver cutlery was in use, making the three long dining tables glitter like fish scales in the candlelight. The Casket of St. Emery had been brought out and placed in the center of the hall—a large, beautifully carved trunk the size of a rowboat.

I sat by myself. It was my own fault—I'd become sullen and moody, and the other scholars were wary of me. I don't think they suspected me of stealing the gold, though. Since the young servant, Thomas, had disappeared at the same time as the money, everyone assumed that *he* had stolen it. I was immensely relieved, though worried about what the Enemy had done to him.

"You promise you didn't kill him?" I whispered into my wineglass, so nobody would see me talking to myself.

"Of course," said the Enemy, taking the seat opposite me. "I have to fulfill your wish to the letter. '*Hide* him somewhere,' you said. So that's what I did."

I met the eye of one of the other scholars across the hall and forced the warmest smile I could manage. He'd been a good friend of Peter's and had helped us with the manuscript we'd been working on before Peter died: a collection of old legends and myths from the early years of the City. He looked away without smiling back.

"You've made them all hate me," I said. I was so tired these days, and barely aware of what was happening around me a lot of the time.

"You've done that yourself," said the Enemy. "You shouldn't have helped my father."

"I had to—those moneylenders would have killed him."

The Enemy smiled. "That's not why you did it. You felt *guilty*."

"Now just you listen—"

But I was cut off by a sudden knocking, loud and insistent. The other scholars looked around, startled.

"Whatever is that racket?" one said.

The master held up his hand and everyone quieted down. In the silence, it was clear where the noise was coming from:

The Casket of St. Emery.

Two of the younger scholars went to investigate. They undid the locks that sealed the lid of the casket shut and flung it open.

A young man burst out, gasping for air. I recognized him at once.

It was Thomas.

14

BEFORE THE DROWNING
OF THE WORLD

Seth and Ellie held hands as the rest of the world rushed up to meet them.

The street was a tiny sliver of cobblestones below. The wind howled in Ellie's ears. Her stomach churned. The street was not so tiny anymore.

Save us, she thought. *Save us from the fall.*

Their feet met resistance, and Ellie's body seized up. She felt one single moment of terror—it hadn't worked!

But it wasn't hard cobblestones they'd hit. Beneath them, something sagged and split.

They dropped like stones through wet paper.

And were caught a second time. Again, the surface tore and, above her, Ellie saw the ragged remains of the first sheet of canvas that had broken their fall. They fell again, and again, and each time her heart exploded in her chest.

The final layer of canvas did not tear. They bounced off it gently and toppled onto their backs. Above them were four punctured circles of canvas, letting in a trickle of sunlight from the street above. They'd fallen through a perfectly round hole in the street, into a narrow tunnel. It looked like part of the sewers.

Ellie's body felt weak, her mind empty. She lay motionless, until a sharp sting of fear forced her to get up. She stepped in a puddle of brown silt, which she hoped wasn't sewage. Seth leaned against the wall, breathing hard.

"What just happened?" he said. "I don't understand—you said there weren't any entrances to the sewers near the tower."

"I made this hole," she said, lying quickly. Seawater dripped from her hair.

"You made *this*?"

"In case I ever had to jump from that tower," she said. "I put a bomb under the cobbles and, um, I blew it up while we were falling."

Seth narrowed his eyes. "That doesn't make any sense, how could you—"

"Look, we need to go before the Inquisitors find this," said Ellie, pointing at the hole above them. It was as wide as a church door, torn straight out of the cobbled street.

She pulled Seth with her along the narrow, slimy tunnel.

"But why did those fireworks go off?" said Seth.

"Um, I mean . . . uh . . ."

"Ellie, I can tell you're lying. This has all been Finn's work, hasn't it? Why are you trying to protect him?"

"Look, I'll explain everything when we get back to the workshop, all right?" she said, hoping to buy herself more time. Seth looked unconvinced. "But, hey!" she cried, happy to change the subject. "You did it! You controlled the sea! It was so incredible, Seth."

Seth frowned, rubbing the back of his head. "It didn't feel incredible. I think it nearly killed me. I couldn't focus. All I felt was that . . . anger. I thought I was completely alone, drowning. Until I saw you."

He stared at her, and Ellie shuffled her feet, feeling her cheeks go slightly hot. "Oh, well, I'm glad the flash-bang got your attention." She cleared her throat. "Come on, we should go."

She fished a small metal box from her pocket and removed a match, drawing it sharply against the wall. Sparks leapt from the end, soaking the tunnel with a flickering orange light. She led the way, the sound of rushing water not far ahead.

"We'll be able to take the sewers back," Ellie said, pulling a compass from her pocket and squinting at it. "My second workshop isn't far from here, and I know the way from there to Orphanage Street."

"You have a second workshop?" said Seth as they descended a set of slippery stairs.

Ellie nodded. "It's hidden in an abandoned ruin, right next to the sea. Anna and I built it last year so I could start working on my underwater boat. It's a boat that can go underwater," she explained.

"Yes, I figured that out."

Navigating the sewers was no simple task—they were not, in most places, supposed to be navigated. They were a meandering labyrinth of stone and rusted metal, crafted together from the ruins of storm drains and long-abandoned streets. Only in certain tunnels were there walkways alongside the sewage flow. Even then, they often had to hunch over. The stench of sewage was everywhere, and Ellie felt like it would linger forever, not just in her clothes but in her hair and on her skin.

After many long minutes they entered a chamber much larger than those before it. Ellie lit a fresh match, holding it up to reveal their surroundings.

"This looks more like a crypt than a sewer," said Seth.

"It *is* a crypt," said Ellie. Sewage water passed disrespectfully between worn old tombs, their bases thick with moss. "These people all died before the Great Drowning.

The sewers were built around them."

At the far side of the crypt they found an old toolbox, a beaten copper helmet, and a tattered, moldy sweater. Inside the toolbox, to their relief, was a rusted oil lamp, which Ellie filled with whale oil from a flask in her pocket. They did not stick around to wonder what had happened to the toolbox's owner.

They carried onward, through what must have once been a wealthy family's mansion. Before the Drowning, there had been so many people that they had built streets on top of streets, so that many ended up buried and forgotten. Ellie and Seth climbed giant marble staircases and hurried through dank-smelling wine cellars. Once, they stumbled upon the bones of a killer whale, scattered on the floor with no clue as to how they'd gotten there. Minutes later, Seth pointed out a vast mural on the wall. They were inside what looked like an old church.

"What's that?" he said.

Ellie held up the lamp, washing the gloom from the mural. At its center was a gigantic, shaggy wolf, lying dead in the snow. It was old; its dark coat grizzled and its teeth worn and broken. Its mouth was wide open.

And from inside, a glowing woman emerged.

A hundred other people and animals had gathered around, seemingly to greet the woman: humans dressed in furs and feathers, bears and eagles and snakes and goats, bowing before her. The woman had a golden halo around her head, and among the people and animals there were others with halos too.

"Why do some of them have halos and others don't?" Seth asked.

"I . . . I don't know," said Ellie.

She leaned in close, admiring the delicate brushstrokes of the woman's face. The paint was faded, seemingly ancient, yet the intense, passionate look in her eyes and her slight smile had survived the centuries intact.

"This must be from before the Drowning," said Ellie. "I've never seen anything like it in a church before. There are paintings of the saints where they have halos, but why would an *animal* have one?"

She inspected a gray horse with a black mane and a glittering halo of gold leaf. Then something clattered in the far distance, echoing through the tunnel.

"Come on," Ellie whispered. "We should keep going."

But Seth kept looking back at the mural until it was sucked up again by the gloom, his eyes full of wonder.

Soon, the sewers became cramped passageways that climbed up and up. They heard water dripping in unseen places.

"Your second workshop's not actually in the sewers, is it?" Seth asked cautiously.

"Of course it is! I mean—it *is* in the sewers, but there's no sewage running through it," she added, seeing Seth's look of horror. "It doesn't smell or anything."

Seth looked unconvinced. They hurried along a more spacious tunnel where there was a slight, fresh breeze. They could hear the crashing of waves against stone. Finally, Ellie led Seth through a rusted metal door, and they were dazzled by a dim haze of daylight reflecting off the sea.

They'd emerged into a small, gloomy ruin that smelled strongly of salt and seaweed, but was fresher by far than the sewers. It had a high limestone ceiling from which long stalactites descended, and one of the walls had crumbled away completely, the floor falling sharply into the sea beneath. To one side were four workbenches surrounded by heaps of tools and scrap metal. It looked like someone had emptied a small portion of Ellie's workshop inside a dilapidated building and made no effort to rearrange the result.

"I can tell you've been here before," said Seth.

Ellie scowled at him, then collapsed against a rock. Her damp clothes still clung to her body, but she was too exhausted to care. She watched as Seth explored the workshop. He paused to look out to sea, then glanced below.

On a low stone quay, propped up on large wooden

trestles, was a clunky, inelegant contraption, about the size of a horse-drawn cart. It looked like a very large turtle, made from leather and metal, with a massive propeller on its front and a large rudder extending from its back.

"That's the underwater boat," Seth said. "Does it work?"

"No."

"What's wrong with it?"

"It sinks."

Seth's shoulders dropped.

"Well I am *trying* to fix it," said Ellie crossly. "In case you haven't noticed, I've been a little busy trying to figure out how to keep you safe."

Ellie frowned at the underwater boat a little longer. She had first had the idea to build it when her brother was still alive, so that she could show him the sea. But like so many of her machines, it lay discarded and broken. How many times had she promised Anna that she'd fix it?

Anna!

In the chaos of their escape from the Oystery, Ellie had forgotten all about her. She had to get back to Orphanage Street, to make sure she was okay.

"We need to go," she said, picking herself off the ground. Then she noticed Seth inspecting a cupboard that was overstuffed to the point the wood had buckled. He reached for the latch.

"Seth, don't!" she cried.

The doors burst open and a hundred things cascaded to the floor.

"Oops," said Seth. "You're so messy. Sorry, I didn't think—"

"Clearly," Ellie snapped, kneeling to gather it all up, her cheeks reddening. She grabbed a framed self-portrait of her mother, a teddy bear and—her breath caught—a blanket that had belonged to her brother. She hurriedly stuffed them back in the cupboard.

"You forgot this," said Seth, picking up a slim book that had landed beside him.

"Give that to me, please," Ellie said, her voice strangled.

Seth frowned at it, running his fingers over the lettering on the spine. "I've heard this name before," he said. "The Inquisitors mentioned it when they had me in the keep."

"It's really boring. You don't want to read it. Why don't you try one of these instead?" Ellie went to grab a book from a workbench.

"But who was he?"

Seth held up the book, revealing the title:

THE DIARY OF CLAUDE HESTERMEYER

Ellie felt a hot coal roll around in her stomach. "Honestly, it's really not—"

"Ellie."

She sighed. "All right. Claude Hestermeyer was the Vessel. The last one to be found. Twenty-three years ago the Enemy broke out of him and tore off Hargrath's arm."

15

A VISIT FROM HARGRATH

It took them an hour to get back to Orphanage Street, winding through the underground tunnels. Seth read Hestermeyer's diary by the dim lamplight, while Ellie strained to see the dial of her compass. He seemed to have much better eyesight than she did.

"Why do you have his diary?" Seth asked.

"What?" said Ellie distractedly. "Oh, that's not the original. After Hestermeyer died, some of his colleagues at the university had a handful of copies printed. When the Inquisitors found out, they confiscated almost all of them, because they thought they were the work of the Enemy itself. They must have missed my mom's copy, though—I found it a few years ago, in among all the books she left to me."

"Have you read it?"

"Of course," said Ellie, swallowing. "Many times."

At last they came to a moldy staircase, leading up to a rusty iron door that opened into the basement of Ellie's workshop. The floorboards were rattling; someone was banging furiously at the front door.

"That must be Anna!" Ellie said eagerly. She motioned for Seth to hang back in case it wasn't, or in case there was someone else with her. She hurried to the door, pulled it aside, and Anna burst in, red-faced and breathless.

"Ellie! You're okay!" she said, hugging her tightly. Like Ellie's clothes, hers were still damp, and she had taken off her shoes and socks. Her nose wrinkled. "Ugh, you smell terrible."

"We've been in the sewers," said Ellie as Seth crept from his hiding place.

"YOU!" Anna cried, marching toward Seth. He watched warily as she stalked toward him, then looked all the more surprised when she hugged him.

"You saved us, you freak!" she cried happily. "Ugh, *you* smell terrible too. So what happened? You . . ." Her smile wavered. "You ran off."

"I went to rescue Seth," said Ellie. "He'd gotten himself cornered by an Inquisitor."

"Oh," said Anna, chewing her lip. "I could have helped."

Ellie shook her head. "It was too dangerous," she said.

"Oh. Okay," said Anna glumly. "So . . . how did that fire start?"

"I've no idea," Ellie lied.

Anna scratched her head. "But you were yelling something at me back at the Oystery. About not being safe. You knew something was about to happen."

Ellie stared at Anna a moment too long. "I didn't. I . . ."

Anna let out a big sigh. "Why won't you tell me?"

Ellie was unnerved by the gentleness in Anna's voice. It was like she was trying very hard not to shout, or cry. Her cheeks had gone pink.

"You always keep secrets from me," she said.

"What secrets?" Ellie felt her temper rise. There were more important things at stake here—why was Anna being so difficult? "Look, I can't let you get hurt."

Anna touched Ellie's sleeve. "You don't have to protect me."

"Yes, I do!" said Ellie, yanking her sleeve away. "You nearly got caught in that fire!"

"We *both* nearly got caught in that fire, and you didn't rescue me from it—*he* rescued us," Anna said, pointing at Seth. "I want to help."

"No, Anna," Ellie said firmly. "It's my job to protect you."

Anna sighed. "It's really not." She dropped her voice. "I'm not your brother."

Something hot flared in Ellie's chest. "Get *out*," she snapped, her whole body trembling. Anna took a step back. "I don't want your help. Get out!"

Anna's brow crumpled to a hurt little frown. Her mouth opened and closed.

"But . . . but I—" She looked at Ellie, then seemed to decide something. Her eyes bulged. Her lip curled. "Fine," she said. *"Fine."*

And she marched from the workshop, rubbing a hand across her face.

Ellie locked the door behind her, then slumped over the nearest workbench, her forehead thudding against the wood.

"Ellie," Seth said sternly.

"I don't want to talk about it," Ellie groaned. Her whole body was exhausted, and her mind was too. It was like someone had drilled a hole in her head and let all the energy drain out of her. She flopped onto the ground.

"Finn started that fire, didn't he?" said Seth.

"I said not *now*, all right?"

The front door rattled. It was an unfamiliar knock; the hair on Ellie's neck stood on end. Seth clambered up a bookcase and hid in the library, and Ellie crept to the front door.

"Lancaster," came a low voice.

Ellie's stomach twisted. *Hargrath.* She stayed utterly still, praying he would go away.

"Let's not play games, Ellie. I've got an ax. Don't make me use it."

Ellie rolled her eyes at this obvious bluff. Who carried an ax around?

There was a deafening crash and a sharp edge of metal broke through the door, spraying splinters.

"All right, all right!" said Ellie, unlocking the door and pulling it aside.

Hargrath towered above her, his black hair neatly parted. He regarded her blankly with his deep, dead eyes. "You're soaking wet," he said, stepping inside. He set down the ax and picked up a microscope from a workbench. He turned it around in his hand. "What's this for?"

"It's like a very powerful magnifying glass," Ellie said resentfully. "It lets you see even the tiny animals that live in seawater."

Hargrath grunted, then tossed the microscope back on the bench, where it rocked on its side and fell over.

"What do you want?" said Ellie.

Hargrath picked up one of Ellie's wheeled, exploding distraction devices, weighed it in his hand, then put it back again.

"I met your mother once," he said casually. "Nice

woman. Clever, obviously. Very clever. So did you make that . . . that magnifying thing?"

Ellie bristled. "No. She did."

Hargrath nodded, idly inspecting the floorboards. "Of course, of course." His eyes drifted lazily up to her. "Why do you smell of the sewers?"

"I was fixing a drainage machine, down near St. Epstein's Spire. It got . . . messy."

Hargrath rubbed his chin, then gestured toward the basement. "You returned through that door?"

Ellie stiffened. "What?"

He pointed at the floor. "Wet footprints," he said. "Also there seem to be two sets?" He looked up enquiringly.

"I was . . . I was with Anna. My best friend?"

Hargrath looked at Ellie for many long moments. She tried to hold his gaze but her whole body was trembling.

"Where is he, Ellie?" he said.

"Where is who?"

Hargrath opened the door to the basement and looked down into the darkness. Ellie prayed that Seth had remembered to hide the mattress he slept on. Hargrath closed the door, then stared at her, letting the silence fill the workshop until it was suffocating.

"You realize . . . whether you protect him or not, he will die. Either by the hand of the Inquisition, or the thing that lives inside him. By helping him you only doom your-self as well."

Ellie's cheeks were hot, and surely red. She swallowed.

Hargrath knelt down, his dead face inches from hers. "I warned you before," he whispered. "You don't know what you're dealing with. I was like you once—young, bold. Foolish. I thought I was the hero from some bed-time story. I raced to the top of the Clocktower of St. Angelus, eager to confront the evil beast. But instead I found Claude Hestermeyer. He looked tired. So thin. So . . . pathetic. And then"—Hargrath snapped his fingers—"he fell apart. Just like that. His skin, his flesh, his body was . . . discarded, like rags in the wind. And—underneath—this thing. This creature. It lives inside the boy as we speak, growing stronger, waiting to emerge. And, when it does, it will bring destruction you cannot imagine."

For a long moment, Hargrath seemed to forget where he was. His hand trembled and his eyes flickered in his skull, as if seeing memories play out in front of him at a rapid pace. He growled and closed his eyes tightly. When he opened them again they were ringed red. With a creak of leather, he turned to show her the empty left arm of his coat. "I *know*, Ellie. You don't want to be there when the time comes. So tell me," he said, "where is he?"

"I told you," she said, "I don't know."

Hargrath studied her. "You hold some influence over him, don't you? I saw that much on the roof of St. Bartholomew's Chapel. You could use that influence for the good of the City. You could convince him to turn himself in."

"I haven't seen him since the day you arrested him," Ellie said.

"Is that so? Then perhaps you can explain why a girl matching your description was spotted fleeing the Oystery earlier? And perhaps you can also explain why I found this just now, close to where the Vessel was last seen?"

From his pocket, he pulled a small, wheeled device with a key sticking from its back, placing it next to its exact replica on the workbench. Ellie's whole body shuddered.

Why didn't it explode?

"You will bring the Vessel to me," said Hargrath. "Or lead *me* to *him*, by noon, three days from now. In return, I won't mention your name to the High Inquisitor. You will walk free. I will hand the boy over or kill him myself if necessary. And then . . ." He took a deep breath, looking longingly into the distance. "They will sing the name of Killian Hargrath. Defender of the City. Destroyer of the Enemy. They will call me a hero."

"They already call you a hero," said Ellie bitterly.

But Hargrath was lost in thought. Finally, he looked at her. "If you do not give him to me, I will inform the High Inquisitor that I found this . . . *toy* at the scene of the Vessel's escape. I will have you arrested. I will have your workshop torn apart. I will make your life an unendurable hell until you tell me what you know. And, when the dust settles, you will be dead, and your mother's legacy"—he picked up the microscope from the workbench—"will fall to nothing."

He dropped the microscope to the floor and stepped on it with his huge black boot, crunching through metal and glass.

"Good day, Miss Lancaster," he said, then he bowed and marched from the workshop.

Ellie stared dully at the broken bits of microscope.

"It was supposed to explode," she said in a hollow voice. "Why didn't it explode?"

"Ellie, are you all right?" said Seth, leaping down from the library.

"I'm fine," she said. Her voice sounded like someone else's and her body felt very cold.

"Are you sure?"

Ellie hobbled toward the nearest workbench, her legs like lead. She laid her head down, resting on one cheek. "Yeah. Yes, I'm okay."

She glanced up at Seth, who was looking down at her skeptically.

"No," she said quietly.

Seth bit his lip. "We'll figure something out," he said. "We'll go back to my first plan—find the *real* Vessel. Maybe Finn can . . ."

He paused, and for a moment was frozen still. Ellie straightened up, watching him nervously.

"Seth, what's wrong?"

He looked at her. "Finn," he said.

Ellie swallowed. "What about him?"

"Why is Finn going to such lengths to protect you? Why do you matter so much to him?"

"It's . . . it's complicated."

Seth picked up Hestermeyer's diary. "But the things he's done. Saving me from that bonfire, starting that other fire at the Oystery. They're *impossible*." He stroked the cover. "It's just like in here. Hestermeyer makes a wish, and impossible things happen."

A horrible, icy pain gripped Ellie's chest. She slumped to the floor. Seth knelt down next to her. Ellie was sure she was about to be sick.

"You keep saying I'm not the Vessel, but you've never explained how you know that," Seth said quietly. "The only way you could be so sure is if you know who *is*. Ellie, is Finn the Vessel?"

Ellie closed her eyes, not wanting to see the look on his face when she told him. She took his hand in hers and hoped he would not let go once she'd said the words.

"No, Seth. Finn is the Enemy. I'm the Vessel."

16

THE VESSEL

The words lingered in the air. Long seconds went by, or maybe minutes, and there was just a huge, terrifying silence. Ellie felt somehow the world had changed, now that she'd spoken the truth at last.

She let go of Seth's hand, pulling herself up and stumbling to the sink for a cup of water.

"You're the Vessel," he said. It wasn't a question.

Ellie's fingers trembled so much she had to use both hands to raise the cup to her lips. She'd never told anybody, not once. She'd never spoken the words, not even to the mirror.

"I shouldn't have said anything," she said. She sipped, put the cup down, and found the water hadn't helped her thirst. She felt a stab of worry, and couldn't bear to look at Seth, afraid of what she might see in his expression. "I shouldn't have told you."

"Why not?"

"Because I'm the *Vessel*!" she said. "I'm evil."

"You're not evil."

"I am!"

She looked at him out of the corner of her eye. He took a step toward her and she shied away, holding up her arms to hide her face. It was strange, being looked at for the first time by someone who knew what she really was. Her skin prickled under his gaze.

Seth looked thoughtfully at the ground. "You asked the Enemy to save me from the fire in St. Ephram's Square. Then the Enemy tried to kill Anna with that fire at the Oystery. And, when we jumped from the tower, you asked it to save us again. So it made that hole in the ground."

"Which means he has another wish of his own to make now," said Ellie. "He'll probably fling someone from the top of a building. Something like that."

"When did it happen?" Seth said quietly. "When did you first see it?"

Ellie swallowed. "Three years ago. I came back here one day, and there he was. It was quite nice at first."

"Nice?" Seth choked.

"I was lonely. I'd just lost my brother—I liked having

someone to talk to. He helped me with my machines."

"And you've managed to keep it a secret for three years?"

Ellie nodded.

"But"—Seth looked her up and down—"you don't seem . . ."

"Like the Vessel?" Ellie gave a tiny, humorless laugh. "Pale, tired, easily scratched and bruised?" She pulled up the sleeves of her coat to show him the many crisscrossing, scabbed-over scratches, the patches of purple bruises. She winced as the fabric brushed against them. "Still, at least my hair isn't falling out yet. So . . . are you going to turn me in to the Inquisitors?"

Seth frowned. "No. Why should I?"

"Because I'm the *Vessel*, Seth. Don't you get it? It's not like I stole a fish or threw a stone at a cat. I have the Enemy living inside me—if the Inquisitors knew what I was, I'd be dead! The whole *City* would want me dead!" She turned from him, shaking her head. "You don't understand."

Seth laughed bitterly. "Oh, I understand," he said. "The whole City *does* want me dead."

Ellie looked at him. A tiny seed seemed to crack open in the pit of her stomach—in a way, he probably did understand.

"And I would be dead," he continued, "if you hadn't saved me, again and again."

"I saved you for now. But Finn's still got a wish to make,

and he's not going to waste it, trust me." Ellie gritted her teeth. "I hadn't asked him for anything for over a year. A year! Not one wish."

"What did you ask him for before?"

Ellie looked around the workshop. "Stupid stuff, at first. Mostly I asked him to help me fix my mom's machines. When something broke, he'd mend it for me. The owner would be delighted. And then, a few weeks later, Finn would use *his* wish to break it again. It didn't help my reputation; people said my workmanship was shoddy. But I couldn't fix the things myself. I'm not smart enough."

"Ellie, you made a boat that goes underwater."

"By sinking," she said. "Most boats can do that if you put a hole in them. I'm a fraud."

"But you've lasted three *years* as the Vessel. Hestermeyer barely lasted three months," said Seth, pointing at the diary. "And it's not like you're dangerous."

"I might not be dangerous now. But I will be. Every time I ask for Finn's help, I get weaker. And he gets stronger. Soon . . ."

She put a hand to her chest. She felt light-headed, her body a brittle shell. She stumbled toward her bedroom.

"I need to lie down," she said. "You can come in. It doesn't matter now."

She swung the door open and drifted inside her bedroom. Seth followed.

Ellie's bedroom was a sad, empty place. The bed was plain, the bare boards were covered with pencils and pencil shavings, and little hills of candle wax. A solitary window close to the ceiling had been boarded over haphazardly, wooden planks hammered into the wall. The only color in the room came from a single red sock that lay forgotten in one corner.

"Who is . . ." said Seth, looking around. "What are these?"

There were at least three hundred black-and-white drawings stuck to the walls, sketched in pencil or ink or charcoal. Three hundred faces, three hundred boys, each one a little different from the next. A crooked nose here, cheeks freckled there, straight hair or messy hair or a dimpled chin or a chicken pox scar.

"They're my brother," said Ellie, flopping down on her bed.

"All of them?" said Seth, confused. Then he nodded to himself. "You're trying to remember what he looked like."

Ellie wrung her hands. "I can't really picture him anymore," she mumbled. The drawings terrified her, but she felt somehow they were necessary. "Look, Seth," she said, "I'm the Vessel. I really am."

"I believe you."

"Well"—Ellie crossed her arms—"you clearly don't. I shouldn't have expected you to understand. You've only been in the City a few days, after all. You don't know how serious this is."

Seth tensed. "They put me in a cage, Ellie," he said. "They tried to burn me alive. I know what this means."

"Then why aren't you afraid of me!" said Ellie, digging her fingers into her hair. "You *should* be. I'm dangerous, Seth. I'm a monster."

Seth leaned back against the wall. Ellie was infuriated by how calm he was.

"You're the only person in the City who isn't trying to kill me," he said softly.

"What about Anna?"

"Oh, Anna is definitely trying to kill me," said Seth. "On the way back from the cathedral, she spent the whole time whispering to me about her collection of poisonous plants, and how she hoped none of them ended up in my breakfast."

Ellie laughed, and it was like a brilliant blue flower sprouting suddenly in the sand. She felt exhausted, yet there was a great relief filling her body. Seth *did* understand. He understood, and he was still here.

"Is that why you saved me?" said Seth. "Because you knew I was innocent?"

"Partly," said Ellie. "I'm sorry, I should have been trying harder to figure out who you are. I've just been so worried about what Finn was going to do to you."

Seth paced over, catlike, moving a wrench from the bed so he could sit down next to her. "There must be something we can do," he said.

"There is. I can turn myself in before the Enemy's ready to take physical form."

"But if you die, the Enemy will just claim a new Vessel, right?"

"Eventually, yes, but what else can I do? If the Inquisition doesn't know I'm the Vessel, they'll keep hunting you."

"You're *clever*, Ellie," said Seth. "You can figure out a way to beat the Enemy."

Ellie scoffed. "Hestermeyer couldn't stop the Enemy, and neither could any of the others before him. And most of them were adults. Every single Vessel before me has died horribly, either because of the Enemy or the Inquisition."

"But you have Hestermeyer's diary to help you, so you won't make the same mistakes he did. And I can help you too. So can Anna."

Ellie shook her head fervently. "No, not Anna. I don't want her getting hurt."

"The Enemy tried to kill her today," said Seth, getting off the bed and crouching down in front of Ellie. "She deserves to know the truth."

"Why?"

"Because she loves you."

Ellie turned her head aside. She opened her mouth to protest, but instead found herself thinking of the time that Anna had looked after her in the orphanage, when she'd had a fever. She remembered Anna chasing orphans from the bedroom to give Ellie peace and quiet, and how she'd cleaned vomit from Ellie's hair.

"I'll talk to her," she said. "To make things right. But I'm not telling her. I have to keep her safe."

"She wants to help you, Ellie."

Ellie clenched her fists. "But you saw what she was like when she thought *you* were the Vessel. What if . . . what if she can't even look at me?"

She tucked in her legs, hugging them tight. Tiny drops of bright blue were spattered across her bare arms, from when she and Seth had knocked over a tin of paint while playing with the net-cannon. An awful thought occurred to her.

"You're not going to leave, are you?" she said.

"No," said Seth.

"You could, though, you know? I'd understand."

"I'm not going anywhere," said Seth firmly.

Ellie managed a weak, grateful smile.

"So what do we do now?" said Seth.

Ellie thought awhile, then shrugged. "Like you said. We figure out a way to stop the Enemy. Before . . ." She took a deep breath. "Before he can kill me."

FROM THE DIARY OF CLAUDE HESTERMEYER

I didn't wait to hear what Thomas had to say. I left the hall, and the university. I left behind my colleagues and my study and my life.

I walked through the City I loved, as calmly as I could, absorbing myself in the majestic gray buildings and the towering statues, drinking in the smells of the sea. In the Markets of the Unknown Saint I passed that charming young Killian Hargrath, who had grown up on the same street as me and had recently joined the Inquisition. He bowed and wished me a good evening and I did likewise, thinking to myself that if he knew the truth, he would arrest me without hesitation.

The same was true of my family. We had never been close, and I was sure they would turn me over if they thought there was money in it for them. I was a wanted criminal now.

"At least they don't know I'm the Vessel," I said, shivering in a cold alley by the Oystery.

"Yes," the Enemy agreed. "Well, until they find your diary."

A chill gripped my chest. "No!" How had that slipped my mind? "It's still in my office!" I cried.

"Oh dear," said the Enemy, shaking his head sadly. "Well, you're not going to be able to get it now."

I paced up and down the alley. If I didn't do something, my secret would be revealed to the whole City. I had to buy myself more time.

"I'm not going to get it," I said. "*You* are."

The Enemy smiled. "Are you sure you want me to do that?"

"Yes—get it! Now!"

"Fine," he said. And just like that, he pulled my diary from behind his back. "Here you go."

I took it from him eagerly, pressing it to my heart.

"Though I wouldn't be too relieved," said the Enemy. "They'd already read it."

My stomach lurched as if the ground had vanished from under me. "No . . . no, they can't have."

"They raided your office for the money and found the diary on your desk. Pretty foolish place to leave it, if you ask me."

"No, they can't! They can't know I'm the Vessel!"

But even as I said this, a bell somewhere began to toll, somewhere high, high above, at the peak of the City.

The bell of the Inquisition.

17

HIS NAME

Ellie stumbled down the orphanage corridor. Her coat was like a curtain of lead wrapped around her, yet she felt if she removed it her body would fall to pieces. Her legs could barely keep her upright, but she had to keep going. She couldn't leave things with Anna the way they were.

She paused at the entrance to the games room and saw Anna sitting in her usual armchair. Her jaw was clenched, her eyes red. The other orphans were keeping their distance.

The floorboards seemed to sway beneath Ellie's feet, like the rope bridges at the Oystery. She steadied herself on the back of Anna's chair. She could hear Anna's loud, angry breathing.

"I don't want to talk to you, Ellie," Anna said, staring straight ahead. Her voice was low and hoarse.

"Anna, I . . ." Ellie's lips were dry and her mind was messy. "I'm sorry about what I said."

Anna wrinkled her nose. "I'm done with being lied to. I'm done with you treating me like a child." A tear fell down her cheek.

"I'm sorry," Ellie said weakly. "I was only trying to protect you. Because"—she drew in a deep breath—"I love you. You're my best friend."

Anna crossed her arms fiercely. "Well you're not mine."

Ellie's heart twisted. She picked up the clockwork mouse lying by Anna's foot. She wound the key, then held it up high. A hush fell over the room.

"Five pennies!" Ellie cried. She hurled the mouse at the floor and the orphans gave chase. The walls resounded with the sound of hammering footsteps and high-pitched, ghoulish squeals.

Only, to Ellie, the noise was a tinny, distant ringing, somewhere in the back of her mind. She knelt down and clutched Anna's hand.

"I'm the Vessel," she said.

Anna looked at her, her eyes wide, the anger gone from her face. She stared at Ellie for many moments. Ellie's hand trembled in Anna's. They were oblivious to everything but each other.

"Please," Ellie mumbled. "Please say something."

Anna's hand fell from Ellie's, then her gaze did too. She

swallowed, and frowned, and looked down at her lap. A sob pressed painfully against Ellie's chest.

"Anna?" she whispered.

The room had gone quiet again. A matron was standing in the doorway, looking from Ellie to Anna.

"What's going on?" she said. "Anna, is something the matter?"

Anna blinked. She looked at the matron, then back at her lap. The other orphans watched with wide, worried eyes.

Look at me, Ellie thought. *Please look at me.*

Anna frowned. She took a deep breath.

She reached out her hand and took hold of Ellie's.

"No," she said. "Nothing's the matter."

Ellie smiled, then found that tears were streaming down her face. It was as if a tightly wound valve in her chest had come undone. Anna's hand felt so good on hers, as warm as summer sunlight.

Ellie glanced around, and noticed the other orphans were watching her with open mouths. She realized how strange she must appear to them, still damp from the sea and smelling of the sewers, her face puffy from crying. She shivered, and a horrible thought scuttled into her mind. What if they knew? What if they could see? She pulled her coat around herself. Her breathing heaved out of rhythm.

A hand tugged at her arm, and Anna led her swiftly from the games room. Ellie shuffled after her like an awkward ghost.

"Come on," Anna whispered. "Let's find somewhere quiet for you to sit. There must be an empty bedroom."

She led Ellie along the corridor, flinging bedroom doors open and shoving her head inside, only to be greeted by laughter or shouting or sleepy protests.

Anna growled. "What are they all inside for!"

While Anna opened more doors, Ellie let go of her hand and drifted farther along the corridor, drawn toward one door in particular. She heard a squeak of hinges behind her.

"Anna, Ibnet's been eating paint again!" came Fry's voice. "I just caught him!"

There was a mumbled complaint, like someone talking with their mouth full. Fry's head poked out of the door.

"Oh look, it's Ellie! Can we have a go in your underwater boat now?"

Anna shoved Fry back inside and shut the door.

Ellie reached out, running her fingers down the door of her old bedroom, down the carving of the boy and girl in the boat.

"Ellie?" Anna called from along the corridor. "What are you doing? I don't think you should go in there—you *never* go in there."

But Ellie had already turned the handle and was step-ping inside.

The bedroom had been left largely intact, though both the beds had since been made, the sheets lying uncreased and unfolded for three years. The walls were different too. Once, they'd been covered in drawings; now there were just nails sticking from the stone.

The bed on the left had a small pile of books on top and a quilt blanket with little whales stitched onto it. Carved into the end of the bed was a name.

ELLIE

The bed on the right had a box of chipped pencils and chalk shoved underneath. A dried paintbrush lay beside it, its splayed bristles coated in green paint.

"Come on." Anna tugged at Ellie's sleeve. "You don't have to be in here. It'll only upset you."

"Yes, I do," said Ellie. She deserved to be upset.

There was a quiet rustle of fabric.

Ellie looked down at the bed on the right. She covered her mouth with both hands.

The sheets shifted and squirmed. They had swollen like bread in an oven, and now a bundle of a person lay inside them.

"Ellie?" said a tiny, pained voice. He sounded thirsty.

"I'm here," said Ellie, taking a step toward the bed, reaching out a trembling hand. "I'm here."

"Where are you?" said the voice.

"Ellie?" Anna said fearfully, gripping Ellie's sleeve.

"I'm here," Ellie said again.

"Where are you?" said the voice. "Why aren't you here?"

"I *am* here," Ellie pleaded. The shape in the sheets rolled over, and Ellie heard a slight tinkling of metal. She crawled onto the end of the bed.

"Ellie?" Anna sounded terrified. "What are you doing?"

"I'm cold," said the voice. "Where are you?"

"I'm *here*," Ellie moaned. She reached out to touch the person beneath the sheets, but, as she did so, the mound seemed to collapse in on itself, and the sheets were flat again.

"No!" Ellie mumbled. She grabbed at the sheets and a cold hand reached back out, clutching her wrist so hard she screamed.

"You *weren't* here," Finn hissed, rising from the sheets with wide, piercing eyes. Ellie slapped his hand away and staggered backward off the bed. Anna stopped her from falling.

"*You*," Ellie spat. "Get out. Get out of his bed!"

"Ellie, who are you talking to?" Anna whispered.

Ellie gripped Anna's shoulder. "Don't worry," she said. "He can't hurt you. He can't hurt you."

Finn laughed, his musical voice filling the tiny bedroom. "Can't hurt her?" he said, then kicked the footboard of the bed. "I *can* hurt her. Can't you smell the smoke on your clothes? I can *kill* her. And when I do, you'll have failed her. Just like you failed him."

"Get out," Ellie said weakly.

"Do you remember, Nellie?" Finn said, looking to the ceiling as if lost in thought. "His little cries of pain, as he lay here suffering?" His eyes snapped down to her. "What am I saying? Of course you don't. You weren't here! Do you think he called out for you in those last moments? Do you think he wondered where you were?"

"No," said Ellie. "I . . ."

Finn pushed his face into hers. "He *did*, Nellie. Believe me. I see everything. He was so *afraid*. You couldn't fix him, so he died. Alone. And afraid."

"No," Ellie moaned. "No."

"But don't worry," he said, straightening up proudly. "You don't need him anymore. Because you've got me."

"You're *not*," Ellie spat through gritted teeth. "You're *not* my brother."

"Really? Why, what was your brother called?"

He tilted his head forward, flashing a devilish smile, the trinkets around his neck jangling. He pointed a finger at the wooden footboard of the bed.

There, carved into the wood, was a name.

FINN

18

THE PEARL

"Ellie, what's wrong? What just happened?" Anna said, following her into the workshop.

Ellie tore off her coat and slumped down by a bench, hugging herself and shivering. "He's being a beast, a *beast*," she said.

"What's going on?" said Seth, appearing from behind a bookshelf.

"I don't know," said Anna, her voice more high-pitched than usual. "We were in her old bedroom and she started shouting—I think the Enemy was in there with us."

Seth looked at Ellie. "You saw Finn?"

"What?" Anna frowned. "How could she have seen Finn?"

Seth glanced at Ellie. "Finn is the Enemy," he said quietly.

Anna wrinkled her nose. "Finn was her *brother*."

Seth's eyes widened. "What?"

Ellie could feel him watching her. She avoided his gaze, her cheeks prickling.

"Finn was your brother's name?" he said.

Ellie risked a glance up. Seth was looking at her, his eyes full of understanding. Ellie's stomach coiled, and she rested her head on her knees. She couldn't bear to look at him.

Anna sat down next to her and put a hand on her shoulder. Ellie drew in a deep, ragged breath, then leaned in close. "I'm sorry," she said, her voice breaking. "I'm sorry I never told you. I thought you'd . . . I thought you'd hate me. That you'd be afraid of me."

Anna gripped Ellie's shoulder tighter.

Finally, Ellie found the strength to look up at them. "The Enemy calls himself Finn, like he called himself Peter with Hestermeyer."

"But you said you couldn't remember your brother's face," said Seth, looking back at Ellie's bedroom door, "and that's why you have all those drawings. How can you not remember your brother's face if the Enemy looks like him?"

Ellie wriggled uncomfortably. "I've started to think that the Enemy's version of Finn is, well, a lie."

"What do you mean?" said Anna.

"Well, everyone always says that my brother's nose was like mine." She touched her nose for emphasis.

Anna nodded authoritatively. "They were both bent at a funny angle."

"And they say our hair was the same color. But the Finn I see now, his nose is straight, and his hair is like the color of gold, not old straw like mine. I think the Enemy shows me—what's the word?—an *idealized* image of Finn. That's why I've been doing those drawings. To see if I can remember my real brother. But I can't. All I see is the Enemy."

Ellie stared at the floor. "Anyway. None of that matters, I suppose." She looked at Seth. "We've got three days to find a way to prove you're not the Vessel."

"Three days?" Anna yelped. "Why?"

Ellie grimaced. "Hargrath knows I've been helping Seth. He's given me three days to turn him in, or else he's going to make me suffer too."

Anna let go of Ellie's arm and chewed her thumbnail.

"It *does* matter, though," said Seth somberly, fixing his eyes on Ellie.

"What?" said Ellie.

"The Enemy must have a reason for looking like your brother. And maybe, if we knew that reason, we could find a way to beat it."

Ellie opened her mouth to protest, but Seth held up a hand.

"I don't think anything's going to convince the Inquisition that I'm not the Vessel. But"—Seth smiled tentatively at them both, trying not to look too pleased with himself—"I found something while you were out."

He raced up into the library.

Anna huffed. "Nothing good ever came out of a library. He's picked up bad habits from you."

"I was so pleased when I realized it!" came his excitable cry from above. "Most people wouldn't, I don't think."

Anna rolled her eyes. "He gets *that* from you too."

Ellie gave a tiny laugh, and something in her chest loosened ever so slightly.

Seth hurtled down the spiral staircase, holding Hestermeyer's diary.

"Look," he said, pointing to the numbers at the bottom of each page. "Eight pages are missing."

Ellie took the book from his hands. "That's odd."

"You probably tore them out by mistake," said Anna dismissively.

"I don't think so," replied Ellie, inspecting the binding. There weren't even any scraps of paper left under the stitching, as there always were when a page was torn out of a book. It was as if they'd simply vanished.

"Well, who took them then?" said Anna.

"What if it was the Enemy?" said Seth.

Ellie felt a flash of memory. For a moment, she thought she might be sick.

"But why would it do that?" said Anna.

Seth tapped his knuckles against the book. "Because this diary is the *only* reliable record about being the Vessel, right? Hestermeyer said at the beginning that he was going to write down everything he learned. What if the Enemy took the pages because they contained something it didn't want Ellie to find out?"

Anna grabbed the open diary and squinted at it. Ellie rubbed her face, over and over.

"Ellie, do you remember what was written here?" Seth asked gently.

Ellie shook her head. "I don't remember reading those pages at all. I'd never even noticed they were missing."

"Could the Enemy have taken them in response to a wish you made?"

Ellie shivered, like cold water was filling her lungs. She nodded, embarrassed and ashamed.

"Three years ago, there was a new matron working in the orphanage. She found a pile of my brother's old drawings in the art room. She threw them out. She didn't know what they were. So I . . . I asked Finn—" Ellie looked up at Seth and Anna. "I asked the *Enemy* to get them back for me." She folded her arms. "I never worked out what he did in response."

Seth leaned forward. "Ellie, listen. If the Enemy used a whole wish just to get rid of those pages, whatever was in them *must* be important."

Anna lifted herself up onto the workbench, kicking her heels against the side. "Can't you just make a wish to bring them back?"

"We can't give him more power," said Ellie. "Every time I ask him for help, he gets stronger and I get weaker."

Anna stopped kicking her heels and looked at her lap. Her mouth twitched.

Ellie looked at Seth, a tiny ember of hope flaring in her chest. "But this isn't the only copy of the diary."

Seth frowned. "You said all the other copies were confiscated by the Inquisition. Where would they have put them?"

Ellie thought for a moment. "Maybe they're in the Inquisitorial Keep?"

Seth's lips paled.

"I've seen Inquisitors in all sorts of places lately," said Anna. "There are all these big buildings around the City that I'd always thought no one used, because their windows were boarded up and their doors were locked tight, only lately they've been swarming with Inquisitors and guardsmen."

"I've noticed that too," said Ellie. "Their doors have shiny silver locks."

"If I was an Inquisitor, and I wanted to keep something safe," Anna continued, "I'd put it in a boring-looking building where no one would suspect forbidden things were hidden."

"But we don't know how many of these buildings there are," said Ellie. "Or *where* they all are."

"Yeah, but we could find out," said Anna.

"How? There are only three of us and we've got no time."

Anna waved a hand dismissively. "The orphans'll find them all in an afternoon. Then we can break into them, one after the other, until we find the other diaries."

"Break in?" Ellie exclaimed. "How do we do that?"

"I can do it!" said Seth and Anna in unison, then turned to each other.

"You?" said Anna, appalled. "You can't go outside—everyone wants to kill you."

"I can be stealthy—I could break into a building easily."

"Yeah, unless you get attacked by a glass of water. Or the voices in your head make you start screaming."

"Those voices are the *sea*," said Seth, touching his head. "And they're not so bad since I figured out how to control the water."

"But what do you know about being stealthy?" Anna

said. "You just turned up, like, yesterday, stinking of whale guts, and now you're acting like you're some sort of expert thief."

Seth pointed up at the library. "I can figure it out—I've been stuck in here for ages with nothing to do but read. I'm probably the smartest person in the City now."

Anna blew a curl of hair from her face. "Oh, you're so full of—"

"Shut up, both of you," said Ellie. Anna and Seth fell silent. "Anna, it's a good idea to use the orphans to find all the buildings. Let's start with that."

Anna nodded fiercely and marched toward the front door, while Seth stuck his face back in Hestermeyer's diary. Ellie looked at them both and felt the knot in her chest loosen a tiny bit more.

Ellie spent the next morning and afternoon wandering the streets alone until her legs ached. The City was unnaturally quiet. There was no cheerful haggling at the market stalls, and far fewer children than usual. The ones she did see were hiding in doorways, playing half-hearted games of dice. The only happy faces she saw all day were Fry and Ibnet's, who waved to her from the roof of a courthouse, overjoyed at being enlisted to help, even if they had no idea what it was about.

As Ellie walked, she examined the buildings, looking

for boarded-up windows and silver locks on doors. Finally, on Erskine Street, she passed a large group of men standing outside a tall, empty-looking house secured by a heavy silver lock. They were animated and angry and seemed to have been drinking. They were yelling up at the building.

"The Enemy has destroyed my livelihood!" a fisherman cried, his hand wrapped up in bandages and his beard singed.

"Do your jobs, you fools!"

"Why haven't you caught him yet?"

They yelled until their faces were beetroot-red. Then, the silver lock rattled and the doors swung open. Five Inquisitors walked out and the men scattered in all directions. One of them tripped and fell and was dragged inside the building.

Her heart beating in her throat, Ellie fished out a map of the City from her pocket and marked an *X* in pencil on Erskine Street.

She wanted to spend the whole day searching, but had to return to the workshop several times to let Castion's sailors in. After the fire at the Oystery, dozens of oyster-catchers had been pulled from the sea, their copper shells warped and blackened, their crablike legs twisted. Now they'd been brought to the workshop, so that it resembled a battlefield, strewn with the bodies of mechanical creatures.

"Poor little things," said Anna, reaching out and waggling one of the legs of an oyster-catcher. The end snapped off in her hand, and she winced and patted the machine in apology.

The sun had set, and the three of them had gathered in the workshop. Between Ellie, Anna, and the orphans, they'd found eight Inquisitorial strongholds scattered across the City. They were all unremarkable buildings, on quiet streets. There was one in the Salvation Markets, and another not far from Orphanage Street itself. There was one nestled among the mansions of the Merchant Guilds and another right by the sea, near the Warrens.

Seth spread out a map of the City and floor plans of the buildings, which Ellie had pulled from the library. An oil lamp sat at one corner, bathing the maps orange.

Seth picked up one of the floor plans. "How do you even have these?"

"My mom," Ellie said. "She wanted to completely rebuild the sewer system. She had plans drawn up of almost every building in the City."

They stared at the layouts of the strongholds. Ellie had hoped it would be obvious which of the buildings might contain the confiscated diaries, but the plans offered no clues. All eight of them were big, with thick walls and narrow corridors.

"So," said Anna, "we've got tonight and tomorrow night before Hargrath comes back, so all we have to do is break into four each night."

"Anna, the chances of us getting caught are high enough breaking into just *one* of these buildings," said Ellie.

Seth began toying with one of the broken oyster-catchers. "What if we watch them tonight, and try to figure out which one gets used the most?"

"We can't watch all eight at the same time," Anna said. "It's too dangerous for the orphans to be outside after curfew."

Ellie sat back, exhausted. "I didn't think there would be so many. We can't search them all—there's not enough time."

Seth fumbled and nearly dropped the oyster-catcher he was holding.

"*Please* don't make them any more broken," Ellie pleaded.

Seth grimaced. "Sorry." He examined the machine. "What's wrong with this one anyway? It doesn't look burnt at all."

Ellie reached for the oyster-catcher. Sure enough, it had only one small scorch mark on its copper shell. She wound the handle in its back, but it still didn't work. She bit her lip and shook it slightly. There was a faint rattling from inside.

"Ellie, what should we do?" Seth asked.

"I'm thinking, I'm thinking," she said.

She picked up a screwdriver and pried open the panel on the oyster-catcher's belly. After a moment of prodding around she found something hard trapped between the cogs. She grabbed a long pair of tweezers from her pocket and pushed them inside. Seconds later, she plucked out a beautiful silver pearl.

"Do you know what a pearl is?" she said, holding out the glimmering sphere for Anna and Seth to see. "It's an oyster's way of protecting itself. If a tiny parasite gets inside the shell, the oyster builds this shiny coating around it, so the parasite can't hurt it. Isn't that amazing? It takes something horrible and dangerous, and turns it into something beautiful."

She held the pearl up to the lamplight, rotating it slowly. It looked like the moon in miniature.

"I wish I could do that to the Enemy," she said.

She looked at Seth, who gave her an uncertain smile, then back at the little pearl. Strange, how secretive the pearl was, tucked inside its oyster shell. You'd never know from the outside that something so beautiful was hidden in there.

A vague idea niggled at the back of Ellie's mind. She looked at Seth again, and tried to chase the idea through her swirling thoughts. But just as she was on the cusp of grasping it, someone knocked insistently at the door.

"Ellie?" came a voice from outside. "Ellie, it's me."

"Castion," Ellie whispered.

Seth rushed off to the basement, and Anna hurriedly gathered up the maps and floor plans, and hid Hestermeyer's diary. Ellie unbolted the doors and Castion hobbled in from the darkness, carrying a large burlap sack. His usually magnificent red velvet coat seemed drab, like it had been soaked in the rain and not dried properly. As he stepped into the lamplight Ellie caught sight of his face. He looked older than she'd ever seen him; she could have sworn there was more gray in his beard, more lines beneath his eyes.

"Forgive my late visit," he said. "Oh, hello, Anna," he added, and gave a small bow.

"Sir, is everything all right?" Ellie asked.

"Oh no, nothing to drink for me, thanks," said Castion distractedly, looking around the workshop. "I think this is the last of them," he said, passing over the sack of blackened oyster-catchers.

"Thanks," Ellie said.

Castion nudged a stool out from under a workbench with his narwhal-tusk cane, and sat down with a sigh.

Ellie shared a worried glance with Anna. "Is something the matter, sir? Are you okay?"

Castion grimaced as he readjusted his mechanical leg. "You know, I'm not sure. Once upon a time, I would have

come to your mother for advice. Now . . . the City is lack-
ing in wise people to talk to."

"Oh." Ellie felt a weird twist of surprise. Did Castion
want her *advice*? She wasn't sure she had ever given an adult
advice before. She looked at Anna, then jerked her head
meaningfully toward the door. Anna frowned rebelliously.

"Aren't you on potato-peeling duty tonight?" Ellie said
loudly, and Anna scowled and slouched from the workshop.

An awkward silence filled the air. Ellie felt stiff and
unsure what to do with her hands.

"I can't stop seeing it," he said. "When I close my eyes, I
keep imagining the destruction . . ." His eyelids flickered,
and for a moment he almost seemed afraid.

Ellie frowned. Lord Castion wasn't afraid of anything—
there were rumors he'd once leapt onto a flaming ship to
rescue his sailors, after an entire barrel of whale oil had
caught fire; that he'd weathered more storms than any
other whale lord, and faced down every fearsome creature
of the sea. The only time she'd seen him look so frightened
was when she'd asked him if he'd ever seen the Enemy.
She remembered the distant, pained look in his eyes, like a
child recalling a nightmare. It was the same look he wore
now.

"You've seen it," Ellie said. "You saw the Enemy, the
day Hestermeyer died."

Castion nodded.

But the Enemy had been destroyed that day, at the top of the Clocktower of St. Angelus, when Hargrath lost his arm. So the only way Castion could have seen it was if he had been there too. Which meant . . .

"Sir," Ellie asked. "Did you used to be an Inquisitor?"

Castion was silent, long enough for Ellie to know the truth. Her heart thudded hard in her ears. "That's how you really lost your leg, isn't it? The Enemy took it."

He let out a sigh. "You are your mother's daughter," he said. "Yes, that's how I lost it—the same day Hargrath lost his arm. I had only joined the Inquisition a year earlier. I was patrolling with Killian—sorry, Hargrath—and five others, when we saw Claude Hestermeyer at the top of the clocktower, looking down at us. Hargrath ran in first. He was actually *smiling*. We were so young; we thought we were about to become heroes. I raced after him. I wanted to reach Claude first."

"Why?"

"I wasn't thinking straight. I just wanted to help."

"Were you and Hestermeyer friends, sir?" said Ellie.

Castion gave her a pained smile. "Dear friends. We studied together at the university, if you can imagine me in a library," he added, with a small, forced laugh. "But I dreamed of slaying monsters, so I joined the Inquisition."

"What was Hestermeyer like?"

"Exceptionally kind. We grew apart after I left the university, and further still after Peter Lambeth died. When I found out Claude was the Vessel, I thought . . ." He tapped his cane against the floorboards. "I thought somehow I could save him. I even found him once, days before he died, hiding in the sewers. I pleaded with him to turn himself in, before it was too late. He didn't listen. The next time I saw him, on top of the clocktower, it *was* too late. I ran up the staircase. I found Hargrath in two pieces, and the rest of my friends all dead. And Claude Hestermeyer, well, he wasn't there anymore, just the Enemy. We fought. I won. I don't know how. When I woke up I was on the surgeon's table, and my leg was gone. I knew I wanted nothing to do with the Enemy—not even to speak of it. So I told the High Inquisitor it was Hargrath who'd killed it. He wanted so much to be a saint, it seemed for the best."

He was silent a long time. "I hope you never see it," he said finally, his voice barely more than a whisper. "I hope you never do."

"Sir, why did you think that you could save Hestermeyer?"

Castion grimaced. "Because I had to. I felt like it was my fault, for not realizing sooner that he was in pain. I thought, maybe, if he saw me, he would remember the good man he'd been, not the evil he'd become. That if I could give him something *real* to hold on to, like the memory of our friendship, then the Enemy couldn't claim him. But I was foolish. It was too late for him—the moment he became the Vessel, he was doomed."

Ellie's chest tightened painfully.

"But then," Castion continued, "over the years, I have sometimes caught myself wondering . . . Why did the Enemy choose Claude? He was filled with sadness and guilt after Peter Lambeth died. Is that the weakness the Enemy exploited? How it wormed its way into his soul? I wonder sometimes—if I had been a better friend to Claude after Peter died, maybe it would have been different? And these days, with the Enemy among us once again . . . it's all I can think about."

Castion leaned forward on his stool, staring at the ground.

Ellie took a deep breath. "Sir . . . have you read Hestermeyer's diary?" she asked. "Maybe it would help you to feel better about what happened."

"The diary?" Castion looked up sharply. For a moment Ellie thought he might chastise her for even mentioning it, but he just shook his head. "I tried. I was one of the Inquisitors who went to collect Claude's things from the university. It was awful, going into his office after he was gone."

Ellie's heart was so loud she could hardly hear her thoughts. "So you took the diary?"

"Yes. His diary, his papers, all his belongings. There wasn't much."

"Where did you take them?"

"An Inquisitorial building," Castion said distantly, lost in memory. "Where the possessions of all the Vessels are kept. I tried to read the diary first. I thought it would help me remember my friend. I sat on the edge of the water-front, listening to the gentle waves. And I tried to read it, but . . . I couldn't. Not without seeing that *thing* in the clocktower."

He put a hand to his mouth, his brow crumpling. "Poor Claude. So I handed his belongings over. My last act as an Inquisitor. I resigned the next day. It wasn't long after that I met your mother, and she made me this." He tapped his cane against his metal leg. "She was a great comfort. My life started to get better from that point."

Castion's eyes were wet. Ellie swallowed, rolling the hard little pearl between her fingers. "You still remember him, though, from before he was the Vessel?"

"Yes," he smiled.

"Just like you remember my mom from before—"

Castion reached out and put his hand on her shoulder. "Yes."

Ellie felt the heavy weight of Castion's hand. "Maybe it's okay to let your happy memories cover up the bad ones," she said. "Maybe you should concentrate on the good memories, until the painful ones get worn away."

Castion rubbed his forehead, closing his eyes. "Yes, yes, I should. Thank you, Hannah," he said, then gave a sad laugh. "I mean Ellie. You're right, thank you."

He glanced around at the hospital of broken oyster-catchers, then blinked down at the sack he'd brought with him. "I hope you aren't working *too* hard," he said, an edge of worry in his voice. "You look—"

"Tired? I am," Ellie said. She had grown even paler since asking for Finn's help the day before at the Tower of the Serpent. She could feel the hot lines of exhaustion under her eyes, like curls of ash. "But I'm okay," she lied.

Castion smiled weakly and stood up, nudging his stool back under the workbench. He bowed to her. "You let me know if there's anything more I can do to help," he said, inclining his head toward the oyster-catchers.

"Thank you, sir," said Ellie, and Castion strode from the workshop.

Ellie found herself breathing heavily. She clattered over to the door of the basement and banged on it hard. A moment later, Seth appeared.

"Come on," she said. "I know where the diaries are."

19

THE OTHER FORTY-FIVE

Only one of the Inquisitorial strongholds was next to the sea, like Castion had mentioned. When Ellie pulled out the plans, they found a map of a three-story building. The largest room was at the back of the second floor, and was probably the best place to keep paper documents.

The building was next to the Warrens, right on the Salvation Waterfront. It wasn't near any entrances to the sewers, so they would have to approach it in the open, sticking to the darkest alleyways. The front door would probably be guarded, but fortunately the plans showed that the lowest floor of the building was below sea level, and accessible by a submerged staircase. Ellie had an idea for how to get in that way.

Ellie, Seth, and Anna waited until two in the morning,

then crept down toward the Warrens. The streets were eerily silent but for the occasional bark of a dog. Down one alleyway they heard footsteps and had to hide in a doorway as a guardsman marched by. As they set off again, Ellie brushed the alley wall, and something wet coated her fingers. She looked up and saw three words scrawled across the stone, glistening in the moonlight:

KILL THE VESSEL

Ellie pulled at her shirt collar, her throat tightening.

The Inquisitorial stronghold reared out of the dark in front of them: a bleak, gray-green slab of a building, furry with moss. Its windows were boarded up like all the others. The gargoyles on its roof had since lost their heads.

They snuck across the street and around the side of the building, three darting shadows. The sea was wild; thick ripples of froth danced angrily in the moonlight. Seth looked down at it.

"Are you frightened?" said Anna.

"Of course not," he said, then swallowed. Ellie gripped his hand.

"We can try the main door," she said softly, "if you don't want to do this. Maybe the guard will be asleep."

"No," said Seth. "No, I can do this."

The sea thrashed, flecking their faces with stinging salt

water, making Seth wince. Ellie squeezed his hand.

He closed his eyes. He frowned, and the sea swirled and crashed up the side of the building. Ellie felt water leaking through her socks. Seth's face twisted to a snarl, then a look of pain. The sea started bubbling up toward them.

"It's okay," Ellie whispered. "It's okay, Seth, we're here."

Anna took hold of his other hand. Seth drew a long, deep breath.

And the sea began to sink.

Down it went, farther and farther, as if a huge glass bowl were being lowered into it, pushing the water aside to form a dark, curved wall. As the sea receded, it revealed two staircases, exposed to the air for the first time in centuries. One set led down to some broad, slimy flagstones. The other rose up, into a dark hole in the side of the building.

The sea stopped sinking. Wisps of blue had formed on Seth's skin, but they didn't swirl as they'd done before. Seth looked deeply asleep, though he was standing upright.

"Is he in a trance or something?" said Anna. She waved a hand in front of his face, then clicked her fingers.

"Stop it," Seth grunted. "I'm trying to . . . concentrate."

Even as he spoke the water rose three inches toward them, before Seth focused and lowered it back again.

"I think we might have to carry him," Anna said.

Ellie put her hands under his arms, Anna took his legs,

and together they hauled him down the first staircase. The stone was slippery with streaks of algae, and occasionally crumbled beneath their feet.

Ellie risked a glance up. The top of the wall of water was now high above them. If Seth lost control, it would sweep in and drown them. They carried Seth up the second staircase, into the belly of the Inquisitorial stronghold. All Ellie could hear was the ominous silence of the water, and Anna's heavy breathing. She couldn't hear Seth at all. She kept watching the little blue wisps on his bare neck, praying they wouldn't turn violent. She held her breath until at last they rose above the top of a thicket of mussels that indicated the high-water mark.

They set Seth down, and Ellie squeezed his shoulder. "Seth, you can stop now," she whispered. "We're above sea level."

She pulled a canister of whale oil and a small lamp from her pocket. She struck a match, revealing Seth's tired face—his eyes unfocused, his lips dry. He shook his head, and as he did the sea came crashing down and swept up the steps, stopping just below their feet.

"You did so well," Ellie told him.

"Did it work?" Seth said distantly.

"Well, we didn't drown," said Anna, gazing at Seth with the reverent look she normally reserved for vicious weapons. "What does it feel like?"

"Like I'm a tiny voice," Seth croaked, "trying to shout at this massive, dark thing, to tell it what to do. Only it shouts back. And its voice is so much louder."

"But you moved it," said Ellie. "You didn't lose control."

Seth smiled. They climbed the last few steps, coming up against a wide metal trapdoor. Ellie tried to push it open, but it didn't so much as shudder. She moved the lamp around until she spied a tiny keyhole.

"You do know how to pick locks, don't you?" said Seth.

Ellie shrugged. "I've studied diagrams—I understand the theory." She pulled two thin pieces of metal from her pocket, then stared at the keyhole. "Um . . ."

Anna groaned. "Move over," she said. She snatched the lock-picks from Ellie's hand, slid them into the keyhole, then rattled them around inside.

Click.

Anna grinned mischievously in the lamplight, then went to heave the trapdoor open. Ellie touched her arm.

"We need to make sure there's no one up there," she said. She passed the lamp to Seth, then eased the trapdoor gently open, peering through the crack. A musty, damp smell seeped from inside, but no sound or light.

Ellie motioned for Seth and Anna to stay put, then climbed up. Her heart clanged inside her head. A shred of lamplight revealed cracked walls and empty candleholders. A floorboard creaked beneath her boot. She paused and listened.

Seth's large eyes watched her from the trapdoor. She beckoned, holding a finger to her lips, and they climbed up to join her, Seth easing the door shut behind them.

They stood in a long dark corridor lined with oil paintings—portraits of austere, white-haired men, who looked like they thought themselves very important. They crept on, passing many wooden doors with tiny barred windows, like prison cells. Ellie wondered if anyone was locked inside, moldering away in the dark.

Ahead, a gray stone staircase led to the floor above. Ellie looked back at Seth and Anna and they nodded at her, their faces resolute and determined.

A floorboard creaked overhead.

Ellie's heart lodged in the base of her throat. The three of them huddled together in the nearest doorway, and Ellie took the lamp from Seth and closed all the shutters, drowning out the light.

She counted to ten, then opened the shutters on the lamp halfway, and they crept on toward the staircase. It was so narrow that she could feel the chill from the stone wall on her cheek. At the top, they paused again. Ellie poked the lamp around the corner, illuminating the new corridor. She counted eight doors on either side. She raised the lamp up higher, revealing a large pair of double doors at the far end.

A shadow stepped across the beam of light. Its head turned toward them.

Ellie wrapped her arms around the lamp without thinking. It was so hot that she almost dropped it, and Anna grabbed it to keep it steady.

"Go back," Ellie whispered as the light bounced drunkenly in the cramped stairwell. *"Go back! Go back!"*

They fumbled on the steps as Seth tried to move backward. But he couldn't turn in the tight space. Ellie took a step toward the corridor, twisting to give them more room. A face appeared before her; large bright eyes and gleaming white teeth. Ellie fell back into Anna.

"What is it?" Seth whispered. *"What's happening?"*

Finn was smiling down at Ellie from the top of the stairs, his golden locks like fire in the lamplight, his eyes swimming with joy.

"What an adventure this is!" he said, his voice dancing up and down the corridor. "And just think—at any moment an Inquisitor could walk out of one of these doors, and you'll have no choice but to ask for my help!"

"Go *away*," Ellie whispered, shamefully aware that Seth and Anna could hear her talking to someone only she could see.

"Why so mean?" said Finn, resting his fists on his hips.

"It's not fair to be mean to me. Remember—I have a wish to use. And if you're not going to be fair, then I can be *very* unfair. All these walls, why, I could melt them away, just like I did when you jumped from that tower. Then the Inquisitors will see the three of you together. You'll all be executed. And it will be entirely your fault. You're always saying it's your job to protect Anna. But then, you said the same thing about me, and look how *that* ended."

Ellie took a deep breath, feeling the corners of her eyes itch. Ice shards stabbed her chest.

"You wouldn't do that," she whispered. "You need me alive."

A warm hand touched Ellie's arm. "It's Finn, isn't it?" said Seth. "Ellie, ignore him."

Ellie stepped around Finn, but he followed after her.

"Oh, so brave, Nellie," he said, puffing out his chest and putting on a deep voice. "Marching into the belly of the beast. But if you keep this up, you're going to get people killed, believe me."

"Then what should I do?" Ellie murmured. "If I let you win, you *will* kill people."

A floorboard creaked loudly beneath Anna's boot, and they all froze. Ellie held her breath, listening for footsteps behind closed doors, for the scraping of chair legs or the clink of swords against scabbards.

Finn leaned on Ellie's shoulder. "What do you even think you'll find in Hestermeyer's diary?"

"A way to stop you."

Finn shook his head, and his necklace of trinkets jangled. "But why do you want to stop me? I can give you the thing you want most."

From far below, there was an eruption of sound that sent a chill down Ellie's spine and into the pit of her stomach. A grown man's scream of anguish, like from a pain deep inside his bones.

Ellie hurried on toward the double doors ahead, praying none of the other doors would open. She extinguished the oil lamp and reached out a trembling hand for the doorknob.

But the doors didn't open.

No, she thought. *Please.*

She groped in the dark for Anna, slapping both lockpicks into her palm. Anna bent over, fumbled to find the lock, and slid them into the keyhole.

There was a rattle of a doorknob behind them, and the squeaking of rusted hinges.

With a sharp intake of breath, they pressed their backs flat to the double doors, gazing into the darkness. Ellie pushed her thumb through the hole in her coat sleeve, nervously gripping the frayed cloth.

A shadow emerged from the furthest doorway, silhou-
etted by a sliver of light from inside. Anna's hand reached
for Ellie's, squeezing it tight, her palms damp with sweat.
Ellie's other arm lay across Seth's chest. She could feel his
hammering heartbeat.

The Inquisitor reached back into the doorway, collecting a lamp from inside the room. Anna's hand gripped
tighter.

"If he looks this way . . ." Finn whispered. Ellie could
see his gleaming smile out of the corner of her eye. Seth's
fists were clenched, prepared to run or fight. Anna's breath
was loud in Ellie's ears.

Then the Inquisitor turned his back to them and headed
down the stairs.

Ellie's vision swam with specks of silver. The three
of them slid down the doorframe, then Ellie felt Anna's
sweaty hand pushing against her cheek, knuckles knocking against her teeth as she shoved Ellie's head aside to
access the keyhole. Ellie heard the lock-picks rattling by
her ear, then a quiet *click*. Anna eased the door open and
they hurried inside.

Though they were surrounded by darkness, Ellie
could feel the immensity of this new room. The air was
colder and smelled of sawdust and old paper. She relit the
lamp, illuminating a chamber that looked a lot like her

workshop, if someone had tidied up. Stretching into the darkness were rows of shelves piled high with wooden boxes, leather chests, neatly folded clothes, and stacks of tattered books.

"Oh, it's the Inquisitors' closet," said Anna.

"What sort of things have you got in your closet?" said Seth, pointing to the nearest shelf, where there was a taxidermy seal with its eyes missing.

They moved between the shelves. Ellie spotted dusty bottles of wine, and framed portraits, and a child's rocking horse. Here and there, large brass plaques had been fixed to the shelves. On those plaques were names:

18: OLIVIA CLAXTON
4: ANDREW URWIN
11: MERL STANTON

The possessions had not been stored in any particular order, and there were stretches of shelf that lay empty, presumably until a new Vessel died to fill them. The smaller the number, the more worn the possessions: the clothes yellower, the paper crumblier, and the metal rustier.

13: MARTHA ORR
28: RIVER BOWDITCH

Ellie stepped over to River Bowditch's shelves. She picked up a small shirt, unfolding it across her front. It had a dark red-brown stain in the middle. She winced and put the shirt back down, inspecting some of the other items: a toy rabbit with a button nose, and a bow made from a crudely curved stick, with a string running from one end to the other.

Ellie felt a twinge in her gut and turned away from River's possessions. She searched the other shelves for Hestermeyer's name. Brass plaques glinted in the lamplight. How many of these people had been real Vessels? Ellie thought. How many had been wrongly accused, like Seth? Glumly, she wondered which of these empty spaces they would put her possessions in. They'd need a lot of shelves.

41: FELIX KERNAGHAN
29: PATRICK HUNTER

"Ellie, look at this."

Seth's voice called to her from the darkness. She found him at the edge of the room, between the rows of shelves.

A huge, sprawling mural was painted up the wall, all the way to the ceiling. On it were many craggy yellow shapes, floating in a faded blue. Her eyes fell on a particularly large one, near the top. Two words were written on it:

THE CITY

"It's a map," said Ellie, wondering why Seth was so interested in it.

"Yeah," said Seth. "But it's different from the one in your workshop."

Ellie held the lamp up, illuminating the top of the mural. She saw the many smaller islands that lay off the coast of the City: the hunting islands, where wild wolves and boars ran free; the farming islands, where endless fields of crops were cultivated. They were a few days' sea journey at most from the City.

Ellie lowered the lamp: a week's journey, two weeks', a month's. The islands vanished, the sea now vast and empty, beyond the reach of even the boldest whale lord. Nothing but blue.

And blue.

Then new islands appeared.

First came a tiny islet, unlabeled. Then another, and another. Then a jagged shape the size of a hunting island. Ellie lowered the lamp farther.

And found a new shape. Even larger than the City.

Ellie stared. "What is this?" she said. "How can there be another island that large? There are no other islands like the City. This has to be a mistake."

She looked left and found Finn at her side, staring at it intently. She didn't like the hungry look in his eye.

"I don't think it's a mistake," said Seth darkly. "I think it's a secret."

Ellie felt a great, creeping weight on her shoulders as she stared at the island.

"Ellie," Anna's voice whispered through the dark. "I've found him."

Ellie's stomach flipped, and she hurried to Anna's side, two rows over, beneath a towering bank of shelves filled almost entirely with books.

45: CLAUDE HESTERMEYER

"Can you see the copies of his diary?" asked Ellie.

"No," replied Anna. "I've got something better." She held out a small, worn, leather-bound brown book with no title. A thrill shot up Ellie's spine. "I think this is the *original*."

Anna put it in Ellie's hands. Ellie turned the pages carefully and familiar phrases leapt out in shaky, careful handwriting. This was it—Hestermeyer's own diary. She turned, and turned, and turned.

Then her finger curled beneath a page and found . . . a gap.

"No," Ellie breathed. "No, no, no!"

She looked at the left page, then the right one. The exact same section was missing.

"*No!*" she cried, flicking the pages back and forth, back and forth, as if the vanished pages might suddenly reappear.

Merry, tinkling laughter filled the room. Finn rubbed tears from his eyes.

"Oh, Nellie, if only I had a mirror!" he giggled, his cheeks rosy red. "You should see yourself. You look so surprised!"

"What did you do?" Ellie whispered.

"*Nellie,*" Finn scolded her. "Work it out! How many of those drawings of mine did I rescue for you? There were loads of them—hundreds even! I didn't just take those pages from *your* copy of the diary. I took them from *every* copy."

He laughed so hard he began to wheeze. Ellie turned away, clutching her hands to her ears. She found it was difficult to breathe.

"It's okay," said Seth, putting a hand on her shoulder. Her mouth was dry; she could barely speak. It wasn't okay.

"The pages are gone," she managed to gasp finally. "They're gone."

"It's okay," Seth kept saying.

"He can't win," she whispered. "I have to fix this. I have to stop him."

"We will, Ellie. We will."

"But *how*?" Ellie moaned. A sob was curled up painfully in her chest, and she was struggling not to let it escape. Finn was still emitting tiny giggles as he got his breath back.

"Oh, Nellie. Oh, dear Nellie. You're too much fun. Did you really think a few pages in a book would give you the secret to destroy me?"

Ellie glared at him. "If they couldn't, then why did you go to so much effort to get rid of them? You *do* have a weakness, and Hestermeyer found it."

Finn looked at her a moment, and his small smile vanished. He licked his lips and bared his teeth in a wide, hideous grin. "If he knew my weakness," he said, pointing to the shelves, "how come I still killed him?"

Ellie turned from Finn to hide her face, afraid that he was right.

"Ellie?"

Anna's voice was hollow, and a little confused. She was holding up a pile of yellowed, tattered pages. A title was written across the top in a neater, more confident hand than the writing in Hestermeyer's diary:

FORGOTTEN MYTHS AND LEGENDS
BY
CLAUDE HESTERMEYER AND PETER LAMBETH

"What is it?" Seth asked, frowning down at the pages.
Anna looked at him seriously. "I think it's about you."

The Great Drowning destroyed nearly everything. All that survived were four immense arks—*Salvation*, *Immutable*, *Revival*, and *Angelus*—and the people who lived in them. The legend goes that one of the gods, still sympathetic to humanity, had warned these people that the Drowning was coming, and they had built these arks so they might survive.

Three of the arks were lost, sunk by storms or perhaps the Enemy. The fourth—the *Angelus*—came eventually to the Last City, the only human construction that still rose above the waves. The ark itself was pulled to pieces, and used to build new, smaller ships. These then left in search of food, and other islands where the people might grow crops.

There are many strange tales of what these early explorers discovered. Our favorite is about a farmer called Clara Biswick. She couldn't write but told her story to all who'd listen. It was eventually written down and found its way into the university library. Perhaps because Clara was a simple farmer, or a woman, it was never given much thought, and soon gathered dust. But we think it worthy of repeating here.

Clara and her family had braved the seas to reach the tiny island of Adrastos. They found the soil to be rich, and perfect for farming. By autumn, they'd gathered a generous harvest, and soon were trading goods with passing whale lords and merchant ships.

One day, Clara was tending the potato field when she heard the sound of her three children shrieking. She raced to the water's edge and was met by the sight of an enormous dead shark which had washed ashore. Her children were climbing all over it, prodding its lifeless blue eyes and admiring its many teeth. Clara ordered them down. Then her youngest son started to scream.

The shark's skin was expanding, as if it had a huge air bubble inside. Something pushed out from between the shark's gills, causing Clara to gasp and her children to scream even louder. It was a human hand.

Clara grabbed her knife and cut into the shark's side. The children watched in terror as Clara pulled a blood-drenched, naked boy from the side of the shark, with light brown skin and dark blue eyes. He was scared, and shivering, and kept repeating the same sentence over and over again:

"Where are my brothers and sisters?"

Clara took the boy home, and he was washed and fed and put in a bed, where he slept fitfully. The next day he seemed full of energy but had no idea how he'd come to be inside a shark. In fact, he didn't remember anything at all, though Clara said he was "remarkably quick-witted." He was prone to long periods of sullen thoughtfulness when he would stand on the beach, staring out to sea.

Within weeks, the boy had become a part of the family. He would help with the farm work, the heavy lifting and wood-chopping. He liked to go out fishing in the boat. Clara's children were especially fond of him and worked harder too in an effort to emulate him.

Then, one day, the two youngest children went out fishing without permission, determined to bring back a feast. On the other side of the island, Clara and the boy were hunting a wolf that had been eating their goats. The boy turned to Clara suddenly.

"Your children are in danger," he said.

They raced across the island as fast as they could, but by the time they arrived they found a freak storm battering the coastline. Clara screamed in terror, knowing instinctively that her children were caught inside it. She raced for the other rowboat, then turned to see the boy, his arms raised toward the sea, his eyes entirely dark blue. He walked steadily into the surf, and the sea thrashed and recoiled, like a wild cat being lashed into the corner of a cage. Later, Clara said that it was as if the sea and the boy had become one, yet that they also seemed engaged in some great war with each other.

Finally, the sea rose in a tremendous wave that swept across the shore. When the wave subsided, Clara got to her feet, and saw her two sons crawling across the sand, coughing up seawater.

Of the other boy, there was no sign.

20

THE BOY WHO GOT LOST AT SEA

"That's *you*," said Anna, looking at Seth.

"It can't be," said Seth distantly.

"But he could move the water, and he came out of a sea creature, and he said the exact same thing you said the day we found you—'Where are my brothers and sisters?'" Anna took a deep breath, frantically rereading. "He's *exactly* like you. Well, except for this 'remarkably quick-witted' part."

Ellie blinked, reading the words again and again. Finn's laughter still rang from the rafters—it had changed from a childish giggle to a harsh, hacking laugh.

"It . . . it does seem to be describing you," Ellie admitted.

There was another agonized cry from deep below. Seth and Anna tensed, looking to the door.

"You heard that too?" said Ellie, and they nodded.

"Whatever they're doing to that poor man, they might not be doing it for much longer. We should go while they're distracted."

Ellie put Hestermeyer's original diary and his manuscript into a waterproof bag made of dried seal intestine. As they crept from the chamber, Ellie spared a final glance for the map on the wall, and the mysterious unlabeled island close to the floorboards, before it was swallowed by darkness.

They scurried along the corridor as quickly as they dared, down the staircase and through the trapdoor. They huddled together at the top of the stairs. Seth looked down at the sea, closing his eyes. It took him longer this time—Ellie guessed he was distracted by what he'd seen in the manuscript. At last, the waters fell away, and Ellie and Anna carried Seth down the steps. Ellie saw the intense concentration on his face, his brow furrowing as if he were haunted by a nightmare. Then his eyes opened.

"I . . . I can't hold it," he panted.

They were right at the bottom of the stairs now, on the slimy flagstones. Around them the dark waters rippled, held back only by Seth's power. Ellie felt a jolt of panic. If the water crashed down on them now it would dash them against the side of the building or sweep them out to sea.

"You can, Seth," she urged him.

Seth gave a low growl and closed his eyes again. The

wall of water trembled. Around Ellie's ankles the sea rose, soaking her trousers.

Then it started to sink. Ellie and Anna sighed in relief, then carried Seth up the steps. With a hiss of released breath, Seth relaxed and the wall of water collapsed, smashing against the buildings below them. Seth was shivering, his skin so icy that they had to wait a few moments, warming his hands on the extinguished lamp.

They crept along a cobbled path by the waterfront, toward an alley that would take them up to Orphanage Street. The wind bit at Ellie's scalp, parting her hair like an icy knife. On their left rose the Warrens: the cracked husks of three hundred buildings, their rooftops gone and their insides scooped out by fire. To their right, sitting just offshore, was a tall, moonlit castle, with many pointed towers and a squat, circular amphitheater nestled at its side. It was called Celestina's Hope, after the first saint, and could only be reached at low tide, by way of a thin line of rooftops that poked above the sea, like a row of huge stepping-stones.

All of a sudden, Seth stopped. "It can't have been me. In the shark, I mean. Can it?"

He looked at Ellie, and she thought there was something almost pleading in his eyes.

Ellie swallowed, staring at her feet. She was finding it hard to think. She pushed her hands deep into her pockets, right down to the seams, and her fingertips brushed something small, and round, and hard.

She took out the pearl and rolled it in her palm. It jogged something in her memory. *Strange, how secretive the pearl was, tucked inside its oyster shell.*

"I don't think you were swallowed by that whale," Ellie said. "I've looked at drawings of whales' throats. They're actually quite small—there's no way they could swallow a person. And even if they could, if you were inside for longer than a few minutes, you'd die of suffocation."

"But I *was* inside one," said Seth. He marched ahead, his energy seemingly returning. Ellie hurried after, glancing nervously around. The path had led them through a collection of crumbled statues from before the Drowning. It was a forest of stone: a hundred men and women and animals, cavorting motionlessly in the dark. They cast odd, jagged shadows, and Ellie had the strange feeling they might start moving at any moment.

Seth sat down, leaning against one of the statues, looking out over the sea, and the line of rooftops that led to Celestina's Hope. "I *was* inside one," he said again.

"I don't think we should hang around here," said Anna, eyeing the stone animals all around them. Something tugged again at Ellie's memory.

"The mural," she said.

Anna frowned. "What mural?"

"Seth and I saw it in the sewers when we were coming

back from the Oystery. It was of this dead wolf, only there was a woman climbing out of it."

Seth looked up at her. His eyes narrowed.

"Who was she?" said Anna.

Ellie took a deep breath. "I don't know. But she had a halo around her head. That usually means someone is a saint. But this mural was old, from before the Drowning, before there *were* saints. Maybe halos meant something different then."

"Like what?" asked Seth.

"Well, nowadays people believe the saints protect us," said Ellie. "But back then, people thought it was the gods. What if that's what a halo used to mean?"

"But why would a god be coming out of a dead animal?" said Anna.

Ellie bit her lip. "Isn't that sort of what the Enemy does? It comes out of the Vessel. Maybe the other gods had Vessels too. Only maybe *they* waited until the Vessel was going to die anyway, instead of killing them—remember how the wolf in the mural looked really old, Seth? They were probably much nicer, those gods. Why else would the Enemy have drowned them?"

Seth stood up, watching Ellie warily. "What are you saying?"

"I'm saying Anna's right. It *is* you in that story. The

shark had sea-blue eyes too, just like the whale you came out of."

"But . . . that happened hundreds of years ago," said Seth. "I'm not hundreds of years old."

"Your body isn't," Ellie said, looking him up and down. "But what if a part of you is?"

Seth turned away. "So . . . you mean . . ."

"I mean the whale I pulled you out of was a Vessel. Which means that you're a, well . . ." Ellie couldn't bring herself to say the word.

"You're a god!" Anna whispered excitedly.

"No," said Seth, glaring at Anna. "I'm not."

"But it's the only explanation that makes sense," Ellie said softly. "The Enemy wasn't the only god to survive the Drowning."

"I'm *not* a god," said Seth, turning angrily to face them. "I'm a boy. I'm me."

"I think you can be both."

"No!" Seth cried, and a wave surged over the water-front.

"Seth, you need to stay calm," said Ellie, watching the water spill between the cobblestones by her boot.

Seth sat down again with a sudden drop. "I can't be . . ." he mumbled, his chin resting on his chest.

"Why not?" Ellie asked.

"Because, that means my brothers and sisters . . ." He looked out to sea, his eyes glistening. "That means they're dead."

Seth bowed his head, shaking gently. Ellie took a step toward him but didn't know what to do. The sea rumbled. Waves washed against the waterfront. Then the sea growled, and a larger wave crashed over the side. Ellie and Anna hopped aside to avoid getting their feet wet. Seth didn't seem to care; he shook and shook, and the sea crashed and raged ever more wildly. Massive waves rose high above, far out toward the castle, smashing against each other like monsters battling on the horizon.

"I don't think it's safe for him to be this angry near the sea," said Anna.

Ellie knelt down next to Seth. "I'm so sorry," she said, anxiously watching the waves. She wished she knew what to say to make him feel better.

She clutched his arm. "Seth," she said.

His eyes opened, his expression mournful, lost. "I don't even remember their faces, Ellie," he said.

"I know," she said, thinking of the hundreds of drawings of her brother in her bedroom. "I know. But you remember that you loved them, don't you? It's obvious you love them, otherwise you couldn't feel strongly enough to do this." She pointed at the raging, furious sea.

She squeezed Seth's shoulder, and he looked out to the

horizon. He watched the waves, and took deep breaths, and the seas began to settle.

He was silent awhile. Ellie and Anna sat on either side of him, and together they watched the moon drift slowly across the sky.

"What have I been doing all this time?" Seth said. "Have I just been . . . lost at sea?"

Ellie shrugged. "The Enemy moves from Vessel to Vessel. Perhaps you do too? Maybe you've been going from one sea creature to the next, looking for your brothers and sisters, for centuries."

Seth frowned and stared down at the sea. He let out a deep sigh.

Ellie glanced into the shadows and noticed Finn sitting cross-legged beneath a statue, grinning his toothy smile.

"Did you know about this?" she whispered.

Finn giggled. "Of course!" he said, rocking back and forth. "How else could he move the sea? My brothers and sisters had all sorts of gifts: controlling the weather; creating music out of thin air; causing dead soil to bloom with life. They were very tedious."

"Is that why you want to kill him?"

Finn rolled his eyes. "Don't be stupid," he said. "I want to kill him because he's putting you in danger. I thought I'd been very clear about that. Besides, if I kill him, he'll be back again soon enough, bursting out of some rotten dolphin or walrus or whatever."

Ellie turned away in disgust. A drop of rain landed on her face, then another. She looked up and saw dark clouds swirling around the moon.

"We should get home," she said. "A storm's on the way."

Then Seth grabbed Ellie and Anna by the shoulders.

"What are you doing?" Anna hissed, putting an arm out protectively in front of Ellie.

"Someone's coming," Seth whispered through gritted teeth.

Then Ellie heard it too. Footsteps. From along the seafront. Heavy, clomping footsteps.

"Let's go," said Seth. The three of them raced through the forest of statues, hiding behind the flank of a bull.

Twenty feet away, a man was striding along the water's edge. He wore the long sealskin coat of an Inquisitor. Ellie could hear Seth and Anna's quick, wary breathing, like they were ready to run or fight at a moment's notice. They watched him pass by.

"At least it's not Hargrath," Anna whispered.

Out of the corner of her eye, Ellie noticed one of the statues turn suddenly in their direction, revealing a wide, demonic smile that shone in the moonlight.

"Yes," said Hargrath. "That would be *most* unfortunate."

21

THE SHARK IN THE THEATER

"Seth, get away!" Ellie cried.

There was a ring of metal as Hargrath's sword swung toward Seth. Seth leapt aside, and Ellie threw a flash-bang at the ground between them, closing her eyes against the sudden burst of blazing light. Hargrath grunted and pressed his arm to his face.

"Here, Matthews!" he roared, stumbling haphazardly. "I've got them!"

He charged blindly forward, whacking Ellie in the stomach with his flailing arm. She cried out in pain and tumbled over the edge of the seawall, landing hard on the rooftop below. Anna leapt down to help Ellie to her feet, and Seth came too, narrowly avoiding another sweep of Hargrath's sword.

"I *told* you this was a bad idea," piped Finn's chiding

voice. He was also standing on the rooftop. "This one's really got it in for me," he added, pointing up at Hargrath. "Okay, so I tore his arm off. But in my defense, he *was* trying to kill me at the time."

Hargrath loomed over the edge of the seawall, raindrops spilling down his greatcoat. There was no way past him.

"Come on, we'll have to try and lose him in there!" said Ellie, pointing to the ruined silhouette of Celestina's Hope. She took Seth and Anna by the hand and raced away across the moonlit rooftops that poked from the sea, vaulting the gaps between them. The skies rumbled, and in the distance was a flash of lightning.

Seth put a hand to his head, wincing. "It's getting louder. The storm is here."

Ellie looked around nervously; if the storm whipped up the sea, it might drown the bridge of rooftops. And she was counting on being able to get back to the City this way, once they'd lost Hargrath in the ruins of the castle.

"That's a dead end, Lancaster!" Hargrath yelled as he chased after them, his boots smashing through slate and sending shards spinning into the sea. He was gaining on them: there were three rooftops between them, then two.

Then one.

Seth turned to face Hargrath.

"What are you *doing*?" yelled Anna.

"Seth!" Ellie cried.

Seth raised his arms. Hargrath skidded to a halt, sword held up in defense. His hand was actually *trembling*, his eyes wide and hate-filled. Then he let out a chilling, anguished howl and charged at Seth, sword raised over his head.

The muscles in Seth's arm twitched. Dark patches moved across his skin, like smoke in the wind. A waist-high wave smashed into Hargrath's side. He screamed in frustration, then was pulled into the sea, vanishing from sight.

Seth laughed, like he was surprised how well it had worked. He turned to Ellie and Anna, grinning.

"Not bad, right?"

Then his face contorted in pain and he dropped to his knees.

Ellie and Anna helped him back up. His skin was ice-cold, his eyes unfocused. Deep booms of thunder exploded in the clouds—the storm was on them now. The sea twisted in agitation. Seth jerked and twitched, and a low growl came from his throat that he didn't seem able to control.

"It's so loud," he groaned, hands on his temples. "It's so loud."

"We need to get him somewhere warm," said Ellie. "Let's get back to the workshop."

"We can't," said Anna, pointing. "We have to lose *him* first."

The other Inquisitor, Matthews, was running along the

line of rooftops toward them, his sword drawn. Ellie and Anna each put an arm around Seth and helped him shuffle toward Celestina's Hope. They climbed a huge staircase, beneath the gaze of towering statues. They struggled through ankle-deep puddles of seawater; the rain was falling so hard that Ellie and Anna had to shout at each other to be heard.

"We should hide!" Anna cried.

"No!" yelled Ellie. "I have a plan!"

"Come on, Nellie," said Finn, popping up atop the battlements. His velvet waistcoat was dry and fluffy, and he didn't have to shout. "Why don't you just ask me to kill him?"

The rain drove painfully into Ellie's scalp. *"No,"* she said. "If I ask you to kill him, then you can kill someone else."

"I take it back. You're *no* fun, Ellie Lancaster."

"Are you talking to the Enemy?" Seth said, lifting his head groggily.

"Um, yeah."

"Tell it to go drown itself."

Finn glared at Seth, his lip curling. "And tell *him* that I had a really enjoyable time drowning his brothers and sisters."

There was a splash of footsteps behind and they turned

to see Matthews gaining on them. Seth raised a trembling hand but Ellie pulled it down.

"*No*, Seth," she said. "Save your strength."

They ran up a long flight of crumbling stairs that wound around the side of the castle, finally coming to the top of the amphitheater—a large, open arena surrounded by tiers of stone seats that rose steeply around the sides, like a place where gladiators might once have fought. Now it was filled with water from the tide, like a giant rock pool.

"If we can get that Inquisitor to follow us around in a circle," shouted Ellie, "then we can go back the way we came!"

"That's a terrible plan!" said Anna.

"Have you got a better one?"

They raced around the perimeter of the amphitheater. The clouds writhed as if in pain, and waves crashed hard against the side of the building. Ellie turned her head and caught a flash of lightning reflected from Matthews's sword. He was following them. Ellie smiled. Her plan was working.

There was a hysterical roar, and something huge and dark and soaking wet hurled itself over the edge of the theater, knocking Ellie flat on her back.

She looked up. Hargrath was lifting Seth high into the

air by the neck, choking the life out of him.

"NO!" Ellie cried, rushing to her feet and batting uselessly at the immense Inquisitor. She felt a hand in her pocket, then Anna shoved her aside, stabbing the point of a screwdriver into Hargrath's arm. He roared, dropping Seth into the water-filled arena below. Without even looking at her, Hargrath smacked Anna over the edge, then grabbed Ellie's hair and hurled her down too.

Ellie's stomach flipped as she crashed hard into the water. She spluttered and swallowed salt, then pulled her head up above the waves.

"Ellie!" she heard Anna say. "There's something—"

But then the water snatched Ellie down again.

"What?" she cried, coughing as she broke the surface.

Anna swam toward her. "There's something in here with us!"

Ellie looked around frantically. A dark shape rippled through the waves. Then a fin, poking above the water.

"What's that?" said Seth, paddling close to Ellie and Anna.

Ellie felt the water move as it went by. It was big: the length of a person between its fin and its tail. It turned sharply, tail swishing as it swam away from them.

"It's fine," said Ellie, her voice trembling only slightly. They clung to one another, kicking hard to stay afloat.

"Sharks aren't nearly as dangerous as people think. They only get vicious if they smell blood."

High above them, Hargrath wedged his sword between his side and the stump of his arm, then drew the palm of his hand along the blade.

"No!" Ellie cried.

Hargrath stretched out his hand and squeezed it into a tight fist. Three thick drops of blood fell into the water.

For a moment, the shark just kept swimming. Then its tail thrashed violently, spraying water in all directions. It circled them, again, and again, and again.

Then it turned, arrowing straight toward them. Ellie saw its beady black eyes as they rolled back to reveal the whites beneath. She tried to grab for Seth's hand, but a sudden, almighty force pulled her and Anna out of the shark's path.

When Ellie looked back, she saw that the shark had been swept to the far side of the amphitheater, pinned against the audience seats by a glistening wave. Seth burst from the water next to Ellie. Dark, swirling patterns raced across his skin.

"Enough," came Hargrath's voice from high above. He reached into his pocket and pulled out his dart-gun, pointing it at Seth.

"DIVE, SETH!" Ellie cried.

"No, don't bother," said a lazy voice right next to her. Ellie turned to see Finn, not so much treading water as floating in it like a jellyfish. "Hargrath's time is up. He knows too much."

Ellie stared in horror. "No . . . no, Finn. Don't do it."

But Finn just smiled.

There was a sickening ear-splitting crack, like a mountain being torn open. Dust sprayed in all directions, and Ellie saw Hargrath and Matthews vanish through the stone beneath them.

She scrambled for the nearest step. She tried to get a grip, but it was too slick; her fingers slipped and scraped the stone. Then the water shifted underneath her, like she was in a huge bathtub being sloshed from side to side. It lifted Ellie, Anna, and Seth onto the steps, and they scrambled toward the top.

Ellie looked down, and gasped. A massive hole had been torn from the stone of the amphitheater. A perfectly round hole leading down to the sea.

"I can't see them!" she cried.

Seth staggered to the edge, looking into the waters and gritting his teeth. It was a moment before Ellie realized he was *feeling*, not seeing.

"There," he said at last, his voice hoarse, pointing out to sea.

Two tiny figures were being swept away from the City, pulled in sickening twists by ferocious waves.

"I'll bring them back," Seth muttered wearily, and then fell to his hands and knees. Anna pressed her hands against his shoulders.

"Are you okay?" she asked.

"I . . . can't," Seth mumbled. "It's too loud."

Ellie turned to Finn, who was watching the sea with an amused smile.

"Do something," she told him. "Save them."

Finn gave a small, surprised laugh. "You want me to save Hargrath? But he knows you're helping Seth now. He'll see both of you executed. Are you sure you want me to save *Hargrath*?"

"Yes! Save him. Save both of them!"

At this, Finn closed his eyes tight, savoring her words. "No."

Ellie froze. She couldn't breathe. "What?"

"I won't save them. I refuse."

"No, no you can't."

"He dies."

"But you'll have no wishes left!" she shouted. "You have to save them. Think how much stronger it will make you!"

"I'm not going to save them."

"No. NO!" She balled her hands into fists. "Finn, please! PLEASE!"

But already Finn was gone, and Ellie could only watch as the two tiny figures were swept out and out to sea, vanishing completely beneath dark waves.

FROM THE DIARY OF CLAUDE HESTERMEYER

I am living in the sewers.

Twice in the last week I've had to ask Peter for help. Just hours ago, three Inquisitors found me while I was hiding in a tunnel. One of them was an old, dear friend of mine and Peter's, from back at the university. He pleaded with me to turn myself in—there were *tears* in his eyes. But I didn't want to be parted from Peter, so I had him curl rods of rusted metal around the Inquisitors' legs, holding them in place while I made my escape.

I keep this diary close. In my malaise, I forget exactly why it's so important, and I am too tired to go back and reread the last few entries to see if I can find the reason. It is easier to just carry on writing. Peter keeps telling me to throw it away, and once I very nearly did. But something deep inside me tells me I must keep it safe.

In the day, I check the traps I've set to catch rats to eat, and the nets in some of the open pipes that fish occasionally swim down. At night, I wrap myself up as best I can. I seem to be cold all the time these days, a cold that's inside my very bones. Peter offers to help—to light me a fire, or bring me more food, but again a part of me knows that I must not do this.

Still, I am so grateful to have Peter with me. This would be so much harder without him. Last night I couldn't sleep, so we went for a walk. I was angry with him at first, for reasons I can't remember now. But then we talked for long hours, and it was as if we were right back in the university, on our eternal search for truth and knowledge. It felt so good to talk to him again, as old friends.

I often wonder what is going on in the City above. I think a lot about Peter's father. I hope he is all right. I wish I could go up there to see him and tell him his son is doing well.

22

MISSING PARTS

Ellie sat slumped against a workbench, her hair a tangled mess, her fingernails chewed to jagged lines. In her hand was a cloth soaked in the sweat from her forehead.

"I don't understand," she moaned. "This isn't how it's supposed to work. Finn *refused* to help me last night. How come I'm still getting weaker?"

Seth and Anna's eyelids were heavy from a lack of sleep. Anna went to get a fresh cloth. Seth rested his chin on his fist.

"Maybe you're still feeling the effects of the last wish you made, when you saved us from that fall?" said Seth, then noticed Ellie rubbing at a shiny green and purple bruise on her arm. "Did Hargrath do that?"

"No, I bumped into a workbench when we got back from Celestina's Hope."

In her mind, Ellie saw two struggling figures stolen away by hulking waves. Guilt tugged at her chest like a hook. She blinked hard and tore a hunk of bread from the plate Anna had put in front of her. She didn't feel hungry—the very idea of eating seemed unnatural—but she knew she had to keep her energy up. Her arms and legs were clumsy, brittle tubes. Her head was so heavy that it pulled her neck forward.

Anna knelt at Ellie's side, dabbing her brow with a new cloth. On the floor was Hestermeyer's diary. Seth nudged it with his foot.

"What do you think was in those missing pages?" he said. Anna glared at him, as if now was not the time to be asking such questions. Ellie forced down the bread in her mouth. It tasted like sponge.

"I don't know," she said. "And I don't know how to find out." She took a deep breath. "I think I should just turn myself in. Before anyone else gets hurt."

"You're *not* turning yourself in," said Anna, pressing a glass of water into Ellie's hands.

"But if I'm executed then the Enemy can't take a physical form!" Ellie said, her voice cracking. "You don't understand—once the Enemy gets out . . . Once he's"— she took another breath—"killed me. He'll murder and destroy. What if he got into the orphanage?"

"It's not a he," said Anna, in a soft reprimand. "It's an *it.*"

Ellie looked nervously at Seth. "And then there's you."

"What about me?"

"Finn knows what you are—he always has. And once he gets out, he'll want you to suffer especially. Because you're like him. Even though you're nothing like him," she added hastily. "Trust me, I know what Finn's like."

"Stop it, Ellie!" Anna said suddenly.

Ellie looked at her in shock. "What's the matter?"

"It's *not* Finn," Anna said, fiercely crossing her arms, "so stop calling it that. Finn was your brother. He was kind and sweet and never hurt anybody."

Ellie looked at the floor. "Sorry," she mumbled, the words "kind" and "sweet" circling her thoughts. She found it hard to think of him that way.

"You *do* remember him, don't you?" said Anna.

"Of course I do!" Ellie snapped, then closed her eyes. "Sorry, sorry. It's just, well, my brother's dead. *This* Finn is real. And even though he's wretched, and horrible, he's all I have left of him."

Anna's lips went pale. "That's a terrible thing to say."

"But it's true."

Anna flinched and turned away from Ellie.

Seth had started pacing the workshop, left and right and

left again, and Ellie found she wanted to snap at him too. She worried Finn was infecting her with his spite.

Seth spun toward them. "What if we left the City?" he announced. "Right away, in a boat?"

"The Inquisition would follow us," said Ellie. "They'd take the whale lords' ships and chase us across the sea."

"Not if they couldn't see us!" said Anna eagerly. "We could use your underwater boat."

"It doesn't work."

"Then we'll fix it," said Seth.

Ellie laughed bitterly. "I can't even fix one of these stupid crabs." She slapped the oyster-catcher next to her. Then she coughed, and coughed, and coughed some more. She bent over and buried her face in both hands.

"We could go to one of the farming islands," Anna said, patting Ellie on the back.

Seth frowned. "The farmers would turn us in. But that map we saw yesterday—"

"What map?" said Anna.

"In the stronghold. It had the City on it, and all the farming islands, but there were other islands too, far, far to the south. And one of them was big. Even bigger than the City."

Anna frowned. "But the City *is* the biggest island."

"Not according to this map," said Seth.

"But if there were other islands, why would the

Inquisition keep them a secret?" asked Anna.

Seth licked his lips. "Let's find out. We take a boat—at night, so nobody sees us leave—and we sail across the ocean."

"The three of us can't cross the ocean in some tiny boat," said Ellie.

"We can if *I'm* in it," said Seth firmly.

"Finn will follow us. I won't stop being the Vessel just because I'm not in the City."

"But there won't be any Inquisitors there to hunt you," Seth said eagerly. "You won't have to make any more wishes, because you won't be in danger."

Ellie sat up, comforted by the determined look in Seth's eye. She imagined the three of them in some strange new land, where people smiled and the word "Enemy" was never spoken in terror. But even if the people were cruel, and even if the ground was ash, it couldn't be worse than the fate that would find her in the City.

"Okay," she said at last. "Let's do it."

Seth's eyes went wide in delight, and Ellie leaned on Anna's shoulder. Even the act of making a decision left her exhausted. Anna glanced eagerly around the workshop.

"Right, we'll need food and water, maps, and a boat," she said. "And we should take the rifle as well." Seth gave her a look. "You know, just in case there are bears."

Ellie found she was smiling and wasn't quite sure why.

She felt a need to tell them how grateful she was, but wasn't sure what words to say. Instead, she looked down, and her fingers brushed the open pages of Hestermeyer's diary. Seth stopped pacing, watching her curiously.

"What is it?"

"In this entry"—Ellie pointed at the left-hand page—"Hestermeyer suddenly starts talking about the Enemy as if it *is* Peter, like they're the same thing—he doesn't seem to realize there's a difference." She frowned, biting her thumb. "The Enemy appeared to Hestermeyer as his best friend. And he appears to me as my brother. Maybe he always does that?"

"*It,*" Anna corrected.

"How do you think the Enemy chooses its Vessel?" said Seth. "I mean, it's not just random, is it?"

Ellie stroked her chin, while Anna stretched out on her front, flicking idly through Hestermeyer's diary. "*The Enemy is a parasite. Like one of those crook wasps that lay their eggs inside other insects,*" Anna read aloud. She looked up at the jars of dead animals on the shelves nearby. "You don't have one of these crook wasp things in here, do you?" she said. "I'd love to see one."

Seth knelt down next to Anna, reading the diary over her shoulder.

"Parasite," Ellie muttered. She'd pulled the oyster pearl from her pocket, rolling it about in her palm.

Seth and Anna looked up. "What was that, Ellie?" Seth asked.

"He's a parasite," she said.

"*It*," Anna corrected.

"*It's* a parasite," said Ellie. "It feeds off the host to grow strong, so it can break out on its own. But the Enemy isn't a living thing—it doesn't eat. So what's it feeding on?"

Ellie winced as she pushed herself to her feet. Anna hopped up to help her.

"Thanks," Ellie said, tottering over to the many thousand sketches on the wall, plucking down a picture of a crook wasp. "Maybe *that's* why he picked me —because there's something in me that he can feed on. Something that's not in you." She looked at Seth. "Or you." She looked at Anna. "Or anyone else."

She stared at the picture a while longer, but her thoughts were thick like custard. She coughed, and Anna hurried over with the glass of water.

"How did Peter Lambeth die?" said Seth, still looking at the diary.

Ellie hobbled over to him, sipping the water. "I don't know," she said. "Hestermeyer never says."

"Maybe that's what's in the missing pages," said Seth. "Do you think maybe the way he died was similar to your brother? Do you think he blamed himself for what happened to Peter, like you do with—"

"SHUT UP!"

A stab of anger surged up through Ellie's body and she hurled her glass at Seth. It fell short and bounced off a pile of books without shattering. The three of them stared at it as it rolled in a small circle.

"I'm sorry," Ellie said, her eyes wide. "I don't know why I did that." The anger ebbed from her chest, replaced with a horrible shame. She sank to her knees. "I'm so sorry, Seth."

Seth hurried over to her. "It's all right," he said softly. "It's fine, really."

"It's not fine," Ellie said as Anna rubbed her back. "I'm so *tired*," she said, and she felt a sudden urge to cry. "*Why* am I so tired? He didn't grant my wish!"

"We're going to find a way to stop it," Seth said. "We're going to find a way to fix you."

Ellie frowned, staring at her hands. They were so pale, nearly the color of fish meat, apart from a few tiny brown freckles. She wondered if her brother's hands had been freckled too.

She gave Anna and Seth a weak smile, and they smiled back, then started chattering about provisions for the voyage.

Ellie looked down at her ragged fingernails. She had a vague memory that someone used to tell her off for chewing them, but couldn't remember who. Had it been her brother? She closed her eyes tightly and tried to think back, to remember him—the *real* him. But as she did, her chest turned painfully cold, and all she could see was his empty bed.

How would they fix her? The only part she needed was gone.

23

FINN

They spent the rest of the day planning their escape from the City. Anna took Fry and Ibnet down to the docks, searching for a suitable boat to "acquire," and using Ellie's small allowance to buy enough dried fruits and smoked fish to last a month at sea. All Ellie could do, meanwhile, was lie in an exhausted heap in the workshop. At times her body felt like it was made from rock and iron. At other times, like it was made from nothing at all.

She awoke that night painfully thirsty. Her heart was thudding like she'd just sprinted up a hill. She groaned in irritation at her own body—how could she be so awake in the middle of the night when she had spent the day half asleep? She pulled a blanket around her shoulders and staggered into the workshop to get some water.

"Hello, sister."

Finn sat cross-legged and barefoot by the front door, beneath the stuffed sunfish. He wore a white shirt and white trousers, and his hair shone silver in the moonlight. He looked like an angel's wingless child.

Ellie hobbled over to the sink, ignoring him. She turned on the tap, sipped water from her cupped hands, then dried them on her hair.

Long strands fell away between her fingers. They too shone silver.

Ellie gasped in shock and went to check herself in the mirror. She felt a stab of fear—her hair was noticeably thinner. She thought she could see the paleness of her scalp underneath.

"How are you doing this?" she moaned.

Finn crawled over to her on all fours. She could smell him, somehow. Sweet and clean, like freshly laundered clothes. He peered into the mirror, admiring their reflections. He was rosy-faced, with a new layer of puppy fat on his cheeks, his hair arranged in tight, gleaming ringlets. She was pallid, her body skinny and scratched. Beads of cold sweat traced her forehead. Finn smiled.

"Oh, Nellie, you're not looking too good. Can I help you with anything?"

"Shut up," she whispered. She didn't want to wake Seth by shouting.

"*Shut up,*" Finn repeated, in a childish, singsong voice.

"Is that all you can say these days? Gosh, you're really falling apart, aren't you, Nellie? It's so sad."

Ellie put her hands to her forehead, avoiding her hair. What had she missed? How had he become more powerful, even though he'd never granted her wish to save Hargrath?

"Maybe if you were kinder to me, I'd tell you," he said, staring glumly at his feet.

"Talking to you never gets me anywhere."

"Oh, so you're just going to ignore me? Again." He nodded. "I suppose . . . maybe I deserve it? Maybe I deserve it for dying."

Ellie pushed past him, heading back to her bedroom.

"But then," he continued, fiddling with one of the keys at his neck, "maybe I wouldn't have died if you'd stayed with me like I asked."

She turned, and Finn bit his lip, as if wondering whether he'd gone too far. "That's what happened, Nellie," he said, holding out his hands. "I'm not being mean. That's just what happened."

"It wasn't my fault," Ellie said firmly.

"Oh, Nellie. We both know that's a lie."

Ellie clenched her fists, then took a deep breath and kept walking.

"Don't go, Nellie. I want to talk to you. Don't leave me again."

She ignored him.

"*Don't* go," Finn repeated. This time, it sounded like a command. The hairs on the back of Ellie's neck stood up.

"What do you want?" she said.

Finn pawed one foot at the ground. "Well, first I think you should admit that you're the reason I'm dead."

She swallowed. "No."

Finn skipped across the workshop with a tinkle of metal.

"Do you remember the way we used to go out in that little rowboat together, on those summer days when the waves were calm? We'd take a fishing rod, and a net, and a telescope too, and spend the whole day not catching anything, and not caring either. We'd get all red and sunburnt and laugh at how bad we were at fishing, and play that board game we'd built together. And then, one time, I thought I saw a blue shark in the water. And I got so excited that I fell in, and you jumped in after me, and I nearly drowned but you rescued me, and then you promised me you'd never let me get hurt. Remember that? Remember you promised you'd never let me get hurt?"

"Finn, what do you want?" she whispered.

"I told you. Admit it's your fault."

"But *why*?"

"Because then I can forgive you! Then you can stop beating yourself up all the time. Let's put this behind us and get back to the way things were—Finn and Ellie, having fun adventures at sea!"

She stared at him a long time, and he stared back, unblinking. He gave her a little smile.

"I shouldn't have left his side for so long," she said. "But that's not why he died."

"I gave up hope, Nellie! Don't you see? It hurt too much. I needed you. I did."

"I hate you."

Finn looked hurt. "You hate your brother?"

"No, I hate *you*."

"But I'm—"

"You're not my brother," she said sternly. "Your forgiveness means nothing."

Finn turned his back on her. "What did your brother look like, Nellie? What color were his eyes?"

With a stab of panic, Ellie realized she didn't remember. She clutched the blanket tighter around her shoulders. "Green . . . like mine," she said uncertainly.

Finn shook his head. "Oh, Nellie." He spun back around on his heels, staring at her with bright blue eyes. "Your brother's eyes were blue!"

"Stop that," she hissed.

"What? This is what he looked like. Trust me."

"No . . ."

"And remember the way his left ear was crinkled?"

Finn said, pointing eagerly at the rumpled fold at the top of his ear, poking out between his curls.

"His ear didn't do that."

Finn frowned. "Are you sure?"

"Yes," she said adamantly, though she wasn't sure at all.

Finn laughed, a warm, childish music. "He laughed like that though, didn't he? Didn't he, Nellie?"

"I . . ."

"You see, you're better off with me. I'm the only Finn you need."

And he skipped forward eagerly and tried to hug her.

"Get *off* me!" She shoved him hard.

There was a jangling of metal and Finn gave a small "Oh" and fell backward. His skull smacked against the sharp corner of the workbench.

Ellie gasped. "Finn! I'm . . . I'm . . ."

Finn grunted and hauled himself up onto his elbows. His head drooped, his eyes half shut. A dark patch blossomed on the top of his head. Thick red drops pattered on the floorboards, dripping from the curls of his fringe.

"What were you about to say?" he whispered. "Were you going to say sorry?"

"No," Ellie lied.

"Are you going to make it better, then? Will you stop the pain this time?"

Ellie shook her head, sinking to her knees. The skin

on her scalp itched, as if she could feel an echo of Finn's injury. She scratched it, and more hair came away in her hands.

"I . . . I tried everything to save you."

"All I needed was you there with me. I was so cold, Nellie. So cold. I just needed *you*." He crawled toward her.

"You can't know that," she whispered. "You weren't there."

"I'm everywhere, Nellie."

"I thought I could save him."

"You're not Mom, Ellie. I know you try to be—you try so hard. But you're not."

"I thought that . . . if I could save you—"

"That you'd prove you're as clever as Mom was."

"No," Ellie whispered, tasting tears in her mouth. "I just wanted him to live."

"Then why did you leave me?" Finn said. He took her hand, smearing blood on her knuckles. "Do you remember, Nellie? Do you remember promising to keep me safe?"

"No . . . No."

She couldn't remember. She couldn't remember any of it. Not her brother. Not his laugh nor their days out fishing in their little boat. Not the color of his eyes. All she had was *this* boy in front of her.

"Nellie, please. You can have me back—you can have

me back forever. But first you owe me an apology."

"I don't owe you *anything*," Ellie whispered, but she couldn't be sure of that either. A terrible pain stung her chest—an agonizing cold that filled up the brittle, empty shell of her body. She was so tired of suffering. She wanted it gone.

"I can help you, Nellie. I can forgive you. I'm your brother. Don't you want my forgiveness?"

Ellie sobbed, and with it came a sudden relief. "Yes," she said, and just saying the word made her feel better. "Yes."

Finn stared adoringly into her eyes. He pressed his forehead to hers, and she cradled him in her arms. Her dear, loving little brother.

"I'm sorry, Finn," she said, crying as the words spilled out. "I'm sorry I wasn't there for you. I'm sorry I left you alone. I thought I could cure you. It was selfish. . . . So selfish. I should have stayed with you and kept you safe. I should have been there at your side."

She trembled, holding him there in the pool of moonlight. She smiled, moving a curl of hair from his face, admiring his rosy cheeks. She felt his head and found it was mended. The bleeding had stopped.

Ellie laughed. He stared back at her encouragingly, and she thought how sweet it would be once he'd forgiven her. How she would be able to picture the two of them again, in their little boat, her with a net and telescope, and him with his golden hair, and his slightly crumpled left ear, and his brilliant, beautiful blue eyes.

"I forgive you, Nellie," said Finn.

Ellie felt a great warmth sweep into her chest, a joy unlike anything she could ever remember knowing. She laughed and laughed, and tears fell down her cheeks. She held Finn close and stroked his hair, her body untethered, floating up and up toward the great warming sunlight.

"Thank you," she said, squeezing him tightly.

But as she said the words, she noticed Finn's body felt lighter. She wiped her eyes.

"F-Finn?"

She turned his face toward her, but it was still and lifeless. His body was dissolving, flaking away like ash from a fire. She tried to catch it in her hands, but her fingers passed straight through it.

"Finn? FINN!" Ellie cried, trying to hold on to him. But there was nothing to hold. His body had no substance anymore. Wisps of him curled through the air.

And then he was gone completely.

From the Diary of Claude Hestermeyer

I think this is nearly the end.

I've been a fool. I let it get the better of me.

Now my body is at its weakest, little more than a paper shell. I can feel a terrible pressure inside my chest, like something yearning to be born. I can barely hold my pen.

I'm going to let myself be captured by the Inquisition. There is a clocktower near the Great Docks where Peter and I shared many glorious evenings, talking long into the night. I shall go there and try to remember him, then call out until they come to take me.

But first, I will deliver this diary to the university. If I can ensure it is read by others, then perhaps my suffering will not have been in vain. It is my dearest hope that my story will help future Vessels—that it will teach them things I wish I had known from the beginning. Maybe it will even help them to destroy the Enemy for good.

The Enemy mocks me as I write these words. *Give them your book,* it says, *but I will hurt them all the same.*

My life has been too brief, and too full of darkness.

But, for those wondrous years, I was lucky enough to know a soul as golden and as kind as Peter. I wish I could remember him now. All I have is the Enemy.

But I believe, one day, this foul god will overreach itself. That it will step into the mind of someone stronger than me. One who can construct a shield from their love. Or even a weapon. And, on that day, the Enemy will know such terrible suffering.

So I say this to you, dear Vessel, my inheritor: I have faith in you.

24

ANNA'S TALE

"Ellie?"

Ellie stared at her empty arms, where her brother had been moments before. Her breathing was loud in her ears.

"Where . . .? Where . . .?"

She scuttled backward against a workbench. Her shoulders bunched up almost to her earlobes and her teeth pressed together so hard her jaw hurt.

"Ellie, what's wrong?"

Anna was scrambling down from the library, still wearing her clothes from yesterday, her face puffy with sleep. "I heard your voice. Where's Seth?"

"I wasn't talking to Seth," said Ellie. She rolled her head, and as she did, she noticed an odd, crunchy feeling in her neck, like there was gravel between the bones.

"Something's . . . different," she said, and a trickle of ice water dripped into her heart. "I think I just made a very big mistake."

"What do you mean? Ellie, you're trembling." Anna rubbed Ellie's bare arms. "You're freezing too! Wait, were you talking to *it*?"

Ellie nodded. The whole conversation with Finn played over in her head. "For a moment, I *loved* him. Like he really was my brother."

Anna looked like she'd eaten a worm. "Why would you do that?"

"Because I wanted to. It made the pain go away." She rubbed her chest. "For a little while."

Anna's brow crumpled.

Ellie glanced at Hestermeyer's diary, which lay open on the floor. "A parasite feeds off its host—it needs something only the host can give it. I think that's what it's been after all this time. That's the secret in the missing pages."

She scooped up the diary.

"Listen—*I've been a fool. I let it get the better of me*," she read aloud. "That's what he says right after the missing pages. I always thought he meant he'd used too many wishes and made himself too weak. But maybe he realized his mistake was giving his love to the Enemy as if it really was Peter. That's what the Enemy needed—Hestermeyer's love for

Peter. And my love for my brother." Her heart thudded in her throat. "And that's exactly what I've given it."

Anna picked up Ellie's blanket and draped it around her shoulders. "Listen, you're still alive," she said. "So it's not too late."

"But I don't think Hestermeyer lasted long after that. In the last entry, he says he's going to go to the Clocktower of St. Angelus, straight after he gives his diary to the university. And that's where he died. I probably have a day at most."

Anna gave a tiny moan and sat down next to Ellie. "Maybe you need to . . . I dunno, take your love *away* again," she said.

"But how do I do that?"

"Well, if the Enemy tricked you into loving it, maybe you just need to point that love back in the right direction—to the *real* Finn."

"But I can't remember him, Anna," Ellie said, her voice catching. "I can't see his face or hear his voice. Every time I try, all I feel is this horrible pain in my chest. I don't think the Enemy will let me remember my real brother. It's wanted to replace him this whole time."

"Well, we need to jog your memory then—what about this?" Anna picked up a thick black clay tube with a whale carved on its side. She blew into it, and a wet gurgling sound came out the other end. "This was his, wasn't it?"

"I think so," Ellie said vaguely. "But I don't remember him using it."

Anna chewed her lip. "Well, what about his drawings then?" Her eyes darted across the workshop and she grinned. "You keep them in that trunk, don't you?" she said, spotting the metal box by Ellie's bedroom door. She raced over to it. "There you go! All you need to do is look at those pictures, then you'll remember Finn for sure."

Ellie winced at the hopeful look in Anna's eyes as she flung open the lid of the box. Anna's smile faltered, fell.

"Oh," she said, reaching in and pulling out a mass of curled, smudged gray paper, the pieces all stuck together. She looked at Ellie in shock. "What happened to them?"

Ellie looked sadly at the floor, her chest filling with shame. "I put them in that trunk for safekeeping, after the Enemy rescued them for me from the orphanage. But a few months later I saw a seal that had gotten tangled in a net, in a rock pool that I couldn't reach. It was drowning, so I asked Finn"—she took a breath—"I asked the *Enemy* to save it. He emptied all the water from the rock pool. Next time I opened the chest . . . it was full of seawater."

Anna returned to Ellie, frowning thoughtfully. "I'm pretty sure there are still some of his drawings in the storage room in the orphanage."

"Really?"

"Yeah." Anna's cheeks went pink. "I used to go in and look at them sometimes."

Ellie's body deflated with a sigh. "But there are thousands of old drawings in the storage room. You'd need an army to find his."

Anna straightened up proudly. "I *do* have an army. The orphans will help. I'll set them to work in the morning." She put a hand on Ellie's shoulder. "We'll figure out how to beat it."

Ellie almost ran her hands through her hair, then stopped herself in case more fell out. "He looks like my brother so that I'll love him. So how *can* I beat him? I can't stop loving my brother."

"You don't have to. Just stop mixing him up with the Enemy. It's simple."

Ellie gritted her teeth. "No, it's *not*. I told you—the Enemy won't *let* me remember him. So all I have is the other Finn—"

"The *only* Finn, Ellie," said Anna firmly, crossing her arms. "You need to bring him back."

"I can't bring him back. He's dead."

Anna rolled her eyes. "If *you* die, do you think you'd just stop existing?"

"Yes!"

"I mean, you'd be fish food, sure, but you wouldn't be *gone*. I'd still remember you, and so would all the orphans.

And they'd have all your inventions and the toys you made them."

"But I wouldn't be there."

"Yes, you *would*, Ellie," Anna said, and to Ellie's surprise her voice broke. "And when you leave the City with Seth tomorrow, you'll still be with me." She rubbed a tear from her eye.

Ellie stared at her, stunned. "I . . . I thought you were going to come with us?"

Anna looked back at Ellie miserably. "I can't. I can't leave the others behind. You and Seth will look after each other. He's all right, I suppose. But the orphans don't have anyone else."

"But . . . what if we never see each other again?" Ellie said, her voice trembling.

"But I *will* see you, Ellie. That's what I'm saying."

They stood in silence, as Anna's sniffles filled the workshop. She took Ellie's hands in hers and closed her eyes.

"When I first came to the orphanage, I was really angry all the time. I kept getting into fights. Mostly for stupid stuff, like when I put that spider in Agatha Timpson's soup." She smiled despite herself. "That was when Matron Wilkins was still running the place, and every time I got in trouble she'd lock me in that coal cellar on the street until she remembered to take me out again." She looked at Ellie. "You never got put in there, did you?"

Ellie shook her head, though she remembered the smell of the place. Dank, like old vegetables.

"It was *so* cold in there," said Anna. "The walls were covered in this green mildew, and the only light was from the tiny barred hole in the door. I was getting put in there all the time. None of the other orphans would talk to me.

"Then you and your brother arrived. I remember watching you in the art room once, surrounded by little wind-up machines. You always had pencils in your hair. I thought you were mad. But your brother was so friendly, and he was excellent at drawing pictures. The others were always crowding around him—he was good at telling stories too. And he was friendly to me, even though Agatha Timpson warned him to stay away. He would smile at me, and we would talk about sharks. Nobody had smiled at me in such a long time.

"Then one day, Callum Trant pushed me over in the corridor, so I bit his ankle. I was thrown in the coal cellar again and left there for two whole days. I tried to tell myself stories to pass the time, but it was like my brain was numb. I felt like I'd been forgotten. Then, on the third morning, I heard something jingling in the street outside. A stick poked in between the bars and stuck on the end was a bit of paper."

Anna's eyes were wet. She broke into a big smile. "It was a drawing of me, on a ship, with a spear. I was hunting for sharks. I stared at it for hours. It was like I was some-where else." Her eyes focused back on Ellie. "Every time I was put in the cellar after that, Finn sent new drawings through the bars. Sometimes it was just me, slaying mon-sters, but after you and me became friends, it was the three of us, out on some adventure at sea. So even though I was alone in there . . . I didn't feel alone."

Anna looked down at the floor. Tears flowed freely down her cheeks, glistening in the moonlight.

"So even if you sail off with Seth, and even if the Inqui-sition shove all your inventions in their creepy warehouse and burn your workshop to the ground, you'll still be here." She touched her chest. "You'll still be here, all right?"

Ellie pulled Anna in and hugged her tightly. They stayed that way for several happy minutes, until she heard Anna's tummy rumble.

Anna grimaced. "Do you have any food? No, wait, there's no time. I should go and find those drawings." She pulled reluctantly away from Ellie. "Fry and Ibnet and the others'll help. But, Ellie . . ."

Anna looked anxiously at her feet, like she was afraid to speak.

"What is it?" Ellie asked softly.

"You remember how you threw that glass at Seth yes-terday, because he mentioned your brother dying?"

Ellie nodded. Anna took a deep breath. "That was you

who did that, not the Enemy. Maybe it's not the Enemy who won't let you remember Finn. Maybe it's you."

Ellie's chest twisted with a familiar cold shame. Her hand fell away from Anna's. She looked at the floor.

"You were trying to find a way to cure him," Anna said softly. "You were doing everything you could."

Ellie winced. "But if I'd been there with him——"

There was a sharp knock at the door. Ellie and Anna shared a worried look. Who could be knocking so late?

"Ellie! Ellie, are you there? Ellie, you need to wake up."

It was Castion's voice.

"Sir?" said Ellie, hurrying for the door. She pulled it open and found the whale lord looking down at her. His mouth was set in a grim line. "What's wrong?"

"They've found that boat of yours that goes underwater. It washed up by the Greens half an hour ago."

Ellie stared. "But . . . it's been in my second workshop this whole time. It's broken."

Castion grimaced. "I don't know what to tell you. It's there. Some guardsmen found it. And now, well, the Inquisition's turned up."

"What? Why?" said Ellie. Her heart hammered in her temples.

"They think it's suspicious. You should come and explain things to them."

Anna rushed toward Ellie with her coat, a shirt, and a

pair of trousers. Castion waited outside while she hurriedly changed.

"Do you think the storm could have knocked it into the sea?" Anna asked.

Ellie shook her head. "There's no way." She shrugged on her coat. "What have you done, Finn?" she whispered. Boyish laughter echoed inside her mind.

Nothing! said a voice. *How could I have done anything? You said I've got no wishes left, because I refused to help you save Hargrath. And you're always right about everything! Aren't you, Nellie? So, so clever, Nellie.*

"Go ahead," Ellie said quickly to Anna. "I'll catch up."

She opened the basement door an inch and hissed down into the dark. *"Seth!"*

"Mm?" Seth's voice was croaky with sleep. "Ellie? What's wrong?"

"I have to go out," Ellie said. "Stay here. And stay safe."

"Is everything all right?"

Ellie grimaced. "I don't know. I'll be back as soon as I can."

She left the workshop and caught up with Castion and Anna. Castion readjusted the straps of his mechanical leg, then led them along Orphanage Street.

The night air was bitter. A dog barked somewhere in the distance, but the City was asleep, its windows dark. They hurried down the long, broad street of St. Horace toward the waterfront. They turned a corner and the sea appeared in front of them—a line of silver moonlight drawn across the horizon.

Before them were the Greens, named because they were the only part of the City with any plant life, and poorly named at that, for from the narrow stretch of gray, dusty soil barely a dozen dismal apple trees sprouted, twisted and bent over like old men. Beyond the Greens, a wide rooftop rose from the sea. A gathering of silhouettes had collected atop it, each one craning its neck to inspect something in the water. As Ellie got nearer, she saw what was bobbing in the sea beneath them, lengths of seaweed draped from its propellers. The bulky, metal-and-leather form of her failed underwater boat.

The silhouettes resolved into three Inquisitors and four guardsmen. Three of the guardsmen had their crossbows aimed at the underwater boat, while the fourth was holding the reins of a horse, which had a trail of rope leading from its bridle down to the boat.

Castion helped Anna up onto the rooftop, and then Ellie. "Don't worry," he said, noticing the strained look on Ellie's face. "I'm sure we can clear this up."

One of the Inquisitors stepped forward, a young, red-haired man. "Eleanor Lancaster?" he snapped. "I'm told this machine belongs to you."

"Yes," said Ellie in a tiny voice.

"Then tell us how to open it."

Ellie hesitated. "It can't be opened, except from the inside."

The Inquisitor narrowed his eyes. "So what's it doing here, then?"

She stuttered. "I—I don't know. It was in my workshop the last time I saw it. I could never get the thing to work."

"Someone must have stolen it," said Anna.

The horse reared up, whinnying in fright. The Inquisitors and the guardsmen looked at it in surprise, then down at the underwater boat.

There was a noise coming from inside it. A tapping sound.

A hand slapping hard against leather.

"There's someone in there!" a guardsman cried, raising his crossbow higher on his shoulder.

"Ellie," said Castion into her ear. "Tell me what this is."

"The tanks are running out of air," she said, pointing down at the pressure gauge. "Whoever's in there can't breathe."

How delightfully familiar! cried Finn's voice in her head. *A big sea-dwelling lump washing up, with a suffocating person trapped inside!*

"Who is it, Ellie?" said Castion. "Tell me!"

Metal screeched as a poorly oiled wheel turned. The

circular hatch atop the machine lurched up an inch, then was flung open.

A trembling hand reached out.

Oh, you're going to hate this . . . said Finn.

A man hauled himself up through the hatch, his normally neat hair now wild and greasy, his dark eyes wide with terror. He took long gasps of air. Then he saw Ellie, and his pale face contorted with hate.

"You," he whispered. "YOU!"

Ellie shrank away from him, huddling close to Anna. Castion spoke in quiet disbelief.

"Hargrath."

25

THE TRUE SAINT

Two of the guardsmen lowered their crossbows and stepped forward to help Hargrath from the machine.

"Leave me!" he roared, shoving them roughly away. He pulled himself fully out of the hatch, lost his grip, then tumbled over the edge. Castion heaved him to his knees.

"Castion," Hargrath coughed, staring miserably at the whale lord. "It would be you who rescued me."

"Killian," Castion said. "What happened?"

"Step away from him," said the red-haired man to Castion. "This is Inquisitorial business."

Castion gave him a look that could have sunk a ship. "I was an Inquisitor when you were still learning to swim, boy. I have stared the Enemy in the eye and lived to tell of it."

Ellie and Anna backed away from the Inquisitors. The edges of Ellie's vision blurred, her eyes swarming with bursts of yellow and purple. She was shaking as if from a fever.

"I don't understand," she whispered. "You *refused* to save him."

She could feel Finn's satisfied smile in her mind. *No. I refused to save* both *of them,* he said. *Him and the other Inquisitor.*

Ellie took a deep, trembling breath, and tried to remember exactly what she'd said when she made her wish.

"You said: 'Are you sure you want me to save *Hargrath*?'"

Finn giggled. *To which you said:*

"'Save him,'" Ellie whispered. "'Save both of them.'"

A tingling, icy pain crept up her spine, taking root at the base of her neck.

"When you refused," she said, "you were only refusing to 'save both of them.' You *did* save Hargrath."

Finn's giggle became joyous laughter, so loud it made her head hurt. *Exactly! I fixed your underwater boat, then used it to rescue Hargrath from the storm, just like you asked me to!*

Castion grabbed a water flask from one of the guardsmen, tipping it up to Hargrath's mouth. Hargrath's throat bulged as he drank greedily.

I saved his life! said Finn's voice. *Then all I had to do was bring him back to the City when the time was right. Now you're as good as caught. So go on—ask me to save you. One more wish, for old times' sake?*

Hargrath coughed up half the water he'd drunk. He was helped to his feet by Castion, then buckled over again, his body shaking with every heave.

"Ellie? Are you okay?" Anna said. "You're trembling."

"No . . ." said Ellie distantly. "I'm not ready."

I did well, though, didn't I, Nellie? said Finn's voice. *Didn't I do well?*

Hargrath staggered to his feet and pointed at Ellie.

"*She* knows where the Vessel is," he spat. "She was with him! He threw me into the sea!"

He blurted this out with a strangled cry, then shrank into Castion's grip and began to sob.

Castion patted Hargrath uncertainly on the back. "Ellie, what does he mean?"

Ellie opened her mouth, but no words came out. Everything was lost. Castion's eyes widened in dismay. He turned to the Inquisitors.

"Put the City on alert." He took a deep breath. "Tell all Inquisitors to head to the workshop of Eleanor Lancaster on Orphanage Street. Tell them . . . tell them the Vessel may be there."

The red-haired Inquisitor bristled. "I don't take orders from—"

"Do it," Hargrath snarled, coughing up a glob of phlegm. "Do as he says."

"I don't take orders from *you* either," the young Inquisitor snapped. "You're mad, Hargrath. The Enemy broke your mind."

Hargrath grabbed him by the neck, lifting him off the ground. "You know *nothing* of the Enemy," he growled.

The man gurgled as he choked. Castion put a hand on Hargrath's arm. "Killian," he said gently. "Let him go. We must get to the Vessel."

Hargrath dropped the man, who hacked and spluttered on the slate rooftop. Hargrath looked at Castion. He seemed close to crying again.

"Why?" he said, gripping Castion's arm. "Why have you let me tell a lie, all these years?"

"Because sainthood suited you better," said Castion, clapping the other man's shoulder. "I couldn't be the Inquisitor who killed the Enemy. I didn't want anything to do with it."

"You took what was *mine*," Hargrath moaned in a quiet whisper.

Castion smiled sadly. "We both failed that day, Killian. Claude was a dear friend, but I was blind to his suffering. Well, not again. This boy is suffering too. Let us end it for him and stop the Enemy from doing to others what it did to us. Let us . . . correct the past."

Hargrath looked at him miserably, his giant shoulders shuddering, tears coursing down his cheeks. He nodded. "Yes," he said. "Please."

"He's not the Vessel," Ellie said, clutching herself tightly. She was so cold.

Castion looked at her like she was a stranger. He gestured to the Inquisitors. "Keep her close," he said. "That one too." He pointed at Anna.

"What about this?" said one of the guardsmen, gesturing to the underwater boat still bobbing in the sea.

"Forget about that," said Castion, and the guardsman untied the rope from the horse and looped it around a chimney pot instead.

The red-haired Inquisitor grabbed Ellie's arm, making her cry out as he squeezed one of her bruises.

"Get off her!" Anna snapped, then an Inquisitor grabbed hold of her too, twisting her arm behind her back as she tried to kick him.

"Don't hurt her!" said Ellie.

"We'll proceed straight to her workshop," said Castion. "Killian, can you walk?"

Hargrath grunted, wiping tears from his eyes. Castion gave Ellie one cold, distant look, then set off. An Inquisitor ran ahead to raise the alarm and the others marched in silence. Too soon, they were back in Orphanage Street.

"Her keys will be in her coat," Castion said as they stood outside the workshop. The red-haired Inquisitor dug a hand into Ellie's pockets, roughly rummaging around.

"Ow!" he shouted, snatching back his hand. One of his fingers was bleeding. Anna laughed.

"Ellie," Castion said, "unlock the door."

Ellie found her keys and put one into the lock, rattling it loudly in the hope the noise would carry to the basement.

"Ow, this *Inquisitor* is hurting my arm!" Anna yelled at the top of her voice, squirming in the Inquisitor's grip and kicking the workshop door. "Do all *Inquisitors* stink like you?"

Ellie took a long, slow breath, then heaved the door aside.

The workshop lay in semi-darkness, just a glimmer of moonlight to show the way. They walked inside, and there was a metal crunch and a loud curse as an Inquisitor stepped on one of the oyster-catchers. Ellie picked up an oil lamp and a box of matches from a shelf beside the door, secretly pocketing a bundle of fireworks that was sitting next to them.

"Where is the Vessel?" said Castion as Ellie lit the lamp.

"He isn't the Vessel."

"Ellie."

Castion knelt down before her, taking her hand gently

in both of his. "You're my best friend's daughter," he said. His eyes were red around the edges. He looked old and tired.

"I'll be executed," she said.

"I will . . . try to see what I can do for you, Ellie. Given your position, your age. Your importance to the City. I will plead your case."

"She'll hang," said the red-haired Inquisitor. "Or worse."

"Silence!" Castion roared, and the man took a step backward.

Ellie and Castion stared at one another a long while, the workshop quiet save for the mumbled ravings of Hargrath, who'd sat down on the floor. Castion was trembling. He couldn't seem to take his eyes from her.

"Ellie, there's no way to protect him anymore. You must help yourself now."

"No," Ellie whispered. "He's done nothing wrong."

She took a deep breath. A sense of strange serenity came over her, like she was about to dive into the ocean from a great height. Once she let go, everyone else would be safe.

"I'm the Vessel," she said.

There were no gasps, no surprise. Only silence.

Castion straightened up with a creak of leather. "Ellie, lying won't save him. He has to die."

"I asked the Enemy to save Seth," she said. "On the

night of his execution. It brought him to the workshop. When Hargrath chased me into Celestina's Hope, the Enemy threw him into the sea."

Ellie's voice echoed around the workshop. It seemed like someone else's to her. Anna was shaking her head.

"I've been the Vessel for three years," Ellie said.

Castion was still. "That is a very serious lie to tell."

"I'm not lying."

"Miss Lancaster—"

Heat surged into Ellie's chest and she lunged forward. Pain stabbed at her forehead.

"I'M NOT LYING!"

Castion stumbled back, bracing himself against a workbench. The Inquisitors gasped and the guardsmen cried out in horror, pointing their crossbows at Ellie. Anna tried to rush to Ellie's side but was wrenched back by an Inquisitor.

"What?" said Ellie. "What happened?"

Anna's voice shook. "Your face," she said. "There was something . . ."

But she didn't seem able to say what she'd seen in Ellie's face.

Hargrath let out a sound halfway between a laugh and a sob. "It's her," he said. "She *is* the Vessel."

Castion watched Ellie, his eyes wide. He went to put his hand to his mouth, then thought better of it. He closed his eyes, as if willing himself to wake up from a nightmare.

"No," he said quietly, touching one of his silver rings. "Please, no."

Then he opened his eyes and motioned for the Inquisitors to step away from Ellie.

"Inform the High Inquisitor that the Vessel has been found," he said. "Inform him that she was deemed too close to the manifestation. Tell him . . . she was executed at her home."

"NO!"

Anna fought free of the Inquisitor's grasp, but a guardsman scooped her up immediately, fumbling to hold her as she twisted madly in his arms. In the moment of distraction, Ellie retrieved a penknife and the oyster pearl from her pockets, storing both up her sleeve.

"You can't!" Anna cried, struggling desperately. "No, no! *Ellie!*"

"You will understand in time, Miss Stonewall," Castion said, his voice hollow.

Anna kept squirming. "Ellie! Ellie, run!"

"It's all right, Anna," Ellie said softly. "It's all right."

"No," Anna groaned, reaching out for her.

Castion took a step toward Ellie. One of the Inquisitors handed him a sword, still sheathed. Tears rolled down Castion's cheeks.

"I'm sorry, Ellie," he said, struggling even to speak. "I

cannot let that thing win again."

He took a long, deep breath, then reached for the hilt of the sword. When he spoke again, his voice did not tremble.

"In the name of the Twenty-Six Saints and Their Most Holy Inquisition, I pronounce you Vessel, corrupt and diabolical host to the Great Enemy of Humankind. I . . . I sentence you to die."

He drew the sword from its scabbard.

"Please," Anna whispered. "Please."

He held it out to one side, holding it horizontally. The blade glittered in the lamplight.

And for a moment, less than a heartbeat, Ellie wondered about letting the sword meet her neck.

But the Enemy would only return, to plague another poor soul.

She looked at Anna. Their eyes met, and Ellie saw the pain on Anna's face. She couldn't give up. She wouldn't. There *was* a way to stop the Enemy. Her pulse flickered in her fingertips. Blood roared in her eardrums. Her mind spun at a dizzying pace. She pictured the chapel where she'd first found Seth. The cracked gargoyle in one corner. She pictured the underwater boat. And, as Castion's knuckles whitened around the hilt of the sword, a plan flashed in her mind.

"No," said Ellie.

She threw herself to one side and the Inquisitors unsheathed their swords. Another second and she'd be dead.

With a furious shout, Anna shook off her guardsman and leapt in front of Castion. Ellie let the pearl drop from her sleeve into her hand and threw it at a metal plate on the ceiling.

There was a hiss, a crack, and four thunderous explosions. Thick curtains of smoke spewed from metal pipes in the ceiling, and the room was consumed by a smothering blackness.

The men coughed, and the light of the oil lamp was swallowed by smoke. Ellie grabbed Anna's hand, then raced for a rope at the side of the room, cutting it with her penknife.

The traps in the floorboards were sprung. The planks fell inward, dropping the men into the tangle of wire underneath with a chorus of shrieks. Ellie rushed for the door, dragging Anna behind.

"FIND HER!" came Hargrath's shrill cry, amid more shouts of panic and the clattering of metal.

Ellie slid the front door open—

And then they were out on the street.

26

THE ENEMY

A bitter wind was howling. Silver light dappled the rooftops and smoke poured from the doorway of the workshop.

"Run!" Ellie cried, and she and Anna hurtled along Orphanage Street. Ellie's heart was beating so hard she could feel it in her eyeballs. She glanced at Anna and saw she was clutching something in her free hand. Hargrath's dart-gun.

"His pocket was unbuttoned," Anna said breathlessly. "I thought we might need it. Ellie, what do we do?"

Ellie grimaced, thinking through her plan again and again. "I need you to find Seth, and get one of Finn's drawings from the orphanage," she said.

Anna nodded. "Of course."

"And then I need you to bring it to the chapel where we

first found Seth. That's where I'll be . . . hopefully."

Ellie heard the thud of heavy boots from back along the street. "And one more thing. Send Fry and Ibnet to find the underwater boat. The Enemy fixed it so it works now. Tell them to sail it west to St. Corrigan's Observatory as quickly as possible, then to get well away."

"But . . . I can't leave you." Anna had fresh tears on her cheeks.

"I'll find you," Ellie said. "In my other workshop, okay? Now go! And try to avoid the Inquisitors!"

"Ellie—"

"Go!" Ellie cried as they came to the end of the street. Anna wiped her eyes and, after a second's pause, she turned and raced off in the other direction.

"Ellie!" she heard Castion bark, far behind her. "Ellie, stop!"

Ellie willed herself to keep going. Her body felt like it was made from paper and would crumple and tear in the wind. She flung herself around a corner and collided with a cold alley wall.

Nellie, come on, said Finn's voice in her mind. *Give up. Then you won't have to suffer anymore.*

Ellie pushed herself from the wall. "No," she spat. "You're not winning this."

Nellie, please! Finn begged. *You've done so well. I'm so proud of you. But you can't carry on fighting anymore. Give me a body of my own! I can make sure they don't hurt Seth or Anna.*

Ellie clenched her teeth. "All you've ever done when you get a physical form of your own is hurt people."

Her body seemed to have lost any means of warming itself. The wind bit at her arms and face, filling her lungs with the icy cold. The crisp, salty smell of the sea grew stronger with every step she took north.

A low bellow rang out above, like a great beast roused from sleep.

The bell of the Inquisitorial Keep had begun to toll.

They're coming for us now, Nellie, said Finn's voice. He sounded like he was crying.

"Get out of my head," Ellie growled.

But we're one now, don't you see? Ellie and Finn, bound by love. Isn't this what you always wanted?

Ellie flung herself down a broad market street, which still stank of fish. Half-picked carcasses lay scattered across the cobbles, abandoned by the seagulls. Ahead, bleary-eyed city folk crept from their homes, drawn by the sound of the bell. Ellie hurtled down slippery steps into a tight alleyway, collapsing behind a crate. The sound of her own breathing exploded in her ears.

Give up, Nellie . . .

Ellie pointed up toward the top of the City, where the

great bell rang. "This is you," she whispered. "You are the cause of all the pain in this city."

She heard shouts nearby.

"It's that girl. Hannah Lancaster's daughter!"

The clamor grew louder as others took up the cry. Then, a name, screamed out to the sky, trilling amid the clanging of the bell.

"Eleanor Lancaster!"

"Eleanor Lancaster is the Vessel!"

She heard the sound of boots on cobbles. She got to her feet, her body almost toppling forward with every step, her legs frozen to numb, brittle stumps.

"ELLIE!" came a distant shout. Castion.

Nellie, this is my game we're playing, not yours, said Finn. *I've been playing it for centuries, and I've gotten very good at it.*

Ellie turned into another alley and stopped dead. Three people were huddled together outside a small tenement house, their breath rising in the night air. A mother and father, clutching their son between them. They stared up at the sky, as if for some sign that they were safe again.

The boy saw her first.

Ellie recognized him—it was the same boy she'd spoken to on the Angelus Waterfront, the day the whale had appeared on the rooftop. He clutched a little model of St. Celestina around his neck. He screamed.

"It's her! It's the Enemy!"

His wails pierced Ellie's head. The mother retreated toward the door, scooping up her son. The father spread his arms.

"Get away!" he cried, waving his hands, his voice breaking. He turned to his wife. "Inside, both of you!"

"Out of my way!" Ellie shouted, baring her teeth and advancing on them. The man cried out in terror. He reached down and picked up a loose cobblestone the size of a fist.

"Get away!" he cried. He threw the stone and Ellie ducked aside, wincing as it scraped her shoulder.

"Kill her!" cried the little boy. "You've got to kill her!"

Ellie turned, and saw two Inquisitors behind her, filling the width of the alley.

"She's here! SHE'S HERE!"

Nellie, please! Finn cried. *They'll kill you! You've got to ask me to stop them!*

Ellie hobbled on, pulling a lighter and a firework from her pockets, lighting the fuse.

Watch out! Finn shouted.

One of the Inquisitors had caught up with her, throwing out a leg to trip her. Ellie stumbled, fell. Her knees scraped stone. Pain exploded in her shoulder.

She heard the Inquisitor's heavy breathing and forced

herself to her feet. He was barely more than a boy, his eyes wide with horror. He raised his sword and Ellie threw the firework right at him.

She shielded her eyes with her coat as blazing purple lights cartwheeled in all directions, bouncing from the walls and covering the Inquisitor in a cloud of red smoke. Ellie staggered back down the alley but crumpled to her knees. She had done something to her right leg when she fell. Putting weight on it made her want to be sick.

More heavy footsteps were gaining on her. She pulled out another firework, but before she could light it an Inquisitor reached out with the tip of his sword and whipped it from her grasp.

A dark shape crossed the street behind him.

There was a heavy *thunk* and the Inquisitor was enveloped in a net that pulled him to the ground in a tangle of limbs. Seth leapt over the thrashing body, tossing aside Ellie's net-cannon.

"Let's go," he said, taking her hand. His face was smudged with smoke from the workshop, but his blue eyes blazed. They started down the alley, only Ellie found it too painful and had to stop.

"Are you okay?"

"I hurt my leg."

"Come on," Seth said, putting his arm around her. She

leaned on him as they ran. It still hurt, but not quite so badly.

"Where are we going?" Seth asked.

"Back to where we first met. I have a plan. And it involves you."

The sea looked unsettled below the light of the moon. Ellie saw the seawall, nestled beneath a row of abandoned, overhanging buildings. And there, near-drowned by the rising tide, was the Chapel of St. Bartholomew, its roof still sagging from the imprint of the whale, the four gargoyles sitting at each corner. Just as Ellie remembered, one whale-shaped gargoyle was bent at an angle, its base cracked from where the actual whale had pressed against it.

They hurried down the steps, pausing to pick up a length of thick, discarded rope, which Ellie hung around her shoulder. They stopped on the seawall.

"I need a boat," Ellie said, looking down at the sea. She remembered there being three the day she'd rescued Seth from the whale, but now there were just three mooring ropes. She cursed.

"They'll follow us here, Ellie," said Seth.

"I know," she said. "I'm counting on it."

"Ellie, what's—"

Ellie fell to her knees as a new and terrible pain stabbed at her rib cage from the inside. She screamed.

"Ellie!" Seth cried, holding her close. "What is it? What's wrong?"

Something was inside her. Her chest was expanding out of rhythm with her breathing, like something was trying to break out of her. Her body crunched and scraped as she moved her muscles.

"I can feel it," she said. "I'm so cold."

Seth gripped her more tightly, rubbing her arm with his hand.

Ellie shook her head. "The cold's inside me. It's the Enemy. It's almost ready."

Seth helped her to her feet. "Come on, what's your plan?"

"I need something that floats."

He looked around. "What about that?"

Ellie glanced at where he was pointing—a ruined house, with a rotten door attached by a single rusty hinge. She nodded, and Seth ripped it free with a sharp breath.

The shouting in the streets grew nearer.

"Let's get this to the chapel," said Ellie. They carried the door to the edge of the seawall. Seth dropped down onto the chapel roof, and Ellie eased the door after him, then lowered herself down too. She hobbled over to the far corner of the chapel roof, inspecting the whale-shaped gargoyle.

"Ellie, there are people coming," said Seth, his voice low.

"Castion and the Inquisitors. Tie yourself to something—when he gets close I'll hit them with a wave."

"No," said Ellie firmly. "It's all part of the plan."

She dug her penknife into the crumbled base of the whale-gargoyle, using it like a lever. The stone creaked. She pocketed her knife, tied one end of the rope into a loop, then slung it around the gargoyle.

"Ellie, why not use this one?" said Seth, pointing to an eagle at the other corner. "It looks much sturdier."

Ellie shook her head. "I don't want it to be sturdy. I need it to fall into the sea and pull me down with it."

Seth's eyes went wide in horror. "What? Why?"

Ellie risked a look up at the City above. "I need the Inquisitors to see me drown."

Seth gripped her hand tightly. "Ellie, you can't."

"I'm not *actually* going to drown," said Ellie. "You're going to rescue me. You're going to move the sea, and me with it. Just like you did with that shark."

Seth stared at her, his lips going pale. "What if I lose control?"

"You can do it, Seth, I know you can," she said. She shrugged off her coat and laid it in his hands. "There's a ruined observatory a little way east of here," she said. "If you could try and get me close to it that would be great. Once you've done that, you have to get away from the Inquisitors. They may still hunt you, even though they know you're not the Vessel. Head to my second workshop. I'll find you there."

"But what about the Enemy?"

Ellie's chest squirmed again. She pressed it with her hand. "I think I know how to beat it now. I need to take away its power. I need to separate it from my brother."

"ELLIE!"

She turned. Castion was on the seawall now, striding toward her with ten or more Inquisitors, and Hargrath staggering behind. Ellie slid the door to the edge of the roof, juddering it across the tiles. Fingers trembling, she tied the other end of the rope to the door handle. With a groan of effort she heaved the door into the water, where it bobbed like a raft.

"ELLIE!" Castion roared again, landing on the roof, flanked on either side by two Inquisitors. Ellie turned to Seth and smiled.

Then she jumped into the sea.

The water embraced her, strangely warm, as if her body was even colder than it felt. She swam toward the door, clinging to its splintery frame. She looked back to see Castion and the Inquisitors stepping to the edge of the rooftop. Seth had ducked behind one of the intact gargoyles, keeping out of sight.

"Hargrath," Castion snapped. "Your dart-gun, hand it to me."

Hargrath fumbled in his pocket, then gave a tiny moan. "I . . . I don't have it."

Castion cursed and went to grab the rope, to pull Ellie back in. The sea rumbled with a sound like splitting rock and a wave crashed angrily against the rooftop. Castion leapt backward.

"Don't come near me!" Ellie roared, so hard her throat hurt, raising her hand so it looked like *she* was controlling the sea. Seth was still hiding behind a gargoyle, faint blue swirls on his neck. Ellie untied the rope from the door handle and lashed it around her waist.

The slightest shred of sunlight had appeared on the horizon. More and more people were streaming down from the upper City, crowding along the seawall. They watched Ellie and Castion, their faces pale and frightened.

Then, the waterfront was silent, save for the quiet lapping of the waves.

"If you want to end it this way, fine," said Castion. "But please, do it now, before the Enemy comes. Before anyone gets hurt."

Ellie looked down at the water. She took a deep breath, then gripped the rope tightly.

Something heaved against her chest from the inside, making her cry out. She fell forward, hands clawing the edges of the door. Finn's voice spoke inside her head, his every word like a nail driven into her skull.

I will not *let you fake your death, Nellie,* he said. *You are going to die* here, now.

There was a searing pain in her fingers. Something wriggled beneath her skin, pushing against it.

There was another hand moving inside her hand.

Ellie screamed, sobbing in pain and fury, clenching her hands to fists and beating them against the door.

"Bring her in, Castion!" someone shrieked from the crowd. "KILL HER!"

But Castion could only watch in horror.

You can't fight me, Nellie, said Finn, as Ellie's body heaved against her will. *You've no right. You* left *me. You deserve this.*

Ellie closed her eyes, trying to think of her brother, to picture his face. She remembered his blue eyes and his golden locks and—

"No, no that's not *him*," she moaned.

Don't struggle, Nellie, said Finn's voice, like an avalanche in her mind. *Now is your end.*

She tried to picture him in their bedroom, scribbling away with his colored pencils. But instead she heard only a boy's cries of pain and felt a twisting, itching shame. Something writhed in her chest. Ellie placed a hand there and could feel a new second heartbeat pounding against her palm. Her own heart was growing weaker and weaker.

"NO!" she screamed as a fresh spasm of pain coursed through her. She took a cold, shuddering breath and knew somehow that the next new agony would take her away forever. She raised her head from the wood, her gaze drifting from Castion to Seth.

Then she heard a voice crying out her name. Through blurry, tear-filled eyes she glimpsed a blue sweater and a haze of ginger hair. Anna dropped down from the seawall.

"ELLIE!" she cried, rushing to the edge of the roof. She pulled something metal from her pocket, and Ellie saw that it was Hargrath's dart-gun. She aimed, fired, and a glint of metal spiraled through the air toward Ellie, embedding itself in the wooden door with a heavy *thunk*.

Attached to the dart was a piece of paper.

Ellie reached out, her every muscle fighting against her as she pulled the paper from the dart. She unfolded it with trembling fingers.

It was a drawing of a boat at sea, done quickly but very well with colored pencils. In the boat were three people—a girl with ginger hair, a girl with blond hair, and a boy with green eyes.

Green eyes.

The figures were so vividly and lovingly sketched that they seemed a moment away from drawing breath. The blond-haired girl and the boy could not have looked more alike. Their faces were freckled, their hair a shock of messy curls. Both had small noses that curved slightly to one side. They sat very close to each other, looking down and smiling, like they could see something secret. The girl had her arm around the boy's shoulders.

Ellie stared at the picture, and at the boy's face. She heard a voice in her mind, but it wasn't the Enemy. It was Anna.

So even though I was alone in there . . . I didn't feel alone.

Ellie's lips trembled, trying to form a single word.

"Finn," she said.

27

THE BOY IN THE ROWBOAT

Ellie's head tingled, and she was overcome by a strange brightness all around her. It was a moment before she realized that the door she was lying on was no longer a door.

She pulled herself up. It was daytime, and she was sitting in a small wooden rowboat, bobbing gently on the waves. She looked for Seth and Anna, for Castion and Hargrath. But they were gone. Even the City—a towering, jagged beast above—appeared to be made of fog.

Ellie's bare arms were unbruised, her hair cut much shorter than usual. She was wearing shorts and a green cardigan with the sleeves rolled up. The cold inside her felt distant now, like a memory. Sunlight warmed her skin, and dragonflies darted above the water, halting on the lookout for mosquitoes. Ellie touched a hand to her cheeks, finding them slightly sunburnt. She looked up and studied the other person in the boat with her.

He had his back turned, leaning over the side, dipping a fishing net into the sea. He wore dusty black trousers and a gray sweater. He was singing quietly to himself.

"Finn?" Ellie said nervously.

He turned his head.

The boy in the boat had a pale, freckled face, green eyes, and a small nose that turned slightly to one side. His hair was a dirty, sandy blond, and he was wiry and scruffy. He looked an awful lot like she did.

"I think I just saw a blue shark," he said.

Ellie opened her mouth to speak. Somehow, she felt like the words were already there for her, on the tip of the tongue.

"You did not."

His eyes narrowed at the challenge. He turned back to his net. "It wasn't very big."

"Blue sharks aren't very big," she said. The more she spoke, the more comfortable she felt, like she had nowhere else to be but in that boat.

"Mom says she saw one that was nine feet long," Finn said.

"How big was that one?"

He shrugged. "About the same size as me."

"Sharks don't come near the City," said Ellie authoritatively. She liked to show off how clever she was to her brother. She knew how much it annoyed him. "The water's too murky for them."

"You heard Mom say that."

"I didn't! It's my own idea."

"And you're putting on that voice you do when you're trying to prove you're clever."

"I am not!" She hit him on the arm.

He laughed. "You're just jealous because I saw a blue shark."

"It wasn't a blue shark!"

"I think I know a little bit more about sharks than you do," said Finn, staring searchingly into the water. "You scared it off with all your yelling."

He sighed and picked something up from the bottom of the boat. It was a large black tube with a whale engraved on its side.

"You're still trying to get that to work?" Ellie said.

"It *does* work."

Finn wet his lips, then put the tube to his mouth, concentrating hard. At first, a gurgling, rasping sound came out, which made Ellie laugh and caused Finn to frown. He tried again.

This time, a deep and unearthly sound emerged that

made Ellie feel like her very bones were trembling. It seemed to come from some far-off place, rising and falling like music.

It sounded just like whale song.

Finn put the tube back down, watching the sea expectantly, fiddling with the collection of keys and seashells and other trinkets that hung from the chain around his neck. Ellie couldn't help but watch the sea too, hoping for some response.

"It didn't work," she said eventually.

Finn stared down the tube like a telescope. "I don't think you made it right."

"Don't blame me!"

"I'm telling you," Finn said confidently, "one of these days the whales are going to sing back. Look—the shark!" he cried, leaning over the edge.

"Careful you don't fall in," Ellie warned.

"I'm not going to—"

From the other side of the boat there was a tremendous splash, spraying them with salt water. Ellie caught the shape of a dark, glossy tail turning in the water. Finn yelled out and fell backward into the sea.

"Finn!"

Ellie stood, and felt a stab of panic. Where he'd fallen in there was now just a white ring of foam. Without thinking, she jumped in after him.

Water rushed up her nose. The sun above was bright enough that she could see the shapes of buildings below her through the gloom. She cried out Finn's name, only bubbles issued from her mouth instead.

She felt a touch on her shoulder, then her arm, and was hauled upward. Finn dragged her back into the boat. He was laughing for some reason.

"I saw it," he said breathlessly. "It was . . . It was . . ."

He collapsed, his cheeks red. Ellie kicked him in the shin.

"Stop laughing," she said. She glanced at his neck. "Oh, Finn, you've lost your chain in the water! That had your keys to the orphanage on it!"

But Finn was still laughing and didn't seem to care.

"This isn't *funny*, Finn. I was worried!"

He looked at her. "What? Why?"

"Because you're not a good swimmer!"

"Yes, I am!"

"You used to struggle."

"When I was *four*, maybe! I've been practicing."

"When?"

"You're not with me all the time!" Finn snapped. "And in case you didn't notice—*I* just pulled *you* from the sea."

The outburst stunned Ellie to silence and she sat down, hair dripping wet. Finn turned from her, frowning and crossing his arms.

"You worry about me far too much," he huffed.

"I'm your big sister—it's my job."

"No, it's not," said Finn. "We'd have much more fun if you weren't fretting all the time."

"I'd never forgive myself if anything happened to you."

"Well, that's silly. What's the point in letting something like that worry you? Besides, I can look after myself."

"You just fell into the water with a shark!"

The corners of Finn's lips twitched.

"What?" said Ellie. "What's funny?"

"It wasn't a shark," he said.

"What was it?"

He averted his eyes.

"Finn?"

"It was a tuna," he said sheepishly.

Ellie laughed. "I told you," she said.

"It was a *big* tuna!"

Ellie hopped to her feet, bearing down on him and pinching him playfully.

"Hey, stop that!" he cried.

He squirmed and pushed her off and they wrestled until they collapsed on their backs at either end of the boat. Ellie stared up at the sky, taking a moment to catch her breath. The fluffy white clouds were turning gray and the sky was growing dark, even though it had been morning just moments ago. She could feel a strange cold creeping into her chest. She gasped, looking down at her hands. Something was pushing against her skin.

"Finn," she asked. "Is this a dream, or a memory?"

The sky was filling up with more and more swirling black clouds. Ellie's limbs were turning to ice. Something did not like her being there, wherever she was. Something was trying to drag her back.

"No," she said. "Please, don't take me away."

"Ellie?"

A fog was creeping in at the corners of her eyes. Ellie looked at her brother, who was watching her with a look of caring concern.

"I'm sorry, Finn," she said.

"For what?" he said. Somehow, the sun still shone on his face, even though the clouds had blotted it out.

"I wish I could always be there to look after you," she said. "I'm sorry if I ever leave you alone when you need me."

She rubbed tears from her cheeks.

"I'm never alone," said Finn. "You're always with me, Ellie. Even when you're not."

The sky cracked above. Ellie was shivering so terribly that she felt like icy water was being poured down her throat.

"No," she sobbed. "I don't want to go. I'm not ready. I just want to stay here with you."

Finn smiled, his cheeks flushed and his hair soaking wet. He reached out and held her hand in both of his. His grip was so warm. Ellie could feel the heat return to her fingers.

"You have to go," he said. "But I'll be right here when you need me."

And above the sky was dark again.

Her body was cold, weak. Her hair was long and thinning. She could feel splinters of wood in her hands and legs.

Somehow, her fingers were still warm.

Ellie placed her brother's drawing down with great care. She pushed herself up onto her elbows, but all her joints seemed to have rusted, and the effort to hold herself up was almost too much. But she had to. For just a little while longer.

She lifted her head. Castion was still at the edge of the roof, staring at her. It seemed like only seconds had passed.

She hobbled to her feet, the door swaying beneath her, and checked the loop of rope around her waist. She drew a long, deep breath, feeling the wind on her face. She looked at Seth, who watched her anxiously. He clenched his fists and gritted his teeth, concentrating hard on the water.

Ellie gave the rope three sharp tugs. There was a slow, inevitable crunch of stone as the whale-gargoyle toppled toward the sea.

"No!" Anna cried. "ELLIE, NO!"

Ellie stepped off the door, and the sea swallowed her up. She drifted a moment, treading water, then a powerful force yanked at her waist as the gargoyle plunged below the surface, dragging her with it.

Water rushed upward all around, thundering like a storm in her ears. She opened her eyes and saw Finn there before her, his fingers around her neck. Trying to choke her.

Except this *wasn't* Finn. This boy had blue eyes, the color of the sky. But her brother's eyes had been green, like hers. This boy's cheeks were too round, and his nose didn't turn to one side, but was perfectly straight. His hair was too golden, even underwater, and he was not nearly so freckled as the real Finn had been. He seemed to be drowning, as the gargoyle dragged them down, farther and farther into the depths. He looked afraid.

Ellie pulled her penknife from her trouser pocket and sliced at the rope. Her hand moved slowly underwater, but finally the rope came apart. She felt an immediate relief around her waist as the gargoyle fell away.

Ellie looked at the Enemy. It stared back at her with such pure hatred, a look so unfamiliar on her brother's face. She closed her eyes.

And in her mind, she saw the little bedroom she and her brother shared in the orphanage. The walls were covered with his drawings. Some were of sharks and ships and sailors, others of mythical birds with majestic pink and blue wings. But mostly the drawings were of a girl, and a boy, and the adventures they shared.

Her brother lay in his bed, wrapped up in his sheets. His skin was pale, and he was shivering.

Ellie stepped inside the bedroom. And though she was not really there, she sat down upon the bed and rested a hand on his head, stroking his straw-colored curls. She lay on her side and hugged him close, as tightly as she could. And though he still shivered, and though he was still cold, he smiled.

Ellie smiled too, even as she began to struggle for air. Even as her fingers went numb and her vision began to fade. At last, she opened her eyes.

The creature before her did not look anything like her brother—or any human. Its skin was turning gray, its eyes a fathomless black. Its lips were gone, and it had only a small mouth filled with tiny, pointed teeth. Its skull was too big for its pallid, infantile body, and at the back grew to a point from which seaweed-like tendrils sprouted. It tried to scratch at her with brittle fingers and claws. Bits of it were flaking away.

Its mouth opened to scream at her, but the sound was weak and unfamiliar. Ellie put her hand to its head and pushed. The Enemy fell away, sinking down toward the rooftops of the City beneath the sea.

Great beams of sunlight broke through the water around her as the sun rose, throwing the City below into relief: a hundred thousand buildings huddled in the deep. Ellie felt the pain in her chest lessen, her head going light. She found she could only smile. How strange it was to be herself again. She thought of her mom, and of her brother. She thought of Seth and Anna.

Then, drifting to her through the morning light, from some far-off place, she heard the sound of whales.

It almost seemed as if they were singing.

ORPHANS OF THE TIDE

Seth raced through the sewers, squeezing through tight tunnels with Ellie's coat clutched under one arm. At last, he came to the little rusted door to Ellie's second workshop. He slammed it open and was greeted by a familiar mess of tools and broken instruments. Light stippled the ceiling, reflected from the water beneath.

"Ellie!" he shouted, hoping she'd pop up from behind one of the workbenches. He held her coat close. It was extremely heavy, its pockets so full that the stitching was bursting in a dozen places.

"She's alive," he told himself. "She must be."

Seth went to the second door, which led the other way out through the sewers. But it was locked. He scrabbled around in Ellie's coat pockets for the right key, then lost his temper, slamming his fist against the rusted door.

"ELLIE!"

Seth strode back and forth across the workshop, wringing the coat in his hands. Where *was* she? He ran to the edge of the crumbling floor, staring down at the waves six feet below. He closed his eyes and tried to reach out into the water. His mind became a writhing, unsettled place, his thoughts swirling in all directions. He cast his mind farther and farther through the churning ocean, toward the Angelus Waterfront. He felt a ripple as a shoal of herrings swam past him, then the jagged spires of sunken buildings as his mind swept above the rooftops.

At last, he found what he was looking for: a broken, whale-shaped gargoyle, half swallowed by silt at the bottom of the ocean. Dangling from it was a length of rope, neatly cut at one end. But there was no sign of Ellie. He pulled his mind back, gasping for breath.

He tried to recall the moment she had jumped into the water. At the time, he had tried to search for her, casting his mind into the sea, feeling it course through him. But there was so much raging water, and he hadn't been able to find Ellie anywhere. Instead, he had taken hold of the sea in his mind. He had woven a current from the shifting tides, directing it east as Ellie had instructed him. And all he could do was hope dearly it had carried her with it.

Footsteps raced along the corridor beyond the workshop. Seth's heart leapt, and he flew to the door.

"Ellie?"

The door swung open to reveal a breathless Anna. She looked up at him, eyes full of disappointment.

"Where is she?" they said to one another.

"She didn't really drown, did she?" said Anna. "You saved her, didn't you?"

"I tried," Seth said in a quiet voice. "I mean, I moved the sea like she told me to—I made a current, going east. But then the Inquisitors started stomping around the roof and I had to jump into the water to hide."

"Coward," Anna grunted.

"There were *dozens* of Inquisitors! Where were *you*?"

"They dragged me off. For stealing Hargrath's dart-gun. And also I sort of . . . bit an Inquisitor."

"How did you get away?"

Anna shrugged. "Castion made them let me go. He was really upset—the Inquisitors all seemed too terrified to say no to him."

Anna looked down at the coat in Seth's hands. Her voice dropped to a quiet tremble. "But she had a plan. I brought her Finn's drawing like she told me." She swallowed. "She's really not here?"

They stared hopelessly at one another for many long seconds.

"Maybe she got delayed?" Anna said.

She wandered between the workbenches, nudging

scraps of metal with her foot, until she reached the part of the workshop where the floor fell away into the water. She stared expectantly at the sea, then sat down with her legs dangling over the edge. Seth sat next to her, running his finger along the seams of Ellie's coat. He paused on a particular hole in one sleeve and thought about how Ellie would sometimes slot her thumb through it when she was worried.

Anna took the hem of the coat on her lap and stroked it. "She was supposed to show me how to gut a cuttlefish," she said.

They sat in silence for several minutes until, from somewhere far above, there was a low rumble. Seth leapt to his feet, but Anna shook her head.

"Fireworks. They think the Vessel is dead."

Seth's stomach twisted in a horrible knot.

"She's a good swimmer," Anna said, though she didn't sound confident.

There was a splash, and a gurgling sound. They turned to see the leather, lumpen form of the underwater boat bursting out from the water.

"They found it!" Anna exclaimed.

"Who?" said Seth.

"Fry and Ibnet—while I looked for the drawing, they ran to get the boat from where it was tied up by the Greens, to get it to the observatory. That must have been Ellie's plan—for you to take her to the observatory so she could bring the underwater boat here!"

Seth jumped down to the wide stone step at the edge of the water. He climbed on top of the machine, trying to prise off its circular hatch.

"You can't open it from the outside," said Anna. "We'll have to smash it!"

She climbed up to the workshop and grabbed a section of pipe from a bench. There was a piercing screech as metal ground against metal: a wheel inside the boat was turning. Seth stepped back as Anna dropped down next to him.

"Anna." Seth shivered, chilled by a horrible new thought. "All I did was point the current east. I couldn't see Ellie. I couldn't feel her. What if it's . . . what if it's . . . *it?*"

They locked eyes. Seth saw his own fear reflected in Anna's face.

The screeching stopped. The hatch creaked open.

"Stand back!" Seth yelled to Anna, drawing a screwdriver from Ellie's coat and gripping it tightly in his fist.

"*You* stand back," said Anna, racing forward with the pipe above her head. They stood side by side, watching the opening. They held their breath.

A small, skinny hand reached out. It scrabbled for something to hold on to, then fell over the lip of the opening. Ellie's face emerged, freckled, pale, and gasping for breath.

Seth and Anna cried out, and Ellie collapsed over the side of the hatch. She didn't seem able to breathe.

Seth threw down the screwdriver and launched himself onto the boat, taking her face in his hands. He clamped his lips over hers and tried to breathe air into them.

"Get off!" said Ellie, shoving him aside. She took several long, deep breaths. "I think the air tanks have a leak."

She rolled off the machine and clambered onto the stone ledge. She was still wearing the same tattered shirt and trousers, her feet bare. Her hair was so thin that in places Seth could see her scalp. Yet, when her breathing calmed, her eyes found Seth and Anna, and she smiled.

"Thank you both for saving me," she said.

"It . . . it worked," Seth said. "Your plan worked."

Ellie shrugged. "They sometimes do."

Anna stood frozen, her hands trembling around the pipe. Ellie hobbled over and hugged her tightly. Anna's face blanched, and tears fell down her cheeks. She slowly lowered the pipe and wiped her nose on her sleeve. Ellie let go of her and looked up at Seth, smiling at him too. Seth realized there was something different about her.

"It's gone," he said, astonished.

Ellie put a hand to her heart, pressing with her fingers. "No," she said. "It's still there. But it's weaker than I've ever known. And it can't take Finn's form anymore." She smiled. "It's like my brother's keeping me safe."

Ellie brushed herself down then climbed gingerly into the workshop. Anna and Seth shared a look, then climbed after her.

"So what does this mean?" Seth asked, as Ellie searched among the workbenches. "If you asked for its help now, would it still give it to you?"

"I'm not going to put that to the test," she said. "But I think . . ." She put her hand to her chest again. "I think it's too weak."

Seth offered Ellie her coat. She put it on and rummaged about in the pockets. She pulled out a spanner and turned it in her hand.

"I need to fix the air tanks before it can go out again," she said, looking back at the underwater boat.

"But Fry and Ibnet got it to the observatory in time?" said Anna, sounding proud.

"Yes," Ellie said, putting the spanner down and looking fondly at Anna. "Though that's not really what saved me."

Anna smiled, and the tops of her ears turned red. "Well, I guess Seth helped a *little* bit."

"What was on that piece of paper?" Seth asked.

"A reminder," Ellie said. Her coat looked even bigger on her than normal, yet her cheeks had a flush of pink, and her eyes shone in a way Seth had never seen before.

"So . . . you can stay now, can't you?" Anna said hopefully. "Now that the Inquisitors think you're dead?"

Ellie looked at Anna sadly, then shook her head.

Anna took a deep breath. "So when will you leave?" She seemed to be trying her best to sound brisk, but her voice trembled.

"Oh," Ellie said. "Soon, I suppose. You're sure you won't—"

"I'm sure," said Anna, then winced. "How soon?"

"A few hours?" said Ellie.

Anna nodded miserably and rubbed her nose. "You'll need clothes," she said. "And all that dried food we bought. I'll go fetch them from the workshop. Maybe I could bring a fishing rod too?" She looked down at the sea. "We could try catching a cuttlefish before you go?"

"I'd love to," said Ellie.

Anna hurried for the door, then turned and ran back to Ellie, hugging her fiercely.

"I'm not going yet," said Ellie, but Anna kept hugging her anyway.

"See you," she said, slouching toward the door. She gave Seth a lazy salute, and then was gone.

Seth turned to Ellie, and found she was already looking at him.

"So, do you still want my help out there?" he said.

She smiled. "Well, I thought that, if I'm to go off exploring the whole wide ocean, it might be useful to have a sea god with me."

Seth scratched his head. "I'm not very good at being a sea god—I've never even been in a boat."

"Not that you remember," Ellie said.

"What do you think we'll find out there?" he said.

Ellie stared out to the horizon, thinking.

"You must have some idea?" said Seth, but Ellie shook her head.

"Something new, I hope. But to be honest . . . I don't know." She smiled. "Exciting, isn't it?"

ACKNOWLEDGMENTS

This novel was nearly abandoned. I am indebted to the following people for saving it.

To Caroline Ambrose, whose tireless support for writers is awe-inspiring. To your army of junior judges, whose feedback I've laminated.

To my agent, Stephanie Thwaites. You saw straight to the heart of the story, and your vision for its redrafting was ingenious—I couldn't have hoped for a better champion. To Isobel Gahan and everyone at Curtis Brown.

To my editor, Ben Horslen, for forgoing sleep in favor of reading my book, and for squeezing every drop of creativity out of me even when I kicked and grumbled. To Tom Rawlinson, Shreeta Shah, Emily Smyth, Lizz Skelly, Lucie Sharpe, Jane Tait, and the whole team at Puffin.

To Anna Davis, whose scheming set this whole thing in motion.

To Katie, Jonas, and Robert for reading the earliest drafts, and giving such thoughtful feedback.

To my brothers and sister, to my mom and dad. And to

Lise, who made the rest of them tolerable.

Finally, to Anbara, this novel has been ours together, and would be nothing without you. I am so grateful for your patience, love, and unfaltering belief. You have given so much of your time to this story and I will never be able to thank you enough.